MOTHERLAND

MOTHERLAND

TIMOTHY O'GRADY

HENRY HOLT AND COMPANY
New York

Library of Congress Cataloging-in-Publication Data
O'Grady, Timothy.
Motherland / Timothy O'Grady.—1st American ed.
p.   cm.
ISBN 0-8050-1230-3
I.   Title.
PR6065.G75M6   1989
823'.914—dc20   89-39636
                                          CIP

First American Edition
Printed in the United States of America
1   3   5   7   9   10   8   6   4   2

The lines from Dorothy L. Sayers's translation of *The
Divine Comedy* are reproduced by permission of
David Higham Associates © Dorothy L. Sayers
1949, and the lines from Philip Vellacott's translation
of Euripides' *The Bacchae* by permission of Penguin
Books © Philip Vellacott 1954, 1972.

for Elsie McKeegan

I spoke; he moved; so, setting out anew,
I entered on that savage path . . .

Dante, *The Divine Comedy*

I

My mother's rooms smelled of the jungle and of death. I could see, from the doorway, a deep green fungus spreading across the ceiling from the cracked skylight and, along a distant wall, the tentacles of an ivy plant which was growing randomly from the bedroom into the passageway. The air was unusually, in fact quite oppressively hot. Borne along on it amidst wisps of white steam was the smell of humid earth, oddly pacifying, like the smell of coffee beans on the morning air. I could faintly hear from an inner room the passionate sound of a solitary violin. It was playing Beethoven's Violin Concerto. The sound of the violin mingled with the sound of water tumbling steadily and powerfully into water, like a tropical waterfall plunging into a river. Along the passageway that separated my mother's bedroom from the sitting-room were strewn in great profusion the blackened skins of bananas and the tinily fragmented shells of nuts, and the smell from the skins was sweet. There was, too, another smell of decomposition, and it was of flesh. The tropical air was redolent with it. I did not know the source of these smells and sounds, nor whether my mother was there in her rooms or not. From where I stood astride the doorway, my greatcoat hanging open, my breathing nearly suspended and my vast weight passing in rhythmical anxiety from foot to foot, there were signs of both life and abandonment.

I crept in along the wall and looked through the sitting-room door, opening to the left off the passageway. The last of the day's light entered through the windows, cold and grey in its final hour and dimly illumining the room amidst long, ill-defined shadows and the orange glow of the gas fire. The trail of skins and nuts extended outwards from where I stood, added to here and there by scattered brown earth and small piles of black excrement. I followed the lines of earth to two bags of damp peat which slouched on either side of the mantelpiece. It was the warm, embracing aroma of this peat which had reached me at the door, a smell long familiar to me as my mother always kept a supply of it on hand for her collection of plants – the philodendra, the evil-looking liverish-hued aspidistra, the dusty parlour palms and St Bernard's lily. Two of the plants were tipped over and uprooted and they were all failing in the intense heat, as was I.

I walked to the fire and turned it off. Then I looked about me and tried to take the room in, its clutter and its randomness, measuring the ways it might have changed during my absence. Here was the Turkish scimitar hanging on the chimney breast and the mounted chalk-white deathmask of Fintan Lalor on the mantelpiece. My mother's small bas-relief Hindu shrine still stood by my tripod and telescope at the window and placed on its baroque stand by the piano was the horrible curiosity that had always repelled and mesmerised me as a child – the glass box with the stuffed equatorial birds, all of them of livid colours and fierce, vibrant eyes. So omnivorously in recent years had my mother added to her collection of exotica that it had become difficult with my ever-expanding size to navigate the room with safety. So often there was catastrophe, the smashing of a doll's teaset, the overturning of tables, the scattering of censers, snuffboxes, anonymous photographic portraits. Out then would come the expletives. 'Foolish blundering whale!' she would shriek in her falsetto. 'I am going to put you on grains and vegetables for a month. And no *chocolats*!' Always she said it in French – *chocolats*.

Above me on the ceiling I discovered something new. Fixed by sturdy, screwed-in hooks, evenly spaced and set in a row, were three miniature trapezes, with bright blue nylon rope and red-painted bars. They were garlanded with dead grey leaves and vines which twisted down the ropes, ending in dead flowers which hung limply from the bars. I pressed my hands to the side of my head and attempted to still a gathering scream. I paced about the room, taking in air heavily, until I came to a halt before the display of birds in their glass box. They were as ever eerily still in the midst of an action, one the colour of lime with his head cocked to the side, another with his neck extended and beak open and another with his great crimson wings fully arched. So vivid and triumphant in the fading light were these birds that I felt, for the first time since my childhood, that they were about to come to life.

I fled the sitting-room, turning left out the door and left again down the narrow passageway that leads past the kitchen. At the end, facing me, was the bathroom, from which came the sounds of the violin and the tumbling water. The door was white and covered in water and around its narrow opening poured heavy clouds of steam. I reached towards it with my hand and found that it was painfully hot. Just visible through the crack in the door and, beyond it, through the swirling steam, glowing like neon, was the red bar of the electric wall fire. I thought of the fuel bills. My mother had always suffered acutely from the cold, and these were a regular source of financial strain to us. I attempted to summon her in a dry, broken whisper: 'Mother?' But there was no reply.

I edged closer to the door and pushed it open with my foot. I looked over at the bath. The steam swirled and billowed thickly about me, but still I could see that it was empty, save for the water which, as it poured, trickled aimlessly through the overflow drain between the taps. I was relieved, at least, not to find her here for it would have been worse still to come upon her unclothed. There on the small table beside the hand basin I could see that she had arranged the wireless, her violet-scented soap, her pots of creams and treatments. I moved towards it to put an end to the loud, crescendoing music, but I was halted en route. I had suddenly and hideously become aware of a living presence, two round, reddish, closely spaced eyes above a small grey shape, poised by the window ledge. Reflecting the electric fire through the almost opaque steam, they glowed like phosphorescent marbles and seemed overbearingly cunning and certain. The violin played frantically on while the creature and I stared at one another, still as the birds in the glass box. How had it survived in this vandalised, overheated wilderness, and for how long? What was it? Its red mouth slowly opened and it looked ferocious and evil. There was then an hysterical, ear-piercing, utterly inhuman shriek, and it leapt from its position in a strenuously elongated arc past my shoulder and scurried along the passageway. I could see that it was a monkey. It had long

3

arms and a long curling tail and was slightly pot-bellied, but otherwise frail and quite thin. Here was my mother and her intermittent and insensible love of animals. Whenever she indulged it it seemed intensely private and exclusive, particularly of me, and on many occasions it made me feel miserably jealous. I was on the edge of nausea, and I could not gauge how much more of this I could stand.

I ran back along the corridor and around the corner again and found the monkey hanging from the hatrack beside the bedroom door, gently swinging from his tail. He was festooned about his neck with a ring of silver charms and up his left arm was a row of tiny bronze bangles. He seemed more or less unperturbed by my presence, in fact quite proprietorial in the way that he moved about our home. He was busily cleaning the fur around his ears with his uncannily human fingers, clattering metallically as he moved. Once or twice he looked up at me, like a clerk interrupted at his books.

It was then as I was studying him that I smelled again the malevolent odour of rotting flesh, clearly emanating from beyond the closed door of my mother's bedroom. I puckered my lips and began to blow rapidly in light, short gusts, a habit I had retained from childhood. Whenever I was faced with anything, however mild, which made me afraid or insecure I was irresistibly inclined to perform this ritual. I did it even while talking and it gave the appearance that I was being perturbed by a flying insect. The longer I stood there the more violently I blew.

Finally I managed to push open the door just wide enough to insert my head. Here was my mother's room in all its spectacular unruliness. The garish overhead light burned nakedly in the centre, falling upon scattered clothes and stockings, the outspilling junkshop wardrobe, lipstick and pots of rouge, monocles, eyepieces, antique microscopes, upon the great canopied bed and the Chinese screen draped now with dresses and undergarments, behind which she would demurely attire herself whenever I was in attendance. My mother, it may be said, had always been assiduous with respect to personal hygiene, but her room was ever in such disarray with her clothing and other articles that it was as though a kind of mould was growing there. The heavy funereal curtains had been drawn and the circular oak table where my mother always took her breakfast had been pushed from its position by the window to the centre of the room. There, amid a debris of wilted flowers, teacups and papers was Hercules, our pet tortoise. His extended neck lay limply along the tabletop pointed at me and his yellowing shell was curling at the edge. His eyes were open and utterly vacant. He had apparently starved to death, unable to dismount from the table and partake of the food which had kept the monkey alive. I thought of his painful, increasingly exhausting journey around the perimeter of the table, his depleted stomach crying out for food while the monkey prospered on a plenitude of fruit and nuts. The smell was awesome, this brutally ugly smell of death. I drew in my breath and walked to the table, where I wrapped the poor dead reptile in newspapers and then left him outside the front door. He was surprisingly heavy.

I sat in my mother's chair and attempted to marshal my thoughts. I had long been plagued by her inexplicable departures, her pitiable wanderings about the land until she fetched up, confused, disarrayed, in some northern town. That it had happened again during my absence was greatly worse, compounded by the appalling circumstances when last we had been together. The shame of it! It pains me to think of it even now. It had been my birthday, a wind-blasted, icy day, a day which, like my mother's own birthday, had long been conducted according to a strict, invariable ceremony, both of us dressing formally, I in my tuxedo of burgundy velvet and black satin lapels, my mother in a sweeping, olive-coloured gown that reached the floor. This was the sort of thing we did to stem the chaos. Dinner began at eight with artichokes, proceeded to lemon sole and concluded grandly with cake and champagne. The cake was always the same – fudge ripple – and the champagne was always Bollinger. Afterwards we would sing a few songs around the piano and then settle down to play bridge. Just before the bridge, however, while I set up the baize-covered table and searched out the cards, my mother would take herself off to the kitchen and return with a pot of tea and a plate piled high with bonbons, hand made in County Sligo. This was how it had been done for years. On this occasion, however, I had stayed on after work in a public house on the north side of town drinking large gins for many hours. Movement of any kind was difficult enough in recent times as I burdened my frame with yet more rolls of rippling, cascading flesh, but with such a volume of alcohol it had become next to impossible. Upon arriving I had knocked over the hatrack and smashed a china vase filled with roses, roses which had been purchased for me. I was above two hours late. My mother nevertheless managed to play her familiar role quite impeccably and I too got through the dinner well enough, though with a kind of mocking grin which clearly strained her patience. Afterwards we went straight into the bridge. As I sat before the table pushing the cards here and there over the baize my mother entered with the tea and a cellophane-wrapped box of rum truffles, laying it all out in front of me with exaggerated ceremony.

I stared at her in disbelief, my eyes blinking rapidly.

'Where are the bonbons?' I said.

'Couldn't manage to get them today, dear,' she said. 'Try one of these.'

I crashed my fist down onto the table, spilling the playing cards onto the floor.

'You know I can't stand rum truffles!' I roared.

We were at each other then as fierce as cats, screeching and hissing, charging each other with all crimes and misdemeanours, slights and inconsequentialities, plates and bottles scattered and breaking about us, until I reeled out into the night, shaking my fist and threatening never to speak to her again as I slammed the door. I would show her, I thought. She was not the only one who could make herself scarce. A month I was, perhaps two, tending bar in a small hotel and drinking obliviously through the night, until I returned to these rooms, my apologies rehearsed, a small beribboned parcel of Sligo bonbons in the pocket of my coat, to find my mother gone and our crowded rooms given over to this macabre, devastated jungle.

She could be anywhere by now, I thought. I took off my coat and suit jacket and put up my hand to loosen my tie. So fearsome was the heat and so streamingly had the sweat run down my neck that my starched collar had been torn through by the stud and sprung open. The knot of my tie was sitting on my Adam's apple and I could feel the ends of the collar pointing outwards like the horns of a small goat. How long had she been gone? The previous record had been twenty-seven days. Here and there on the table before me were a number of mugs, most of them drained now of their tea, but one, I could see, still half filled, the tea itself scarcely visible beneath an encrustation of dusty, grey-green mould. Could the growth rate of mould be calculated in days? But then this was no use as the climatic conditions in the flat were so unascertainable, as were the domestic routines of my mother. What, then, about the expenditure of gas? Could I learn anything from this? If I could discover how many cubic metres of gas a fire and water heater in maximum use consumed per day, then, by consulting the meter, I could perhaps deduce the day of my mother's departure. But no. My mother always had the fire on full in weathers such as this. It was useless. I was no more capable of the rigours of deductive reasoning expected of the detective than was the monkey.

I had had one rather icy telephone conversation with her a day or two into my exile. Neither of us gave anything away, though I did ask her in a pointed manner how she was passing her time. The implication, of course, was that I myself was passing it in lordly style, having altogether the time of my life. 'Studying,' she said. I knew she was trying to bait me so I refrained from pursuing the matter, but indeed here on the table I could see an assortment of papers, writing implements and other such paraphernalia, strewn about and betraying evidence of exhaustive labours and attentions. The papers were loose white sheets, and on them could be seen my mother's familiar looping scrawl. Some bore lines, paragraphs, fragments of narrative of some sort, but on most of them there had been entered many dozens of words in double columns running to the full lengths of the pages. In the left-hand columns of some of the pages the words were Irish; in others they appeared to be some form of French, connected with the language which I knew passing well, but in unfamiliar, perhaps arcane spellings. To the right of these words, both French and Irish, were columns of what I took to be their English equivalents. The words were not connected by any apparent logical necessity, but I made my way through page after page of them nevertheless, lost for a time in their strange and evocative uniqueness, their succinct music. I take a page now at random and reproduce it here:

7

knot
waterwheel
Spain
glass
daughter
rent
mushroom
juggler
gold
desertion
thunderbolt
twin
club-foot
chess
chapterhouse
oak
martyr
pig

At the far end of the table from where I sat, stacked in a pile surmounted by my mother's hatbox, were three very large and rather antique-looking volumes. The upper two I found to be bilingual dictionaries, one the standard Dineen's Irish-English and the other Anglo-Norman French-English. I am ashamed to say that both had been stolen by my mother from the Pearse Street Public Library. These bore well-worn and functional bindings, but the third of the books was something else altogether, an infinitely more ornate and curious production, massively thick and bound to standards of high opulence and precision. It was covered in dark olive morocco with other leathers of different colours, primarily black and cream, onlaid around the borders in a writhing, intricate pattern, and around the four corners of the front cover were distributed rectangular panels of watered silk – images of the shamrock, the harp, Cuchulainn's wolf-hound and the round tower, painted by hand in grisaille. Emblazoned in gold letters across the centre was the word SYNNOTT, a name then unfamiliar to me. The book had a noble weight and a wonderfully luxuriant aroma. Its leathers were subtly delicate and in the varying colours there was a fine harmony of tone. I never knew my mother to be a collector of books, and I could not imagine how such a thing as this had come to be in her possession. I, certainly, had never seen anything to match it in extravagance, not in the museums, nor even when, so many years ago, I had been in regular proximity to books of the highest quality. This had occurred during a gloomy summer when I was nineteen. My mother had for some years previously been carrying on an intermittent affair with an English piano salesman during his visits to Dublin. I had not noticed his comings and goings affecting her greatly one way or the other – my mother had always lived operatically, whatever the stimulus – but it seems that his effect on her was cumulative because that particular summer she developed an unrestrained obsession for him, packed up her necessaries and pursued him to London, accompanied by me. We established ourselves in a small bedsitter in Chelsea, and while my mother besieged the unfortunate man – who was married, with family, in a respectable part of Chiswick – I took a job as a postboy at Maggs, the antiquarian bookseller's in Berkeley Square. It was my first visit to England and I thought myself lucky then, as I do now, to have passed it in such gentle company. I became quite friendly with a member of staff there, an elderly Dutchman called de Grunz who ran the packing department in a mews behind the shop. He had an appreciation both scholarly and sensual of old books and their bindings, and he taught me a great deal about them, leaving them unwrapped as he sent me off on my messages so that I could peruse them at leisure as I rode around London in the tops of the red buses. The book before me on the table, this book I am holding now, I recognised to have been derived from Grolier, a French collector of the sixteenth century much copied by the Victorians, though here adapted to a Celtic pattern, the interlacing strapwork running around the borders like an entanglement of vines, without beginning or end.

I unlatched the gold clasps holding the covers closed and opened the book to its title page. On the left, facing it, were two twisted bygone figures in woodcut, 'Poetry Reciter and Harper' according to the caption, the rough black lines lending them a contorted and angry

9

aspect, as though they were administering a curse on what followed. The title page itself read thus:

SYNNOTT

The Record of
a Norman Family in Ireland

1169 –

Printed and bound in London
1892

Many hundreds of unnumbered pages followed, all of them original documents, written mostly by hand in at least three different languages and collected it seemed over all the centuries from the twelfth on down to our own. The scripts ranged from a near-illegible scrawl to the beautifully calligraphic, though there was a small section towards the end set in type, the paper here vellum, the ink exceptionally black, the typeface reminiscent of the German incunabula. At the end was a very long section of blanks. What could my mother have been doing with this astonishing artefact? Or what had it done with her?

I let fall its covers and pushed it away. Just beyond it, protruding over the edge of the table from beneath another of my mother's pages, was a long, thin mahogany handle. It was carved into a pattern of leaves and inlaid at either end with rings of ivory. I lifted the page to see what it might be. It was a magnifying glass. Here was my mother and her affectations. Her eyesight was as keen as a hawk's but she doubtless thought the magnifying glass lent her an air of scholarly purpose as she performed her simple translations.

The peace I had sought as I made my way across the city that day to my mother's rooms was now, of course, beyond me. Even sleep, other than that of the most fitful and discomfiting kind, was out of the question. She was gone. I lumbered my way mournfully about her room. If only I had followed her when she had set off in the past I might have established some pattern, a regular destination perhaps, but inertia had long been my calling. I heaved my shoulders up and down as I paced and banged my fist ineffectually against the side of my leg. At some point and with some bulking aspect of my body I collided with my mother's Chinese screen. It teetered for a bit on its little clawed feet and then down it went, raising dust and debris all about it. There behind it was my mother's dressing table with its impossible congestion of mud packs, palliatives, tweezers, pumices, eyelash-curlers, paints, powders, gels and the like. Rising above it was a mirror, and on it was an image. It was my mother. It had been drawn by her in chalk, her creased, angular features and jaded eyes trans-formed here by her hand into an image of perfectly maternal saintli-ness. The lines were full and round and the eyes were modestly downcast. Across her shoulder were inscribed in lipstick the words: 'Love, Mama'. Not since I was a child had I seen such a thing, those evenings when she arranged me on her knee in front of a mirror and traced the outlines of our faces and torsos, drawing in the features and colouring the background with a variety of chalks. Sometimes she would make us look like cartoon creatures, but at other times she would carefully sketch in the background as a landscape of green Italian hills and pines and give to both our faces a beatific, Renaissance aspect. This was the mode she had chosen for the portrait in the mirror. I seemed momentarily to see nothing only it, its pale, tremu-lous lines, floating there like a heavenly visitation, unriddling nothing of its subject's whereabouts, but absolving all, my failings and my crimes. I felt light as a flute note borne on the air. My mother had long known that I was hers entirely, that she could undo any and all transgressions with the merest affectionate gesture – a kiss on the dome of the head, a present I would never use, a *chocolat*. I looked past the mirror, the dusty prints and scattered papers, the clothes and dangling stockings, to the bed, spread over now with receipts, maga-zines, an astrological chart, the bed where, even in recent years, I had settled down to sleep with her, my spreading girth pressed against her back and my arm around her waist like a lover.

I walked out then, across the hallway to the sitting-room. The monkey passed me en route, leaping nimbly from a chair, to the glass box with the tropical birds, along the notes of the piano and finally to his trapezes on the ceiling, where he swung with vigour from one to the other. I walked to the row of windows along the far wall, which, facing northwards, look out towards the centre of Dublin. Though the sky was overcast there was a clear thin line along the horizon which the falling sun had filled with a profound, luminous scarlet, rimmed in orange and giving way to yellow where it met the clouds. All day the light had been brutally cold and grey. Such light is peculiar to coastal towns and, as it gathers towards dusk, grows more isolating and menacing, like a sea in storm. Now the cold and grey had been dispersed by a light suffused with rose, and this light shone down the length of the Liffey and along the rooftops and steeples of the city, illuminating the flat surfaces of walls and the faces in the crowds as they made their way home or gathered around the bus stops. I put my eye to the lens of my telescope and moved along the lanes and wide avenues, over the rugby players in Trinity's fields, Moore's poised finger, Larkin's petitioning hands, the pigeons on the broad shoulders of the Liberator, the cars and buses and bawling newsboys. I found a man then still on a streetcorner among the hastening crowds, his neck straining, his face upraised, the rose light filling the lenses of his spectacles and falling gently upon his white skin, a blush on porcelain. He looked rapturous and devotional. I heard the monkey drop from his trapeze and make his way onto the window ledge beside me, placing his hand on my shoulder for support. We stood together for a long time in this posture, the rose-coloured light slowly fading over the city. It grew first paler, then darker, and as it did lights went on in rooms and smoke began to rise from the chimney pots. It was the time of the day when families congregate together, to eat or discuss the day's events, and it was at this time that my mother always called me into the sitting-room and settled me into a large chair by the fire. We would each have a glass of sherry and she would read aloud to me the news items that interested her from the evening paper. I wondered if she was anywhere in the city which I now beheld, if she was cold, or hurt, or alone. I yearned painfully for her presence, to hold her before me and tell her that although all through my life I had taken from her I

12

truly did love her deeply, that she was brave and true, that she had given me my life and all that filled it. I knew too that I could have no other purpose except to bring her home.

II

I should, I think, try and put forward now something of how I came to be and how, at the time of my mother's disappearance, I was to be found.

Calculating from the time I am writing these words, I was born forty-three years ago at Holles Street Hospital in Dublin. According to newspaper reports the day of my birth was a cold and wintry Sunday, with an unusually heavy snowfall. My mother remembered the labour leading up to it as an uneventful and oddly timeless period of some two and a half days, at the end of which the doctors gathered around her and opened her womb. She remembered the operating theatre most acutely of all, the gleaming chrome cabinets and marble floor, the great crowd of students and doctors massed around her in rubber boots and white masks, the green sheet with the round hole stretched across her middle. There the incision was made and the doctor plunged in with his hands, a sensation she remembered as pressure rather than pain. The doctor said, 'I have the head,' and then a kind of holy silence filled the room, she said, as I was lifted into the air, my eyes dimly open beneath my pile of black matted hair. 'Such an easy passage you had of it,' she would say to me later, sighing. 'No swimming or struggling for you. Just lifted like fruit from a basket.' The silence in the theatre seemed to last a long time, my face contorted in a thwarted scream, my body twisting above her held by the doctor. Then she heard a gasp beside her and someone said, '*Look at his hands.*' She saw them then, my amphibious hands quavering and clutching in the air, a fine pellucid webbing stretched between the fingers. The silence then ended with a great cry from me as the plug was removed from my throat, there was sudden movement everywhere about the room, and there my mother's memory of the event drew to a close.

Beyond that, I have only the scantest knowledge of my beginnings. From what my mother has told me – and she has told me very little as it was an unhappy time for her – we passed the first three years of my life in a small flat in Herbert Place overlooking the canal. I do not know if my father ever lived with us there. I never knew him, and cannot be certain how well my mother knew him either, although I gather, at least, that they were married. She spoke of him only when pressed to the limit of her endurance by my childish questioning, and when she did the version of their life together and his whereabouts which she put to me usually differed wildly from all previous ones. When I was very young she seemed to try to appeal to my imagination with these stories, but as I grew older I believe she only tried to please herself. For some time in my early childhood I believed that my father was the statue of Saint Dominic that resided in the chapel that we used to attend. On Saturday afternoons when my mother went to confession, or on Sundays after Mass, I used, in consequence, go alone to the altar of Saint Dominic and whisper things to him. I told him that my mother was sad because he did not live with us, that I had memorised a new rhyme or that I was learning to count, and on one occasion I supplied for him a list of what I wanted for Christmas. That his plaster visage, with its sallow complexion, its gaudily painted features and oddly unfocussed eyes was immobile and mute did not, for some time, deter me from speaking to him. It was not until years later, when I could distinguish between statues and living people, that I discovered that far from the handsome, kindly image presented by the ecclesiastical sculptors, Dominic was a hard-hearted and rather grim Castilian, whose order became the great enthusiasts of the Inquisition and whose only departure from strict orthodoxy was to confess to one Jordan of Saxony that he preferred the company of young women to old ones.

My father thereafter went on to become many things in my mind. I remember looking out of our bedroom window with my mother at the unused barges parked along the canal bank and she telling me that my father was captain of such a vessel in a distant and wintry place called

Poland. She said that his life was very hard, navigating his cargo through the icy waterways, and we resolved there and then to save our money and send him a warm coat. He was also, at different times and in different places, a tubercular poet, an aviator who had been lost in the air, a perpetually touring tap dancer and the permanent Ambassador to Afghanistan. This last I have come to regard as a delightful touch, just the sort of whimsy which my mother indulged in in the midst of her despair.

Somehow or other my mother managed to merge these diverse spectres into a single image, because I remember maintaining throughout my childhood a constant and properly devout filial love towards someone that I felt I knew. By the time I arrived at adolescence, however, this image had been subjected to the corrosive effects of time, and had fallen apart. I ceased to have any feelings about him one way or the other and came to accept, the way some people accept statelessness, that I had no father. More recently, and for reasons that had nothing to do with an interest in him, I obtained from the Records Office a copy of my birth certificate and on it discovered a few bare facts about him. He was called Lawrence O'Banion and his profession is listed as 'journalist'. He was seven years older than my mother and had been born in Roundwood, a small town in Wicklow. I too am called O'Banion on the birth certificate, but my mother later jettisoned this name because throughout our life together we have both used the name given on the certificate as her maiden name, which was Burke – though this too was later changed and is not the name which I use at present.

My mother let herself out from time to time for shop work or cleaning duties in the big houses in the squares, but we came to the point where life in the city was no longer economically tenable and were forced to abandon the flat in Herbert Place. She was a naturally gifted cook and decided that her most suitable course would be to take up a position as a resident domestic in a large country house. I was at this time only recently in speech and I complained long and loudly to her about this venture into the unknown. To no avail of course. I was cajoled with lies and sweets and indulgences and off we went.

My mother's first position was with an elderly American judge, who had retired after being left a widower to a huge grey house in Kilkenny. He was gaunt and very tall and he wore braces, he had haunted-looking eyes and his mouth, like mine, was usually open and moist, for he suffered from a congenital defect which prevented him from breathing through his nose. Living in the house along with him, my mother and I, were Blake the gardener, the head housekeeper Mrs Hennessy, a young maid called Eileen and the Judge's two teenaged sons, Blair and Henry, who spent their time playing baseball on the immense lawn which led down to the drive. Try as I might I can bring about no pictures to my mind of our arrival at this house or of the first few months we passed there. It was truly an enormous place, the largest by far I had been in at that stage of my life, with its two colossal wings and outlying regions of orchards and sheds and gatehouses, and it was perhaps the house's scale which oppressed me in my smallness. I was well into my fifth year, eight months, I suppose, out of Dublin, before I was able to secure a memory of this house. In it I am running down the seemingly infinite corridor of the upper floor of the west wing, deranged by the house's vastness and its multiplicity of doors and angles and crying uncontrollably for my lost mother. As with all such memories I can see with disturbing clarity not only the frightening elements of the episode, but also the calm moments which preceded it.

In the memory it is an afternoon in spring and my mother tells me that she has to go to the Judge's study to bring him a glass of sherry before dinner. She leaves me sitting on the kitchen floor with an alphabet book and a large bowl of apples and bananas. I remain there for what seems an eternity, and when I can bear it no longer I make for the door from which my mother has exited. This I find to be locked. The door which leads outside, however, is open, and I pass through it into a small gravel yard. A light drizzle is falling. I pass through a hole in the wall at the far end of the yard and race along the front of the house looking for a way in. I cannot reach the handles on the main door, which in any case is too heavy for me, but at the side of the house I find some French windows left ajar. Years later, in a book of memoirs which I came across while working at Maggs, I discovered a photograph of George Bernard Shaw standing before these same windows.

It was an overcast day, but he looked strangely luminous. I go through the French windows into a dark circular room, with a domed ceiling illustrated with figures of men in subfusc cowls and tailcoats and a number of identical doors leading off in all directions.

I choose a door and run along a narrow hall past a dark stairwell towards another closed door. This I find to contain only a dried-up toilet and I retrace my steps to the dark stairwell. I run up the hard wooden steps, but at the top step I slip and tear open the side of my knee on a protruding nail. I watch the stream of blood dribble down my bare skin onto my white sock. I find the sight of it terribly frightening and I crave more desperately the presence of my mother. The landing contains only three more doors, boarded up and padlocked, and I run back down the stairs, but in my bewilderment I pass the ground level and find myself at the entrance to the cellar. There are a few openings at the tops of the walls which look up through cobwebbed grilles to the dull sky, and in the gloom I can just make out the silhouettes of stacked crates of empty bottles. As I try to form some impression of where the room leads, I hear the sound of two bottles clinking together, like a polite toast. The sound is repeated. Then I hear the brutal sound of smashing glass and see a black animal leap to the floor from one of the crates. I briefly catch the weird red glow of its eyes. It was here, I think, that my habit of blowing to ward off fear originated. I suppose I believed I could drive away this animal and even the thought of it with my little gusts of wind. I run back up the stairs, dabbing at the wound on my knee lest the animal catch the scent of my blood and launch an attack. I am now back in the mysterious circular room, where I run frantically around its perimeter until I push through another door into a large, half-derelict entrance hall, with a huge sweeping staircase and yet more doors and empty rooms leading off. I make for a door to the left of the staircase which leads to a complexity of corridors, empty kitchens, cupboards and meaningless rooms of which I remember nothing, for as I run through them, my fear having coagulated into a kind of numb momentum, I have constantly before me the image of my mother, her bright animated eyes, her warm skin, her smell of violet-scented soap. I run hysterically, seeing nothing at all around me until I emerge into the light of the long corridor on the second floor. It is here that the memory becomes most acute and, perhaps, at this distance, most reliable.

The corridor opens before me, its wooden floors gleaming. Along one wall are thousands of leather-bound books, the shelves divided by recesses containing red satin furniture, and along the other side is a series of tall windows reaching nearly to the ceiling. These overlook a walled orchard. The walls are made of round whitewashed stones, and between the crevices are growing the sprigs of ferns and small purple flowers, a nightmare of stones in bloom. I see all this in excruciating detail as I run down the centre of the corridor, crying for my mother, a sharp pain growing under my ribs and my feet smarting from the hard wooden floor. Then, before me, a door suddenly opens and the old Judge steps out, abruptly stopping my momentum with his large, bony hands. He wears his claret-coloured dressing-gown over his trousers and bare chest. The few tufts of grey hair which remain on his large head stand upright and his long, unshaven jaw is hanging loosely open. Behind him I can see, hanging on a hook on the back of the door, my mother's apron. He bends painfully over and blots the blood which still oozes from my knee.

'You are like me,' he says, and the smell of the sherry comes out of his mouth with the words. 'The world is vast and empty, but whenever you move about in it you bump into something.'

Then he gives out a barking, joyless laugh. He means to comfort me, but his grey watery eyes carry such tragedy and grief that I begin again to sob, though this time, I think, for him. I ask him where my mother is.

'In there,' he says, whispering. 'Asleep. She'll be down readily.'

And he takes me by the hand along the corridor and down into the kitchen, where he entertains me with a dazzling display of knife juggling and a quite remarkable trick in which he transfers by means of his pinched fingers the sound of a reverberating fork into a crystal glass, where, when deposited, it sings mightily.

I had journeyed alone through this dizzyingly vast and labyrinthine house, and at the end I had found only a cavity where my mother had withdrawn, lured, perhaps, as I was, into the life of the Judge by his immense frailty. It was, I think, my first experience of being unaccountably separated from my mother, and ever afterwards, whenever it happened again, I was beset by this same complex feeling of loneliness and panic, breathlessness and dread.

My mother and I remained in the Judge's household for many years, until I was perhaps ten or eleven, and throughout that time we had no contact whatever with the outside world. I remember it mostly as a time of tranquillity, when Blake the gardener taught me card games and about the habits of birds and flowers and Eileen, the young maid, taught me how to knit. The Judge and my mother taught me the remedial skills and read to me from the classics, because neither of them believed in schools, and even Blair and Henry occasionally took me fishing in the river which ran behind the house or threw baseballs at me on the big lawn.

Sometime in the middle stages of our time there, however, I began to notice my mother being overtaken by a set of unpredictable and eccentric symptoms, which went on to plague her intermittently throughout our life together. On the first occasion that I recall she was at the sink trimming the fat off a shoulder of lamb and I was sitting on a bench in a tiled recess in the kitchen, slicing carrots over a long wooden table. She had been singing to herself for quite some time, a series of gently melodic airs that I was accustomed to hearing, and then fell into 'She Moved Through the Fair', a song which the Judge often called upon her to sing if he was entertaining or dining formally. I stood back in the shadows and watched, and always I felt very proud of her. She would hold her clasped hands between her thighs, swaying on her seat with her eyes closed, her brow severely creased and her head tilted upwards as she sang.

> *She went away from me and moved through the fair,*
> *Where hand-clapping dealers' loud shouts rent the air.*
> *The sunlight around her did sparkle and play,*
> *Saying, 'It will not be long, love, till our wedding day.'*

I liked the song a great deal and listened to it attentively as she hummed and sang it to herself that day over the sink. I therefore remember acutely when the notes began to disintegrate and be replaced first by sighs and then by stifled groans. I heard the knife clatter into the enamel sink and saw her grip its rim tightly with both her hands. She began to sway backwards and forwards, first absently and then more violently, until she turned to face me, a wisp of her piled-up hair trailing across her left eye. She looked with seriousness at a spot above my head.

'The lenses for Mrs Foster have been improperly ground,' she said, very deliberately and with an odd resonance.

She continued to stare at the wall.

'Did you hear me?' she said.

I sat motionless over the carrots on the long wooden bench.

'I said, "Did you hear me?" Mrs Pearce,' she said again, with menacing force.

'Yes, Mama,' I said.

I had never heard of anyone called Mrs Pearce.

'Well send them back, for God's sake!' she said.

I dreaded my mother's directives when she was in bad form because they were always delivered with equal amounts of vehemence and obscurity, and while I felt the urgency to do something I did not know how to go about it. In this instance of the lenses I just remained on my bench and watched my mother move about the kitchen, rooting in drawers and cupboards, muttering, 'Why should anyone want to see, anyway?' This seemed to exhaust her and she retired to her bed for a profoundly deep sleep which lasted for fourteen hours.

On this occasion my mother escaped detection by the Judge or any of his staff. Young as I was, I covered for her by saying that as she was indisposed it would be best if she wasn't disturbed, and between us Eileen and I managed to serve the dinner. But the malady struck again a year or two later, and this time it was in front of the entire household. It was Hallowe'en, and the Judge had invited everyone out onto the lawn after nightfall to watch the bonfires which were raging on the hillsides and in the fields which surrounded the house. It was a moonless night, and the whole valley glowed with an orange light beneath the black sky. The Judge's sons had constructed their own flaming cone of wood in the drive and were adding to it with maniacal relish, running backwards and forwards from a small copse with armfuls of dead branches. The Judge placed his hand on my shoulder and led me away from my mother towards the fire, so that we stood together within the spill of its light and I could feel its heat tautening the skin on my face.

'See the way fire affects people?' he drawled.

Light from the flames danced over his face and I could see that the thought seemed to please him.

'Do you know the French saint, Joan of Arc?' he asked me. I had heard of her, and knew that she had short hair, but that was all.

'She was placed in a fire like that before an immense and awe-struck crowd and burned until she died. Do you know why? For the purity of her belief. On the advice of God she had gone to war against the English and the English ecclesiastics in consequence tried her for heresy. Ha! "Idolator! Relapse! Worshipper of Belial!" they ranted at her before consigning her to the flames.'

He shook his fist in thunderous accusation, laughing hoarsely. Then he became serene.

'Hallowe'en, you know, is the ancient festival of Samhain, the end of summer, a Celtic New Year's Eve. Celebrated here from druidic times. Extraordinary the way it is re-created so effortlessly. The bonfires are meant to drive away evil spirits which fly about in the air. But I think there is a mistake here, don't you? The punishment of fire has always been employed as a purgation of evil, but I think that on the contrary it attracts it. Look at those boys.'

Blair and Henry were moving in and out of the circle of light, their faces unrecognisably fierce.

'The evil was not in Joan but in those who had selected the means of her punishment, and in those who were lured into the marketplace at Rouen by the prospect of watching the fire devour her body. Their satisfaction was *evil*!' he said with vehemence.

'Interesting from my professional point of view, you know, how the Bishop of Beauvais, knowing full well that Joan would be burned at the stake, made a pious appeal for mercy to the civil authorities as he handed her over for punishment. The civil judge who was on hand never even opened his beak, though it was up to him to pronounce sentence. Crimes punishable by death have historically been crimes against property or against the state. Men of wealth and power, like the Bishop of Beauvais, create a malevolent moral climate, deliver those who resist it into the hands of the law and then disclaim all responsibility. They know that the fury of the ignorant, like the fire, is irresistibly consuming. I and my colleagues on the bench have been servants to these men, more so than Eileen or your mother are servants to me.'

I thought that he had finished here and I made to move away, but he gripped me tightly by the shoulder.

'The practice of public death by burning did not end in the fifteenth century and continues even to this day, though the fire is now electrical and the end more sudden. I once had the misfortune to sit in judgement over such a case and to dispense such a sentence . . . I am still trying to get over it.' The look in his eyes was very like when he stopped me running along his corridor, and I was afraid that he might weep. But he didn't. 'My colleagues take all of that more easily. Some of them even rather enjoy it.'

This is the way I like to remember the Judge, worldly, pedagogic, confessional and overflowing with empathetic mourning. He often chose me as a recipient for his reflections. I do not know why. Perhaps it was because I was my mother's son, and he was beginning to fall in love with her. I never replied, I was never really able to, but the Judge often spoke to me as though I had. On this occasion he turned to me, his fleshy eyes opened wide, his brow arched and his mouth forming an innocently protesting O and said, as though I had disputed what he had put to me, 'Many pure souls have been burned alive, you know.'

With this we heard a terrible cry of pain behind us. We looked back out of the circle of light but found it difficult to discern anything in the darkness beyond. We made our way towards the source of the sound and found there, surrounded by the remainder of the Judge's staff, the writhing body of my mother lying on her back on the grass. She seemed to have been overtaken by a sudden and brutal agony. Her legs were bent at the knees and opened wide. Her neck was arched and among the beads of sweat which stood out on her skin I could see grossly protruding veins. The spectacle terrified me and I let out a cry and tried to run towards her, but Eileen caught hold of me, fixing me fast in her arms and wrapping her cardigan around my shoulders.

Blake was knelt down beside her, dabbing at her brow with his bandana and running his hand over her hair. His face was very tense and he appeared to be struggling with a powerful emotion. When the Judge arrived she looked in his direction but her eyes did not register him. She called out the name 'Tommy' over and over again.

'Help me,' she cried. 'It's killing me. I can't push any more.'

Her body heaved terribly and she cried and moaned in great convulsive bursts. Everyone stood by helplessly watching, understanding nothing. At last she let out a final cry and slumped onto the grass, the tautness of her body subsiding into limp exhaustion. Then she half-opened her eyes, smiling weakly, and whispered towards the Judge, 'I can hear him, just over there.' She pointed vaguely towards the fire. 'Bring him to me, Tommy.' I looked over the body of my mother at the Judge, and I could see his face go suddenly cold.

'Oh my God,' he said, looking at me. He rose to his feet and lumbered absently towards the house. 'Oh my God. Take her to bed.'

Blake took her up in his arms and carried her, and as the light of the hallway fell upon his face I could see that he was weeping. He put her to bed then and I crawled in beside her. Exhausted as she seemed to be by her ordeal, she slept fitfully, thrashing about and on one occasion sitting rigidly up in bed, her eyes wide open, declaiming, 'That damned mill, going night and day!' When she awoke the next morning she was herself again, remembering nothing, as always, of her ravings.

Mrs Hennessy, the housekeeper, at once inaugurated a campaign for the dismissal of my mother from the Judge's service. She found the chilling congruence of my mother's phantom birth with the unholy festival of Hallowe'en too much for her, and she repeatedly urged the Judge not only to send my mother and me away but also to summon a priest to bless the house. The Judge endured her for a few days, at the end of which she confidently presented him with an ultimatum that either she or my mother would have to go. Mrs Hennessy was an obese and florid woman with a sycophantic nature and bandages on her legs beneath her stockings. She had rust-coloured hair which was very crinkly and very sparse, so that through it were visible patches of her dry brown scalp. I remember particularly the way her stomach and breasts seemed to be packed tightly within her plaid dresses. The

Judge, I think, also found her repellent, and he was glad of the opportunity to be shot of her.

Whatever the Judge's attitude towards my mother may have been before, this episode marked a dramatic turning point in their relations. Nothing so moved or alerted him as the tragic, and he clearly perceived in my mother's spell the uncontrollable force which he had pondered throughout his professional life. He took to coming over to our quarters several times a day, his face illuminated with this simple wonder, and thereafter my mother and I spent many evenings with him in his study, sitting for hours on the long leather sofas by the fire, being served from time to time by Eileen with brandies for them and tea and lemon biscuits for me and listening to his stories of the criminals who had been brought before him. He had a generous tolerance for all our foibles, his, my mother's, even mine, and he examined them quite openly with his profound and innocent curiosity. I remember him taking up my webbed hands gently in his own, prodding them and turning them about.

'Ah,' he said at last. 'These are really quite remarkable. Amphibious, you know, means "double life". You're a boy after my own heart.'

He said such curious things in a deeply ruminative manner, searching far within himself for his thoughts, particularly when he pondered his sentencing of a young man to death some two decades previous. But whenever my mother spoke he turned towards her with intense concentration, as though all she said carried an oracular authority. I think that in some way he sought atonement from her. My mother was as taken with him as he was with her and she soon abandoned all pretence of decorum for my benefit during these evenings, regularly taking up a position within the hollow of the Judge's arm, her shoes lost on the floor and her legs doubled up beneath her. These were some of our finest days, when the two of us were drawn together into another's life. At the end of the night my mother and I both kissed the Judge and then went down to our room, where we got into bed together. She often sang to me then and I liked to place my ear in the centre of her back to hear the notes reverberate. She would keep singing until she heard me breathing with the rhythm of sleep, and then she would steal silently from the bed and go to the Judge's room, where she stayed until dawn. This never perturbed me, because the Judge was kind to me and he made my mother happy, so I accommodated her as best I could by closing my eyes and breathing deeply and thereby allowing her more quickly to make her escape.

We stayed in the big house in Kilkenny until the Judge was killed while crossing the road in America by a driverless car. He had been visiting his sister in the city of St Louis. We heard that the brake cable had snapped and the car had rolled silently down a hill, knocking him down and crushing his ribs under its wheels. The news came initially in the form of a cable from the Judge's lawyer, which Blake read to the assembled staff in a solemn, oratorical manner. The message thanked all the staff, told them that their wages would be paid by the Judge's bank in Kilkenny town, and that we would all be expected to leave the house within two weeks. My mother reacted as though she had been violently struck, reeling backwards from the little group in the hallway to a chair behind her, where she wept freely and inconsolably. I was repelled, for though I had seen her seemingly possessed by voices and other beings I had never before seen an adult cry openly like a child and I took it as a more striking sign of lost reason. I was afraid she would be taken from me and that I would be left alone and, in the immediate term, that it would be left to me to cook the staff lunches that afternoon. But my mother recovered, and for the remainder of our days there she managed for the most part to contain her grief within her black clothes and solemn demeanour.

Something else happened to me in those moments that removed me from the disturbing scene taking place around me. When Blake had concluded reading out the cable and just before my mother cried out in pain, a picture of the car that had killed the Judge, red, massive and with gleaming chrome, and of the road on which he was walking, brilliantly white, entered vividly into my mind. I then began to assemble the rest of the death scene myself, with steadily growing fascination, freely taking from what I had heard of America from the Judge, the staff and my mother. I placed a fully accoutred marching band moving over the hill behind the silent car. Along one side of the road were tall trees growing along the muddy banks of the Mississippi

River, which was crowded with paddle-boats and steamers and rafts. In among them were a black man and a young wiry boy who was smoking a pipe. I had never before seen a black man, but the Judge had told me that much of America had been built by men and women of this colour. Along the other side of the road was a pavement down which strolled crowds of people in brightly coloured robes. Set back from the pavement was a row of immensely high buildings of glittering granite, and before each was a flagpole carrying the Stars and Stripes. It seemed a happy, celebratory and very beautiful place.

In the picture there had been a recent rain, but now the sun had come out and everything was gleaming with a diamond-like brilliance. I could see the Judge walking down along the road among the crowd of people in the brightly coloured robes, dressed in the flowing judicial regalia he had described to me and in animated conversation with his sister. I made her out to be more elderly than he, and walking, as he occasionally did, with the aid of a blackthorn stick. He turned in towards the road to cross over to the river bank, and as he did the red car began its silent descent from the top of the hill, just before the marching band. He paused in the middle of the road to point out to his companion a rhododendron bush on the river bank. It was in magnificent purple bloom. The Judge was a great lover of flowers, particularly those with a sweet perfume, and he once told me about the lilacs and dogwood that grow in his home town. I could see the raindrops poised at the ends of the petals.

As the Judge stood thus entranced in the middle of the road, his large head inclined towards his attentive sister, the red car made its way towards him with increasing speed. Members of the band proceeding down the hill and passers-by on the pavement could see the coming calamity and began to shout warnings to him. He appeared not to hear them – nor, strangely, did I, for the vision was mute – and the car made its impact, knocked him to the ground and passed with undiminished speed over his body and further down the road until its momentum was finally dissipated along a flat stretch. I saw the Judge's face closely then, his long unshaven jaw and his moist lips composed faintly into a smile, until a little rivulet of blood trickled from the corner of his mouth and he died. I was aware of nothing else around

27

me as I composed this picture. It grew more absorbing and more exhilarating as it grew more detailed, until finally, even while witnessing in my mind the bloody spectacle of violent death, I felt a tranquillity I had never known before. It was the tranquillity of forgetfulness, of oblivion towards the changing world beyond our skin, such as some people feel in prayer, or love, or at the arrival after great labour of an eternal definition. It is perhaps most evident of all in a crowd unified in a single great belief. But when I reached it, or perhaps when I heard my mother cry, or perhaps thought of the Judge's strange remark about bumping into things in the vast world, the picture disappeared and I became horribly aware of my surroundings and my meagre place in them. I felt reduced by the Judge's death, this sad, towering figure whose final moments I had used to entertain myself, and I knew that I would miss him and that because he was gone there was no longer anyone to protect my mother and myself. I looked around me in some shame and tried, as ever, to remain inconspicuous. But I held on strongly to the feeling I had discovered that day, and I stayed alert for it, the more so as my life grew bleaker. It has visited me many times since then, always welcome and always brought about by pictures in my mind composed of exquisite details. More often than not it has come as a surprise, unsolicited, but as time has gone on I have learned the knack of inviting it so that it responds.

My mother and I left the Judge's house at the appointed time and set about our wanderings. I remember being driven away from the big house in the Judge's long black car, our twine-bound suitcases under our feet. It was very early in the morning in summer, and there was a thin white mist gathered about the trees and fields. Blake was at the wheel with Eileen beside him and as he turned out of the gate onto the main road he looked back at me and said, 'This is a Packard, a great car. It's not many lifts you'll be getting in a machine like this.' There was silence then for a long time and I looked out of the window, thinking with some dread of the unknown world which we now faced, a world I had never experienced. He left us at a lodging house in Carlow, where we lived for a time while my mother cast about for a new position, and that was pretty much that.

So it was that my mother and I entered into a long and itinerant period of some half-dozen years during which we trekked, with intermittent and unpredictable stops, around the big houses of the province of Leinster. I remember this time, and for that matter most of what extended beyond it, as sprawling and indeterminate, like the vast suburbs of London which my mother and I passed through by coach en route to her lascivious piano salesman that summer I worked at Maggs. And, as with that journey, there was about this time a profound weight of tedium on me as I awaited a destination I neither knew nor cared about. Nothing stirred. We remained, as before, insulated from the course of events in the outside world but in this case, without the Judge, we had nothing to replace it.

My mother felt it too and throughout these years I watched her withdraw painfully into herself. Nothing was ever quite the same for her after the Judge died. She took to wearing sack-like frocks in which she stooped slightly, and drew her hair severely back from her face, tying it up in a taut little bun on top of her head. Her eyes no longer focussed with that vivid delight on the here and now, but instead looked wistfully into a distance unknown to me. She tried heroically to keep her grief to herself, but now and then it would spill volcanically over and I would find her slumped in a chair in one of those cold country houses, sobbing and moaning to herself, or, clutching me to her breast as we lay in bed, she would speak about him in a fragmented, obsessive manner until she finally exhausted herself and went to sleep. Once I opened a small book which lay on the table beside our bed and saw scrawled in a shaky hand across the title page the words 'alone, alone, oh how alone'. I was helpless and abject before this terrible grief, all the more because I could see that by myself I could never be enough for her.

In time, perhaps a year or two, these outbreaks of mourning began slowly to diminish and then finally departed for good. But this brought no relief, for in their stead there came, with increasing severity, the eery symptoms of possession which I first began to notice in the middle stages of our stay with the Judge. Passing into a trance by a means which had grown familiar to me, sighing and swaying with growing acceleration, she spoke out of a life which I could not fathom. The words came out of her not with the listlessness which had recently

29

characterised her, but with a sharp gravity, and even anger. They covered many different things, sometimes more than once, but none were familiar to me and I could detect no linking theme. Several times she complained of the presence of guns, though I had never seen any in the household where we then lived. 'Arm yourselves!' she shouted. 'Go on, arm yourselves! Little toy soldiers . . .' There was a vehemence to her at these times which unnerved me, but in time I came to live through them with equanimity, as though they were changes in the weather.

The distinction between the being who inhabited the trances and her own daily life was not always so strictly adhered to. This was particularly true of her fascination with the mechanics of sight. She began to collect from her employers' discarded newspapers articles to do with the eyes, paying particular attention to the failing eyesight of the President, and to advances in the field of optics. A large and hideous diagram in red and blue of the human eye was hung in a frame over our bed. I began to notice too that whenever she travelled to the abattoirs and markets in Dublin for supplies she would return with some object containing a lens – a magnifying glass, a pince-nez, a monocle or opera glasses, purchased from the antique shops off the quays. On my twelfth birthday she gave me a telescope with a fine Zeiss lens and brass fittings, and on clear summer evenings we would take it out into the grounds and look up into the firmament, my mother speaking with knowledge of the principles of refraction and I of my frustration at being unable to pick out the patterns in the stars. The following year my present was a captain's spyglass. 'There's money in collecting, you know,' she assured me.

This dark and remote aspect of my mother's character took a more menacing turn in the early 1960s, when we were stationed at Kildare, not far from the Curragh, where my mother worked for an English horse-breeder called Skinner. Skinner shared his house with his sister Martha, who had come over one Christmas from somewhere in England to visit him and stayed on. I did not take to the sister at all. She had a large bony nose beneath two narrow-set eyes and the worst case of bad breath I have ever encountered, a smell not unlike that of sweat and curdled milk. One morning in winter, after we had been there for about two months, my mother rose from our bed in the faint pre-dawn light, silently dressed and left the room. I thought she might be going to the hens for breakfast eggs, but the sound of her feet on the gravel alerted me that she had left by the house's front door. From the gable window I saw her pass through the main gates and set off along the road, her figure finally vanishing from my sight among the ancient grey trees of a distant orchard. Skinner put his bald head through our door at about ten o'clock enquiring after his breakfast, and I had to tell him that I did not know where my mother was.

I waited for her throughout that long day, wandering around the grounds between trips along the road to the orchard, where I looked down from a hill which led from there in the hope of catching sight of her. Now and then I came across Skinner, who would smile over at me and shrug and then return to his horses. I noticed that all of his gestures seemed to emerge from a cheerful and uncomprehending resignation to fate, a quality I was not to observe again until some years later when I went to London.

That evening Skinner's sister had to pitch in with me to prepare the dinner, a grim concoction of burnt potatoes and tinned Spam. Troubled by my mother's absence and faced with an array of bubbling pots and empty plates, I slunk off at one point to a high stool by the sink, where I sat with my head down and succumbed to my habit of blowing gusts of air through my puckered lips. I was startled from this posture by the shrill bark of Skinner's sister. 'Will you ever stop that damnable puffing!' she shouted. I looked up and saw her pig-like eyes, a square of Spam dangling from a fork at the end of her arm. By this time I had worked myself up into such a state of nervous tension that my natural obsequiousness fell by the wayside and I snapped back at her, 'If you did it we'd all die of asphyxiation.' She looked at me with such murderous coldness that I thought better of taking dinner and I went up alone to our room. There I tried to apply myself to Marco Polo's account of his fabulous adventures in the Orient, the book my mother had set for me that week. We had taken turns reading it to each other over tea at night, and I had taken with great keenness to Marco's tales of his long trek across the Persian sands, of the elephant armies of

Burma and of his ascendancy to the governorship of Hangchow. Now and again I almost felt lost in it all, as when I had invented the Judge's death. But now as I read I had a profound sense of desolation, as though Marco's wondrous story was a standard against which to measure the smallness of my own life. Eventually I had to give it up because the thought of my mother bedevilled all my attempts at concentration, and I could do nothing but pace up and down the room in the hope of tiring myself out. Finally I got into bed, but the coldness of the sheets in the absence of my mother kept me awake. I lay there for an unmeasurable time, shivering, my eyes closed and my knees drawn up to my chest, the terrible silence broken at long intervals by the neighing of a horse or the rattle of a train making its way to Dublin. Cars passed a few times during the night and whenever I heard the gathering sound of their engines I prayed fervently that they would contain my mother. Eventually I came to doze intermittently, but the dream I dreamed offered me no peace. In it the Judge and I were walking along a dirt path that wound its way through a forest. We came to a place where a small ridge rose above us to our left and from this vantage we were suddenly advanced upon by a succession of wild boars which came crashing down at us through the undergrowth. I returned to the dream again and again. The Judge was carrying a rhododendron walking-stick and I remember still the sight of him burying the handle of it into the sloping forehead of one of these beasts, its black blood bubbling thickly around the wood. In the deep shadows of the room the boars had more substance and definition than anything else and, as though in a fever, I was unable to distinguish sleep from wakefulness.

Finally the dawn came and I began again the previous day's routine of wandering aimlessly about the grounds between my vain journeys up the road. There were times when I could not contain myself and I ran into the depths of the orchard to cry. The torment continued on through that night and the next, during which time I slept not at all. I found that unlike most sensations, the pain of missing actually increases with the passage of time and with repetition, reducing its victim through attrition to a hollow ruin.

This is how I found myself on the morning of the third day when

Skinner came up to our room. He announced in uncharacteristically blunt tones that he had received a telephone call from the Station Master in a northern town called Coleraine to the effect that my mother had presented herself there just after dawn. She was confused, he said, but not unwell, and if he paid her fare at an agency in Kildare she would be placed on a train that would bring her home. 'I'll have to go back again at four o'clock to collect her,' he told me. 'Damned nuisance on trial day.' My relief was instantaneous and immense, and of course I could not have cared less about Skinner. From the time I heard his car pass out of the gates that afternoon until I saw it emerge from the entanglement of branches in the orchard, I kept a tremulous vigil at the gable window. When it turned into the drive I ran down into the hallway and was there when my mother came in after Skinner through the door, her hair in terrible disarray and her clothing damp and flecked with mud. She looked over at me with inexpressible remorse and then ran to me and took me in her arms, kissing my face and mumbling, 'I'm sorry, so so sorry, never leave you alone again . . .' Skinner and his sister stood by, both of them with testy expressions on their faces, and my mother then drifted penitently past them, up the stairs to our room for a long recuperative sleep. I slipped in beside her and arranged myself happily along the curve in her spine. Over the next few days I was frequently to see Skinner and his sister in agitated conference, her large nose, reddened with cold, jabbing forward like an angry bird's and Skinner bending politely backwards from the waist, unable to restrain a wincing expression on his face from the odious smell rising in front of him. Finally then my mother was summoned to the drawing room and told that as business was somewhat slack at the moment he was forced to make some reductions in staff and that, regrettably, he would no longer be needing her services, all of this accompanied by a plenitude of shrugs and smiles. Fortunately for him, he said, his sister was there and she had volunteered to take over the cooking duties. After my mother told me this and after considering it for some time I said, 'She burns the potatoes and serves him Spam,' whereupon she threw herself back onto the bed and laughed with an abandon I had not seen since our days by the fireside with the Judge.

33

Over the next three years our residences changed in rapid succession. I cannot remember them sequentially and some of them I cannot remember at all. Whatever force had driven or lured my mother away that winter morning at Skinner's had quickly taken root in her and she thereafter took to disappearing with increasing frequency, always inexplicably, and always coming to her senses in some northern town, where she would make her way to the bus or railway station, penniless and in considerable disorder, and then phone in nervously to her employer for help in getting back. I noticed that as these spells increased, as the powerful urges which led her off to these distant places took a greater hold on her being, the skin which had contained her so severely over the years began to wear away. I had watched her brightness fade and her character withdraw in the wake of the Judge's death, but the process had now become inverted and I saw her emerge with steadily increasing flamboyance. It disturbed me, as though I had chanced to observe the growth of a mutant bacterial strain, brought about by an accident of my doing. Apart from that, I felt that whatever way it was leading her, it was bound to be in a direction away from me.

During this time, whenever she went to Dublin she would contrive to extend her stay overnight, leaving me behind to a grimly sleepless night as I wondered what she was up to. She prepared herself extravagantly for these trips, inflaming her face with rouge and lipstick and untying her hair from the top of her head, letting it fall grandly about her shoulders. She did away for good with the sack-like frocks and took to wearing black again, though without the solemnity of her period of mourning for the Judge. Her dresses now reached to the floor and were festooned with brooches, and when she went out she covered herself with shawls or capes, winding long purple scarves around her neck. Even in her relations with me she was more demonstrative, though less intimate, in a manner that I have since heard described as theatrical.

She eventually abandoned domestic service in 1965, airily announcing her decision to me one night as we lay in bed. The days of servants were over, she said, and it was time I learned of life in the city, though I knew even then that the true reason was that she could no longer bear

34

either the isolation or the indignity of repeated dismissals. We set off by coach a day or two later, and I remember well the painful experience of trailing behind her through the city streets, weighed down by two suitcases stuffed with clothes and assorted lenses, my telescope tucked precariously under my arm. I had not been in a city since I was three, and now I did my best to stay within her shadow as we moved along to our new home. I did not like the pandemonium at all. It was a Saturday afternoon and the pavements were brimming. Sharp-faced, cunning-looking boys, the knees gone in their trousers, darted about like beads of mercury, kicking footballs among the throng of shoppers. I dreaded their caustic attentions and pressed closer to my mother, who paraded magisterially on. At O'Connell Bridge she stopped abruptly and hailed someone who to me was an utter stranger – a silver-haired man wearing tweeds – causing me to collide into her back. I tried to manoeuvre myself behind her so that I would not have to speak to the man, but in doing so my feet became entangled and I fell with my bags and telescope onto the legs of a blind man who was begging on the pavement. He clutched me with both arms around my middle and let out an outrageous curse.

'Guards!' he shouted, and then, to me, 'You'll not get away from me, you great fat bastard.'

Locked in his horrible embrace, the smell from his clothing as rancid as the water fungus in the river below us, I felt infused with incurable diseases. I squirmed to free myself, but his grip was positively vice-like. I began to bawl like an infant. By this time the shoppers had formed a little semicircle around us, with my mother and her silver-haired companion enclosed within it and the whey-faced delinquents jeering mercilessly around the perimeter. He finally managed to extricate me, with my mother standing beside him, poised threateningly with my telescope raised over her head.

When I found my feet, shivering with imagined contamination, she fell on me, dabbing at my eyes and murmuring into my ear. 'Poor petal,' she said. 'We'll get you home and into the bath.'

As we lumbered off with our bags, I could hear the taunting echo, 'My poo-ooo-oor petal,' followed by a shrill burst of laughter. Then, 'Fatty, fatty, fatty!' It was ghastly. I pushed on with my eyes to the ground, still sobbing, but I could feel my mother waving back to the silver-haired man – 'an actor of my acquaintance,' she explained to me.

That afternoon we moved into our small attic flat off Merrion Square, and lived there together for the next quarter of a century. It had a fine south-easterly facing façade, covered in Virginia creeper in a Georgian terrace. I found the height of it diverting, looking out past the mews house in the back with its little stone bust, through the complexity of laneways and long gardens, and finally at the City Centre itself, reposing quietly in the haze. At the beginning my mother took a job as a vegetable cook at a hotel, but she abandoned this after a few months and put it to me that, as I had come of age, I could be out earning a regular salary while she would continue to supply our main source of income – 'from dealing,' she said. In practice this meant that a substantial portion of my unpredictable wages was impounded each week for her to take around the antique shops and indulge her obsession with ocular paraphernalia. En route, she picked up many other things as well – flags, cartoons, tapestries, glittering blades, all manner of curiosities – explaining that she used them in her trading but more often than not finding a niche for them somewhere. Slowly and sporadically the flat filled with this exotica.

As for me, for some time I found it difficult to regiment myself to the demands of life in Dublin. I had passed almost the entirety of my conscious life in the domestic quarters of big country houses, and I was wholly ignorant of the empirical world of cities. Like the early Greeks, who put forward fantastic notions of physics and astronomy derived from metaphysical principles which they had only imagined – principles primarily concerned with aesthetic qualities of beauty and harmony – I had neither an experience of this world nor the instruments with which to measure it, and had in consequence to deduce it from ideas I had nurtured in isolation. In particular I did not understand the workings of money. I knew from my experience in the big houses that it was inequably distributed, but I believed that this was in the natural order of things. I knew nothing about such rudimentary matters as regular wages, income taxes, unions, private property or rented flats. My view of the world was essentially feudal, a benign kind of feudalism in which there was an infinite supply of land, living quarters and wealth which was doled out by its owners and protectors, however parsimoniously, as it was needed. My mother was much the same in this respect, with the result that our shared economy was in a more or less permanent state of turbulence.

From the time we came back to live in Dublin, our paths were inclined to diverge, she going off with a kind of fanfare in one direction, and I staying put, as I had always done. Her obsessions drove her harder than ever, and the spells she took continued to propel her on her unaccountable northward journeys. She took on men with an apparent randomness, at first concealing from me her relations with them, but latterly banishing me from her bed to the fold-down couch in our sitting-room, where I cringed alone, listening to the hideous uproar she made with them. All of this, and the passage of the years, had its effect on her, so that the spectacular redness of her hair faded, growing here and there dry and grey as an old coin. Her face grew harder and more lined, her humour crueller, her enthusiasms more unwieldy, and she looked out at the world with a sharpened hunger and diminished expectations. But, in the grace of her movements and the darting speed of her mind, she never quite lost her beauty and, ever in awe of her, for years I pined dreadfully for the intimacy we had known.

On the evening of my birthday, before it all ended so catastrophically, my mother took a photograph of me. When I returned home from the seaside hotel, my mother gone and the flat transformed into that eery, rainforest wilderness, I discovered the photograph among the ancient ragpaper pages of the leather-bound volume on her breakfast table. It marked a page written in Norman French and dated 21 June 1187, a page which I later found to contain a message of great moment to me. I have this photograph before me now as I write and have placed it on a table, side by side with another photograph separated from it in time by some thirty years. In this older photograph, a miniature for wallets, I appear to be smiling, though it is difficult to tell because my head is inclined towards the ground and the image is out of focus. It is summertime, and I am wearing short trousers and a light cotton shirt. My mother is crouched just behind me and to the side, holding me by the arms, her polka-dot dress pulled up over her knees. There is a bow in her hair and she is laughing. The photograph was taken by the Judge not long before his final journey to America, a time when, in our tentative way, we most resembled a family.

When I compare the two photographs I can see that the quaintly porcine shape I had when I was a boy had spread over the years into monumental dimensions. In the later one I am seated in three-quarter profile at our dinner table, my plump webbed hand extended in front of me. The hand is small and pink and unused. The one eye which is visible in the photograph, large, heavy browed and of darkened lustre, does not seem to be focussed on anything in particular. It is, rather, inward-looking, having the appearance of an acquaintance with the unknown while passively uncomprehending it. The face, in its entirety, resembles somewhat the poet Coleridge. The forehead is high and sloping, topped by a pointed crown and rounding as it descends through my features, like an aubergine. The beard, though closely shaven, is darkly grey in outline among the white, almost transluscent skin. The mouth, finally, is gross and voluptuous and the lips are moist and open, as they always are. It is, all in all, quite a formidable aspect, though I never felt that way about myself at the time.

Looking at the two photographs now I feel I can enter more easily into the mind of the boy than that of the man. I remember the tall grass by the river where the Judge stood with his American box camera, and I remember the warmth of the sun that day and the taste of the pears from the walled orchard which we ate with our picnic. I remember particularly well how, in those few years, a fine day like that could come to me naturally, and how, for all my fears and awkwardness, I listened with equanimity to the Judge's ponderings and revelled happily in my mother's love, her affections that summer boundless and her movements astonishingly lithe. But of the middle-aged man I know almost nothing. His visage in the photograph is clear and immutably fixed, like an ivory statue. I remember his loneliness and I can see his preoccupation, but I cannot feel as he did. For this reason I find him fascinating. Proceeding forward from that photograph, my memories become greatly clearer, more vivid to me by far even than those of my childhood. They are the memories of a long, extraordinary journey. But setting out, before I moved about the land and its past looking for my mother, I knew precious little of myself, hardly enough, in any case, to have formed any distinct memories. I lived only by sensations, and the strongest sensation of all at that time was that my mother had formed that incomplete mind and placed it within that grotesque body, and that, in the end, only she could free it.

III

I first met my guide and mentor the morning after I had come upon my mother's disappearance. It was, I thought then, a chance encounter, something that had just happened to me in the way that things had always happened to me up to then, but I later found out that there was little about him that was merely chance.

The day had begun softly enough. I had slept, still fully clothed in trousers and brogues, in my mother's canopied bed, and was awakened by a gentle movement in my hair. It produced a soft, tickling sensation, as though insects were passing along my head in ranks. The movement was so quietly attentive in character that I was not at first inclined either to move or to feel in the least frightened. I lay on my side and opened my eyes, allowing it to continue. Facing me on the bedside table the lamp was still burning. Beneath it, amid my mother's debris of old pamphlets, ointments and syrups and a jeweller's eyepiece, were my parcel of bonbons and the heavy and opulent volume which I had been studying a little before passing into sleep. I felt pleasantly languid, resigned at least to the singular fate of seeking out my lost mother, and for the time being wished merely to lay on in the halo of warmth which I had created around me in the bed. A dim light from the overcast sky was coming in through the parting in the curtains and I could distantly hear the sound of activity in the streets below. I had no reliable sense, however, of the time of day. Nor had I any strong feeling of compunction about ascertaining it. I concentrated instead on trying to catch my mother's scent on the pillow, but the passage of time had obliterated it, leaving only the smell of neglect, of damp and of dust as in a derelict house.

Finally I rolled onto my back and felt the movement in my hair abruptly cease. I looked above me and there, crouching on the headboard and anchored by his tail to the bedpost, was the monkey, his face inclined towards mine and his fingers flexing industriously over my head. His eyes were very wide and his face seemed grey and anxious, like that of an elderly person in hospital. I reached over to the parcel beside me and handed him a bonbon, which he seized eagerly, gnawing at it and finally crushing it between his sharp little teeth before swallowing it down. His features then recomposed themselves and he looked at me plaintively. He had seemed fit and nimble enough, but I could see that his tiny ribs were protruding through the fur along his flanks. I sensed too that his spell of isolation must have taken its toll on his mind.

After a time the monkey clambered down and made off into the sitting-room, where I could hear him entertaining himself on his trapeze. It was a companionable sound, and I enjoyed listening to it after my period of exile. I too arose then and tugged at the creases in my shirt and trousers. At my mother's dressing-table I passed her brush through my disarranged hair and sat down in the chair before her mirror. I could see a thickening darkness around my jowls and pleased myself with the thought that I would not bother to shave. I gamely removed my tie and collar and released the top buttons of my shirt. I looked more deeply into the mirror then, watching my outsized features bulking beyond the fine chalk lines of my mother's self-portrait. There she was, radiant and serene, held within the circumference of my head. It was, I felt then, as though she had inserted herself into me, one being residing within another, as I once had resided within her, and as I watched her thus her expression seemed to change, the eyes moving a little and the look eerily ironical, mocking even, a look I had seen her cast across bars at men. 'Come and get me,' it seemed to taunt. I moved my head about in a vaguely circular pattern, feeling on the edge of vertigo, and she stayed floating there within me, a ghostly pastel orb in my vastness, lighter than air, so light that she would take me upwards with her into the unknown regions she travelled in. I had felt, up to then, that though she was lost I could still place her somewhere, on a distant country road by an orchard, on a railway platform, even, God help me, in a morgue, but swimming thus within me, a thing more of atmosphere than of flesh, she seemed everywhere and nowhere, alive and dead, all at once.

I saw the monkey in the corner of the mirror and turned to face him. I held out my arms as though to a congregation. 'How can I trace a spirit?' I petitioned generally. I made ready to move off then but as I did my feet became entangled in the straps of one of my mother's brassières and I fell resoundingly to the floor, clutching at the breakfast table for support on the way down but instead bringing down upon me an avalanche of biros, rubbers, nail parings, bread-crusts and inkpots. Some of my mother's papers had become dampened with tea and stuck to me all about my person. That crushing dread which in my mother's absences and since the time I had become lost in the Judge's house had so often come near to destroying me now surged within me and I roared to the heavens. I badly needed air. I got to my feet then and divested myself of the papers. Once again I fled my mother's rooms, collecting the remains of Hercules by the door, down the dank stairwell with the monkey gripped by the hand and out into the uncertain light of day. I panted extravagantly at the top of the little set of stairs that led down to the street.

I had to wait a long time for my breathing to abate, but when it did I was able, as before in my life when things of great moment were about to happen to me, to take in my surroundings with a sudden clarity of perception. I noticed first of all, in a rapid sequence, the resonant thud of a demolition ball, followed by the crisp splintering of dry wood and the raining down of masonry and plaster. To my left, deep within the recesses of the neighbouring house, a windowless shell supported by heavy black beams, I heard an echoing splash, as of a stone dropped into a well. Then I noticed the disconcerted murmurings and the petitioning look of the monkey, whose tiny hand I was crushing in a death-like grip. Finally I could see two figures advancing towards me. They were revealed to me in slow gradations through a cloud of fine dust that had been exhaled from the collapsing house a little way down the pavement. One of the figures was a dog and the other was an elderly man, and they were the only living figures within my field of vision. They moved elaborately but harmoniously, like an early piece of farm machinery, all limbs and rising and falling actions. The man, tall and erect and dressed entirely in black, swung a horn-handled walking-stick vigorously outward as he walked and clenched a long-stemmed pipe between his teeth. His black leather trenchcoat was unfastened and billowed slightly in the breeze made by his progress. The dog, a white poodle, zigzagged at the end of his lead from one border of the pavement to the other, like the beam of a searchlight.

When they came even with our gate the dog pulled up short and began to bark insanely. He made a series of high, bounding leaps at us which were ended abruptly in mid-air by his lead, so that he looked like a paddle ball. He was very ferocious and he wore a bright tartan jacket. The monkey had scaled my leg and was hiding in the hollow of my arm and I cowered back into the alcove of the doorway. I had since returning to the city been fearful of dogs on the streets and whenever I ventured out into them I carried a pocketful of stones with which to ward them off. From my position in the doorway then I could see the old man stop and turn, his head snapping around first and followed with theatrical slowness by the rest of his body.

'Atma,' he said, with courtly politeness, 'don't be discourteous,' and the little dog's growl died away. 'He has an irrational aversion to death,' he said to me, pointing with the stem of his pipe at the bundle containing Hercules and looking me squarely in the eye.

I wanted to move away and set about my business, but I seemed to have been overtaken by a kind of paralysis and could not in any case remember what my business was. The man was positioned a little way along the railings from me but even at this distance his look was so formidable and penetrating that it produced in me the feeling that I had been caught out in a lie. I tried to reach for my keys but found that I could neither move my hand nor even take my eyes away from his. I could as it happened see nothing at all around me only his face. He had stunningly white hair, and a voice such as I had never heard before. It had a mechanical, almost sepulchral sound, like the slow opening of a creaking door. It was also exquisitely melancholic, like his watery blue

43

eyes. I could neither assign him a name nor place him in any memory, but as I stood staring at him thus I had the powerful sensation of having seen him before. I had had such an experience once previously when on a week's holiday with my mother in the town of Bournemouth, on the southern coast of England. She had made an uncharacteristic killing on some jewellery she had bought at a house sale and we spent the proceeds on a room in one of the better seafront hotels. I was perhaps twenty-four at the time. The hotel had a small portico around the side which overlooked a bowling-green and upon which it was possible to take afternoon tea. One day quite early in the holiday my mother and I were seated there on a pair of rattan chairs eating a plate of scones and watching the bowlers at their quiet sport. The women, I recall, wore wide-brimmed hats over their squat, cylindrical bodies and the men bulged brightly about their girths. Their skin was reddened from the August sun and they all wore starch-stiffened uniforms of the most brilliant white. In among them as I watched I noticed a face which I knew well – as well, I thought, as the counterpane on our bed back home in Dublin or the mug from which I drank my tea. I stared at the man in silent consternation as I tried to discover his identity, hearing the bowling balls move over the velveteen lawn and their maddening click as they met their objects. I was thoroughly unsuccessful. What was worse, I saw him several other times that week in the corridors of the hotel or about the streets of Bournemouth, with the result that he was seldom out of my mind and the holiday was more or less ruined. It was not until several weeks later, when I chanced upon him again in Dublin, that I realised that he was the head gardener in Merrion Square. As I remained thus similarly tormented by the old man's face I watched his jaw drop and heard him laugh, a sound like the cawing of a crow. He and his dog then moved away down the road, resuming that strangely patterned and synchronised movement, and I stared after them until their diminishing figures were swallowed by the overhanging trees.

When finally I moved from my spot I did so piecemeal and stiffly, as though I had been encased in a plaster cast. The smell from Hercules was overpowering. It was a complicated smell of decay and the sea and it was quite nauseating. I descended the stairs of the concrete well leading to the basement, the two animals in my arms and the old man's shrill laughter still ringing in my ears. The bins here were scattered about, one of them on its side and another spilling over, and in order to reach them I had to make my way through drifting heaps of leaves and refuse, sodden and clinging from the recent rains. We had, in our little street, long been neglected by the municipal authorities. I let the monkey down to stretch his legs and uprighted the bin. I saw then among the leaves in a corner of the well an envelope. It was cream-coloured, and though lightly mud-flecked it was otherwise dry and clean and therefore newly arrived in its place. Within it I found a small wad of papers, clipped together and running slightly with ink. They were receipts, individually dated and inscribed to my mother from an antique dealer with whom she regularly traded and listing on separate pages the following items:

Etruscan figures	£27
compass	£9
binoculars	£14
brat (with brooch)	£35

The last page listed a collection of books and bore a date two days on from my fateful birthday.

The Anatomy of the Eye	£10
Sir Edward Carson, *Speeches*	£22
Antique volume, privately bound	£1

Antique volume? Was this the book I had come upon on my mother's breakfast table and if so how was it that such splendour and venerable age could be had for so little? What on earth was a 'brat'? The compass could suggest a conscious decision to travel, but otherwise the items seemed sufficiently representative of my mother's eclectic interests so that I despaired of forming them into any coherent picture that might suggest her whereabouts. I folded the pages and placed them in my purse and turned my mind instead to disposing of Hercules. I wanted to make for him as decent a resting place as I could, picking a little mournfully among the tins, the congealing food, the sachets of my mother's breakfast tea, and hollowing out there a small, bowl-shaped hole. It was dirty work and I did not like it at all. Just as I was preparing to cover over the corpse, however, I was startled by a distinct chirruping noise, like a cricket. It made my ear itch. This was followed by a ferocious whistling sound and then a great metallic THWACK! A few inches from my face a gold-tipped stick perfectly bisected the circular opening of the bin.

'May I speak with you for a moment?' I heard.

It was the unmistakable voice of the old man. I turned to face him and he was smiling broadly, though his eyes were fierce.

'Would that be an animal you have there?' he asked.

I admitted that it was.

'A pet?'

'Yes.'

'Of what species is he?'

'He's a tortoise.'

He stood at a distance and lifted open the newspapers with the end of his stick, exposing the blanched, drooping corpse.

'*Testudo graeca*,' he said. 'The oldest living vertebrate. The spurred heel is the sign. What do you intend to do with him?'

I was confused by the question and did not answer.

'What? *Speak up!*'

'I'm burying him in the bin,' I said. 'You saw,' I added moodily.

'The bin? How long has he been in your care?'

I looked at the ground and kicked at the newspapers.

'Fifteen years, I suppose.'

'Fifteen years?'

'About that.'

'Perhaps longer?'

'Perhaps.' I shrugged.

'That's a very great while,' he said. 'Many times longer than the lifespan of most creatures. Do you not think some small ceremony would be in order? Proper obsequies and a decent interment?'

46

'I suppose so,' I said. I was still crouched over the bin while he towered above me, his hands folded over the handle of his stick.

'I know the very thing,' he said. 'Earth and water, they are his elements. It will help you to overcome your grief. Come along.'

He prodded me up the stairs with his stick and we proceeded along the road. I followed him doggedly. He ignored me then for a long time while he looked around himself attentively, now and then sniffing the air. We meandered along twisting streets, wide boulevards and in among the mewses, looking from time to time over garden walls. The monkey grew very tired and I had to carry him on my shoulder. Finally we came upon a square and entered it through a locked gate, which the old man opened with a piece of wire and then closed again behind him. Around its circumference were distributed a variety of trees and shrubs, clogged around their bases with weeds. Inside of this there ran a dirt track, containing within it two lawn tennis courts. One net had slackened to the ground in the middle and the other was torn in half. The grass grew wildly and to the height of my knee, and when I set the monkey down he disappeared into its density.

'Water runs along here somewhere,' announced the old man, making his way along the path, stopping and starting and sniffing as he went. Finally he came to a halt. He spread out his feet and planted his walking-stick into the dirt. 'This will do,' he said. 'There, under that bush. Dig a hole.'

I moved a little morosely on my haunches to its edge.

'Further in,' he said.

I lowered myself further, crawling along on my knees through the muddy earth and barbed weeds until I was well under the branches. I began to claw away at the ground with my fingers but I could make no progress as the soil was stony, and I had to complete the job with one of my brogues. When I had cleared a small circular pit about a foot deep the old man ordered me to place a bedding of leaves along the bottom of it and to set Hercules down facing eastwards, the direction, he said, of the underground current. I removed the newspaper wrapping then and prepared to perform my small office. As I held Hercules aloft to stay out of the path of his rising odours I remembered my mother carrying him towards me many years before in a similar posture, borne on her little velour pillow and accompanied by some grandiloquent recording which she had placed on the gramophone. She had just returned from one of her weekend debauches, her hat askew and her eyes leaden with exhaustion. On such occasions she tended to resort to ceremony to get round me. 'Here you are, my petal,' she sang, 'a nice strong companion for you. I once saw a picture of a Hindu tortoise carrying *three* elephants on his back. We'll call him Hercules, shall we? He's Greek. He can protect you when I go away on my little trips.' Then she laughed with outrageous coquettishness. Hercules then was only about a quarter of the size he attained in his maturity, and he spent much of his time retracted well into his shell, looking out forbiddingly like a hermit in a cave. After a time, though, he grew accustomed to us and I used to enjoy watching him manoeuvre nimbly around the table legs and among my mother's curiosities. Now as I held him his feet dangled limply down and his head swung pendulously, like a ball of lead in a sock. I had always, in the past, been afraid to touch dead things, but now I felt moved to kiss his softening shell before lowering him into the earth. He seemed strangely *mineral* in death. Was my mother's skin now cold like his and passing into dust in some distant, unmarked spot? Were the hands that had fed and nurtured me now putrefying stumps, like Hercules' paws? *Would I never feel their caress again?* Tears began to flow freely down my face as I raked with my fingers the clods of damp earth over Hercules' body. My great frame shook convulsively and a deep uncontrollable wailing came pouring from my mouth. The square around me filled with this sound and I did nothing whatever to stop it. The tears of missing and jealousy and pain that throughout my life had burned inside my head now came flooding out of my eyes and onto Hercules' grave. I wept on and on until I felt that I was finished and then I crawled out from under my shelter in the bushes and presented myself to the old man. He laid his hand on my arm and looked at me with the sweetness of a small child.

'Do you love animals, too?' he said gently, and led me over to a bench. 'It shows, if I may say so, in the way you performed the funeral service for your tortoise. Very moving.'

He took a large handkerchief from his pocket then and dabbed at my drenched face.

'These ceremonies are a great boon to us, don't you think? They extract emotions from within us and place them out so that we can see them and put them to good use. That is because they are so elaborately artificial. *Baptism* is particularly useful,' he said, looking at me keenly. 'It employs water to cleanse and renew at the commencement of a journey. I have known hunters and explorers about to embark on difficult and dangerous missions drench themselves in water in performance of this rite. Any water would do,' he said.

He reached into a leather pouch then which was suspended from his belt and made an eery warbling noise through his pursed lips. The monkey came crashing through the undergrowth to the bench, and the old man dispensed some shelled walnuts in turn to him, his dog and finally to me.

'I commend you your monkey,' he said. 'Splendidly turned out. Really very smart. I admire especially his necklace.'

The monkey was before us, still and distant and looking over to the trees, as though he was listening to music.

'My mother dressed him,' I said.

'Your mother?'

'Yes.' I sighed. 'She has a great sense of style, my mother. It's quite unerring. And she's kind and beautiful and very intelligent.' My voice was rising, the tears brimming again in my eyes. 'I've lost her.'

'Lost her? Did she die?'

'*Don't say that!*' I beseeched him. 'She went away somewhere. I came back yesterday and she was gone.'

There was a brief silence during which I tried to keep the image of her at bay.

'Do you know what a brat is?' I asked him then.

'I do. It is a long black cape-like garment worn by women of our race in centuries gone by. Its specific use was for travelling.'

'Travelling? That's worse yet. When she went away before she couldn't help herself. She'd go into a kind of trance. But this time

49

though it looks as though she intended to go away . . . I just can't understand it. No one loves her like I do. How could she desert me?'

'Maybe there is someone you don't know about,' he said. 'Someone who loves her better. Anyway, no matter.' He waved it all aside. 'Perhaps she is setting you a riddle. A person close to me once disappeared and regarding the dilemma as a riddle I was able, with imagination and guile and systematic thought, to trace her. Perhaps your mother is like her. In any event, I recommend the procedure. Now then.' He looked down the stem of his pipe and scrutinised the monkey. 'Your monkey is looking a little peaky. What have you been feeding him?'

'He was eating fruits and nuts,' I said. 'I gave him a bonbon earlier on.'

He continued to regard me expectantly as though I had not spoken.

I looked at the ground. Well I didn't know anything about monkeys, I told him. I intended to seek advice from the zoo.

'The *zoo*? They will feed him dry pellets. Let me tell you a little bit about your friend. He is native to the tropical forests of Central America and is accustomed not only to their verdure but also to the foods available there. He is happiest in the air because although he is a quadruped he is designed most naturally for brachiation. Note the prehensile tail. Aesop believed monkeys to be the most accomplished dancers among the animals, but your monkey dances in the treetops. He can drop spread-eagled from the top of a tree to the lowest branch. Do you know what he is? *A model of controlled abandon*. That takes acute perception. Watch this.'

The monkey was now sitting on my knee, looking out over the tennis courts. The old man reached his arm around behind the monkey's head to a position beside his left ear and rubbed his first two fingers together against his thumb. Out came the chirruping noise which had startled me when I was poised with Hercules over the bin. The monkey rubbed his ear furiously. The old man rocked back and forth on the bench and produced his crow-like laugh, delighted with his performance. The monkey then became very still and seemed to be thinking.

'Perhaps it's a sound his tropical ancestors heard,' whispered the old man.

He repeated his manoeuvre then, but this time the monkey turned slowly towards him and seemed to smile.

'You see, *you see*,' he said. 'Nothing gets past him. He is shrewder than you. I could do that to you all day and you would think it was a visitation by locusts. But your monkey knows how to *listen*. Sensations do not merely enter his system and die there. He knows how to *use* them. There is nothing that happens to the monkey that does not in some way mean something to him. Do you know that if you shot your monkey with an arrow he would remove it and staunch the wound? You would probably bleed to death. Do you know also that a monkey who was a guest in this country in the eighteenth century once saved a Fitzgerald child from burning and in consequence his image occupies a position of eminence in the family crest? In India the monkey walks with men as their equal. You should sit at his feet and become his disciple. Instead you feed him bonbons and bring him to a place of incarceration!'

When he finished he reclined back into the curve of the bench and closed his eyes. The two animals had stationed themselves on either side of him, like sentries. He seemed to have fallen into a deep silence as he had done earlier when we were walking about the streets in search of a grave for Hercules, and I took the opportunity to study him closely. His hair was as white as spun cotton, but where it gathered in curls at the back of his head it was tinted with gold. Beneath it there descended a long angular face, which ended in moist lips and a heavy jaw. There were lines of age emanating from his eyes and mouth, but they were etched lightly, and his pink skin was otherwise fine and delicate, like a child's. His face in repose had a slight smile and was profoundly serene, like the statue of Saint Dominic which I had knelt before and studied so often in my childhood. I looked into his face in silence for a very long time, but as I struggled again to attach it to a memory I noticed his features blurring gradually and moving about. Soon I could distinguish two ill-defined mouths, two pairs of eyes, two noses. These two sets of features were not the same, though they resembled one another, and as they came more slowly into focus I could see that the second set belonged to my mother. Her face became clearer and swam within his as it had swum within mine in the mirror. Gradually my mother's face floated more freely within the old man's and began to move outwards, until it tore itself away, like the splitting of a cell. It hovered in the air, and her body composed itself beneath it then, dressed in a magnificent bridal gown made of cream-coloured silk. As she stood there at the edge of the dirt track before the bench, I could see that she was young, younger than I could ever remember her, and her hair fell in curls about her bare shoulders. She walked lightly out onto the tennis court, seeming to sway to music which I could not hear, a bouquet of roses dangling from her hand. When she neared the centre the old rotting nets disappeared, the willowy grass gave way to a gleaming wooden floor and a circle of blue light formed around her. Along the edges of the circle I placed a crowd of people in evening dress, past which my mother moved slowly, smiling graciously and lightly touching their hands. Beyond the crowd of people and in the sky above there was an impenetrable blackness.

The old man entered the circle then and everyone's eyes, including my mother's, turned to look at him. He too was younger, his hair brilliantined and shining like onyx, though he was not nearly as young as my mother. He was dressed in striped trousers and tails, and on his feet he wore spats the colour of a pigeon's breast. He advanced towards my mother with his hand extended, and when they converged in the centre of the circle of light they began to dance, a slow waltz, moving in long languid circles past the crowd, who had begun to applaud. My mother's face was lifted rapturously towards his and he beamed with magnanimous pride as they danced on. As before, when I had watched the Judge's death, I could hear nothing, but the tempo of the music seemed to increase, because they moved steadily faster, building in momentum until the dance itself took on a life of its own. It was as though they were gliding on ice. I could not control the speed at which they moved, their utter oblivion to all that was around them, and the fury of their spinning brought a lightness to my head. The entire vision began to blur and break up into small pieces. The darkness encroached inwards until all was swallowed in it and I could see nothing whatever.

I waited for some time in this darkness until I discovered that my eyes were closed. When I opened them again I could see that the grey light in the sky was weakening into dusk, but that otherwise things were as I had left them. I was still staring at the old man, the two animals in place on either side of him, his hair white as before and his features composed into an expression of serenity. Somewhere in his face, however, I detected a small movement, and I looked closer. His eyeballs were moving like a dreamer's beneath the closed lids. *I felt that he was watching me*. I jumped abruptly to my feet and grabbed the monkey from the bench.

'I have to go now,' I said.

'Very well,' he replied. His lids rose slowly like stage curtains and revealed his glittering eyes.

'I don't think I can get out of here,' I said.

'Quite,' he said, and opened the gate deftly with his piece of wire.

I stepped out onto the pavement and looked through the failing light at the emptiness around me. The houses distributed around the square were of the same materials and design as those in our terrace, red brick and stately, and they too stood mutely agape, their windows and doors removed and the ceilings and floors letting in light where they had been plundered for wood. It was an area unknown to me.

'I don't know where I am,' I said.

'Well, perhaps I can be of some assistance,' he said, smiling beatifically, a mocking smile, one that assumed his power and my weakness. I placed myself once again in his charge and we set off in a direction different from that by which we had arrived in the square. We tramped on without speaking for what seemed to be miles, a tortuous, complicated route of dim streets, narrow, walled-in laneways and expanses of tarmac containing tall buildings and, here and there, some gutted cars. The murky grey in the air gave way to the blackness of night as we travelled and the streetlamps, distantly placed along the road, came on, their yellow light bleeding onto the roads. There was no sign of the Animal Gang, with their fierce cries and their strange weapons, nor did we meet anyone else along the way, though a police truck with dark windows passed us and the headlamps threw onto the walls the long shadows of figures moving rapidly to and

fro in the courtyards and alleyways around us. I did not like the
journey at all. There was a foul smell about, of oil and bad meat and
damp, smouldering rags, and I had no sense whatever of the direction
in which we were travelling. Once or twice we were forced to traverse
in the darkness large open spaces, fields of broken brick and mortar,
gathered here and there into small piles from which smoke was slowly
rising and where dogs ran wild. The monkey refused to set foot in such
places and I carried him on my shoulder, twisting my ankles and
stumbling as I went. We were both thoroughly exhausted. The old
man, however, carried on unperturbed, never slackening his pace as
he swung his walking-stick out jauntily and whistled a strange and
incomparable tune.

He spoke only once along the way. It was when we came upon a long
deserted block of government flats, silent and dark like a ghost ship,
with green weeds erupting here and there between the blackened
bricks and blue ceramic tiles. Our little procession halted in front of it.
'An ancestor of mine owned these lands once,' he said. 'He was a very
great man capable of maintaining vast and intricate systems within his
mind. By profession he was an industrialist, but he read Descartes
for the sport of it and his principal aspiration was to be a town planner.'
He looked over at me and laughed bleakly. 'What do you suppose he
would have made of these habitations? Shortly after they were built the
pipes began to leak and the sewage commingled with the fresh water
supply, resulting in an outbreak of dysentery. Many died. It is strange,
is it not, the way the past takes vengeance when it has been violated,
even upon the innocent.' He waved his hand dismissively at the building
as we set off again. 'It is only the wind's home now.'

We entered then into more brightly lit and familiar territory,
passing first of all our district's police barracks, the open area in front
of it starkly illuminated by massive floodlights, its east wall still
collapsed and scaffolded from the bombing it had sustained over the
winter, and then along the canal, where I could see the crouched
figures of boys attempting to remove objects from the murky water.
We then came upon the little row of shops nearest my home. Most of
them had closed for the night, but the café where I occasionally took
my meals was still open, its light spilling weakly out onto the pave-

ment. The familiarity of it pacified me. When we were upon it the old man ordered me to wait and stepped in quickly through the door. He emerged then carrying two tiny paper packets of salt. He was smiling warmly at me, his white teeth sparkling in the light.

'New friends should always exchange salt upon parting,' he said.

He lifted my hand up then and poured a little mound of it into my palm. His eyes widened at the sight of it.

'Interesting hand,' he said. 'A sign of our aquatic past.'

'Yes?' I said, my breath quickening.

'Amphibious,' he said, lingering like an epicure over the word. 'It means "double life".'

Had he reached into my mind? Could he see my past as I saw him before me? The Judge had held my mutated hands in his like they were doves. His words to me then were now echoed three decades later, and whatever it is that separates the present from the past was instantaneously removed. That time we had spent together in such happy amity in the big house in Kilkenny flooded into my mind. It came upon me riotously, like the bursting of a dam, not gently, like a recollection. I heard the amplified lapping of water from the river that ran down along the back of the Judge's house and the monstrously loud buzzing of bees from the flowers on its bank. I remembered the smell of the brandy that wafted on the air about his face and the rasping scrape from the bristle on his chin when he kissed me goodnight, and then walking hand in hand with my mother along the long, dark corridors and the smell of violets on her skin. And I heard too the reverberating sounds of her songs as I used to hear them when I placed my ear to her back when we lay in bed. All these things passed around and through me, but as they did I could see and hear too the real world as it was ranged before me. The monkey was in my arms and we were placed within the fall of yellow light from the café. The old man was nodding at me, turning and walking away. The past had heaved forward, summoned, I thought, by him and held in place briefly by me, and had lived for a little time in a continuum with the present. It all ebbed away then as I looked down along the road after the old man. He seemed to me like a sorcerer, ambling along in his mechanical gait, the fine white wisps of his pipesmoke twisting balletically around one another in his wake and the little dog throwing himself upwards against his leg, like a salmon trying to jump a weir. The night finally took him away from me, and I turned towards home with the monkey, trying hard to quell the unknown exhilaration rising within me.

IV

It was at this point that I began to lose my grip on time, as I had known it. I do not know precisely how or why this came about – it may have been the disorienting effect of the old man, it may have been the arcane researches which I then embarked upon – but I found that the pattern of my life was no longer divided into the familiar sequence of seconds and minutes, days and weeks. In the way that astronautical engineers can create space without gravity, I seemed, now and again, to be living in space without time.

Time was a subject upon which my mother and I had always exercised quite a high degree of precision. In the days when she was a domestic we had both fallen unthinkingly into the temporal routine of the household, serving up meals at the appointed hours and learning to pace our leisure according to the intervals between. This regimen was not in the least relaxed when my mother retired and we moved up to Dublin. It was, if anything, intensified. The more unfathomable our life together became – the more she rouged her pallid cheeks, the higher grew her pile of lenses and spyglasses and the more frequently she set off on her wanderings – the more it came to be governed by an infinitesimal punctiliousness with respect to time. We began each day by synchronising our watches and concluded it on the stroke of midnight by brushing our teeth together and climbing into bed, punctuating the hours between with pre-arranged telephone calls to each other, meals announced by handbell and a prescribed evening ritual for each day of the week. Each Friday night at ten, I remember, we tuned into a dance programme on the wireless and waltzed for an hour together around the sitting-room carpet. It was, I suppose, an unnatural fastidiousness, the fastidiousness of the nearly mad. I can still recall the acute discomfort, that feeling of falling into a vortex, very like vertigo, produced by any deviation in the schedule.

In my mother's absence, my life in its sudden formlessness came to resemble that of my companion, the monkey. I remember leaving the old man that night, climbing the reverberating stairwell and falling with profound relief onto the bed. My vast body sank luxuriously into the opal-coloured quilt. My bones ached from all the exertions, but my mind was on fire. Above me, the bare lightbulb hanging from the ceiling was on and there was a profound darkness beyond the window. The clocks on the wall, beside the bed and on the dressing table, even the watch on my wrist, had all stopped, each at a different hour. It amused me to think that these clocks, which had always governed my life with such martial strictness, not only recorded time, but actually *contained* it, and that in stopping so haphazardly, in abandoning their own inexorable laws, they had disoriented the world. I lay on in the bed, thinking too of the wizardy of the old man. He had presented to me a fragment from my past as though it were a peculiar glittering stone he had picked up from the gravel on the road, a thing as present and real as his athletic dog, a thing not subject to the grammar of time. I thought of the inflexibility of the verb tenses, which divided experience into the past, present and future – the irrecoverable, the fleeting and the unknown. I thought too of the Greek word *uaipos*, which carries the dual meanings of time and weather. I came now to sense time as something akin to weather, an encompassing of diversity, and I found that if I lay quietly in the smoothness of the quilt and listened to the musical murmurings of the monkey, more and more fragments from my past came my way, singly and in clusters, so that I could ponder their fine details and place them in different relations, like a child with a sack of wooden blocks. They came forward from a broad territory, not from my life merely, but from my mother's too, anterior to my birth, and even, as my enquiries extended, from the long life of the nation itself. Without them I could not have directed myself to my mother's path of departure from our rooms nor written this account of my journey along it.

While I was thus occupied the darkness beyond the window succeeded to light and then reverted back again, and so on. This oscillating rhythm came to seem to me a kind of leakage, of black into grey and grey into black, back and forth, and I went about my business without reference to it, the electric bulb in the centre of the room glaring on throughout. The monkey, I think, was pleased that I had fallen into pace with him. He was regularly to be found in my vicinity, squatted down before me staring with concentration into my face and now and again erupting into animated monologue, his little brown brow creased thoughtfully and his head moving about like a bird's. He seemed to speak in the full confidence of my comprehension, and I in time came to answer him. Like him I slept and ate not according to the hour of the day, but as the mood came upon me. More often than not we dozed together, my mountainous form lying fully clothed on the bed, the monkey folded in upon himself against my ribs, and when we were hungry one of us fetched food in from the kitchen and we dined together. In these days I grew very close to him, closer, I think, than to any other being in my life up to then, bar my mother.

At some point – I do not know when in the succession of days that followed on from my outing with the old man – I found myself seated at my mother's breakfast table, staring at the large volume that bore the inscription SYNNOTT. My mind had lightened still further in the anarchy of that time, and in the circumstances I found the profound longevity of the book unusually exhilarating, just as, in the museums, I had looked on in wonderment at the bones of the saints in their reliquaries. Its outer design had none of the understated symmetry I had grown accustomed to from the books at Maggs, but was, instead, ingeniously intricate, wayward and explosive, so that each individual tooled line pursued its course through astonishing convolutions to its own unpredictable end. It seemed quite without overall purpose. So tantalising was the effect of this that I could not at first distract my mind from it. Within the book, however, I knew there to be documents encompassing some seven centuries, mysterious documents in a variety of tongues which my mother had travelled in prior to her departure. I opened the cover and passed on to the first full page of text. It was made of vellum, and it gave off a fine autumnal aroma of dry leaves.

59

At the top of the page was a date, 3 November 1169, and beneath it there followed a mass of densely packed prose which seemed to proceed in a continuous narrative for twenty-two pages. It was written out in black ink in a close but impeccable hand. The text, I found, was intermittently inscrutable owing to ruptures in the page and water damage, and the language and even some of its characters were unfamiliar to me, but I determined nevertheless, there and then, to come to some understanding of it. Around the book I cleared a working space in which I placed the two dictionaries my mother had purloined from the library and segregated into two piles, one for each language, Irish and Anglo-Norman French, her translation notes. Taking those words I could decipher from the opening line of the document, I determined from the dictionary that it had been composed from the latter language and I set about, as best I could, making a literal translation. My mother's own word lists were a helpful supplement to my efforts, though, perhaps through haste, I could see that where on average she had translated just under half the words on a given page I, with increased concentration, usually attained nearer to eighty per cent. It was work of a methodical nature, like tillage, and I found it highly absorbing, so absorbing and so prodigiously did I apply myself to it that I gradually lost consciousness of almost everything else around me. Had the monkey not brought me food and pulled furiously at my hair until I agreed to lie on the bed and sleep, I might have become quite ill.

When I reached the end of the first entry I stopped. I did not, of course, have anything approximating a translation. The dictionary was of no help whatever with the syntax, and with that and the missing words I had merely what seemed a random vocabulary. But I had laboured hard over these words, scrutinising some of them for long periods through my mother's mahogany-handled magnifying glass, and so unaccountably hungry was I for the other world which they represented that they were each in their way luminous with meaning to me. I found that if I divided the entry into short sections of up to five sentences each and then repeatedly said aloud the available words, a sense of the author and his message would crudely emerge, like a photograph in a bath of chemicals.

For the first section I was able to compile the following words:

I Hervey Synnott ... seventeen summers ... ...
Meiter, glass-blower ... Flanders ... ... set
down ... ... follow me ... my origins ... my life ... ...
now. ... ... story ... sometimes wondrous ... ...
awful. ... ... Ireland ... 1169 ... ... travels
... talks ... ... tower. I write ... love ... brother
Milo ... ... lord and teacher Bertrand de Paor ...
Bristol ...

From this I determined that the author of the document was called
Hervey Synnott, and that these opening sentences formed a preamble
to an autobiographical account which concentrated mainly on his
coming to Ireland in 1169 and his life there over the ensuing months.
His high rhetorical style, his choice of vellum for writing material, and
the dedication of his labours of composition to his brother on the one
hand and his lord and teacher on the other indicated that he intended
the document not merely as a personal diary but rather as a record for
the benefit of posterity. I felt even then the insistent pressure of his
ancient voice, though I could discern no connection between the book
from which it arose and myself. So, like the dreamer who completes
his dream in the telling, or the historian scribe who refashions the
records while transcribing, I said aloud these and the words which
followed and thereby assembled a narrative. Here, then, is Hervey
Synnott's story as it came to me.

Meiter Synnott, Hervey's father, was a glass-blower from Flanders
who had migrated to Britain in the prosperous aftermath of the
Norman Conquest. He had landed at Bristol in the mid-1140s and
proceeded northwards into Wales, where he established his trade in a
small village in Pembrokeshire, married locally and sired two sons,
Hervey and Milo. When they reached adolescence their father began
to instruct Hervey in the glass-blowing trade and apprenticed Milo to a
local carpenter, and the two boys quickly displayed the skill and
devotion to craft for which their race is widely renowned. Hervey had
dark hair and Milo's was the whitest shade of gold. Hervey loved to

watch green plants growing from the black earth and was happiest sitting in his mother's garden in the summer twilight. Milo had a fierce passion for the sea. He spent his evenings constructing highly detailed model wooden boats and when he completed them he brought them down to a small pool in the field behind their home and moored them at a series of piers which he had constructed along the bank. On fine days in the summer he would lead Hervey down through the field and together they would launch the boats, pushing them out from their moorings with long sticks. Gradually the little pool became as crowded with nautical traffic as the great Channel itself.

One Sunday morning just a few days after his sixteenth birthday, Milo left the house without explanation and did not return. The two boys had loved each other very much and Hervey was bereft in his brother's absence, falling rapidly into a state of lassitude and despair. He kept a watch from the hills around the village and in the evenings he would gaze pitifully into the pool at Milo's beautiful boats. He could neither eat nor focus his attention on the glass-blowing trade, and hideous ulcers began gradually to disfigure his face. After a time he took to his bed and rarely stirred from it. Meiter Synnott had long before that concluded that Milo's love of the sea had finally got the better of him and that he had left home to join a ship as a sailor. He took pity on poor suffering Hervey, who in any case had ceased to be of use to him in his business, and allowed him to travel to the nearby port city of Bristol in the hope of gaining news of his brother. The date of his departure was 9 January 1169, one full year after Milo's disappearance.

1169 was also a fateful year in Irish political affairs. Dermot MacMurrough, the vanquished king of Leinster, had been active in recent times along the western coast of Britain in raising an expeditionary force of mercenaries to travel with him to Ireland and go to war against those of his fellow Celtic clan chiefs who had usurped his lands. He coveted in particular the advanced military tactics and weaponry which had been developed by the Normans and he had already, with the help of Richard FitzGodebert, launched one unsuccessful invasion in the summer of 1167. By the time the poor disconsolate Hervey arrived in Bristol in search of his brother, Dermot was back at his headquarters in Ferns, County Wexford, waiting in tense anticipation while his secretary, Morice Regan, moved again among the Normans looking for recruits.

Hervey's leprous appearance appalled the citizens of Bristol and he was forced to establish himself in a small lean-to in a woodland overlooking the Severn Gorge on the outskirts of the city. There he eked out a tortuous existence over the winter months among the forest creatures, his ravaged skin darkening from woodsmoke and grime and his clothes hanging in ragged strips from his weakening frame. He entered the city only under cover of night, foraging for scraps of food and prowling in a desultory way around the docks, where he enquired among the sailors for his lost brother. They taunted and reviled him, and none of them knew the skilled carpenter with the golden hair.

It happened that Hervey's woodland bordered the baronial estate of Bertrand de Paor, a man of immense wealth and eccentricity, vilified by the local populace for his apostasy but held in awe by them for his extreme cunning and fearlessness. One day after the spring thaw, just after dawn, Bertrand entered the woodland on a mushroom-hunting expedition and came upon Hervey, still asleep under the cover of his lean-to. He tapped him on the soles of his feet and bade him come out. As Hervey rose before him, his spine unable finally to unwind because of the coldness in his joints, his milky eyes looking out from the darkened skin and his mouth hanging mutely open in stupefaction, Bertrand looked upon him not with pity but with nostalgia, the melancholic nostalgia of the newly civilised for the primitive. He collapsed the lean-to with one stroke of his staff, wrapped Hervey within the ample folds of his fur cape and led him away to the warmth and the plenty of his home. This was the beginning of an alliance that was to have the profoundest consequences on Hervey's life.

Throughout March and into April of that year Bertrand de Paor provided Hervey with food and a warm bed in one of his outbuildings in exchange for the performance of some small tasks around the great estate and his submission to such lessons as Bertrand thought suitable for the young man. These included letters and numbers, some botanical and zoological lore, and the great works of antiquity, but excluded the moral sciences and any form of religious instruction.

63

Bertrand found in Hervey a surprising ability to absorb information combined with an inability to place this information into the workable systems of relation known as knowledge. He wondered if his little experiment with the child of the forest might be a failure. The fact was that deep within his soul Hervey still pined for Milo. The ulcers still fouled his face and at night his painful lamentations could be heard pouring out of the loft where he slept. Slowly, like the sap from a tree, his sense and his will to live were passing from him.

One morning as Hervey was in town on some errands he came upon a notice written out in verse and posted on a low wall by the docks:

> *Whoever shall wish for land or pence,*
> *Horses, trappings, or chargers,*
> *Gold or silver I shall give them*
> *A very ample pay.*
> *Whoever may wish for soil or sod,*
> *Richly I shall enfeoff them.*

Beneath the verse there appeared the name 'Dermot MacMurrough – King of Leinster' in an elaborate script, followed by instructions for all interested parties to assemble for a meeting in a dockside inn that same night. The speaker would be 'Morice Regan – Envoy'.

As Hervey continued on his rounds that day he came upon these notices all about the town, publicly posted in conspicuous places and written out in an identical hand, waving mournfully in the breeze that came up the long estuary from the sea. Around some were gathered small crescents of heavy-set men, debating the meaning of the verse and repeating the names 'MacMurrough' and 'Regan' quizzically. Hervey was not aware of the turmoil in Ireland nor of Morice Regan's diplomatic exertions along the coastline, so he did not at first comprehend the signs as Irish recruiting posters. He sensed only in the dimmest possible way that they pointed to some form of exit to an unknown land, a land, he hoped, of peace and forgetfulness, and so painfully agitated had his spirit now become that he would at that stage have cast off to anywhere like a penitential monk in a boat without oars. By midday, when he had returned to the grounds of Bertrand de Paor's estate, he had made his decision to flee.

Hervey was as ignorant of the profound consequences of the action he was about to take as was Dermot MacMurrough of his. Nor indeed did I, as I set out in so amateurish a fashion on my task of translation, sense the meaning that these powerful historical confluences would one day have for me. Hervey would go on to remarkable colonial adventures and become the first protagonist in a story which stretched before me through hundreds of pages in the annals of his family, and the would-be Irish king was to alter his country's history by inviting in skilled warriors loyal to the English Crown. These two fates, the fate of the nation and the fate of the Synnott family, both set into motion by acts of despair, were to mingle and clash in many ways as they wound their way down through the ages before arriving finally at me.

That night Hervey stood in a corner of the inn, beyond the spill of light from the candles on the wall through shame at the blight on his face. The room was a density of men gathered shoulder to shoulder in ranks, and as he stood on his toes looking over their round heads he saw the figure of a man mount a dais. He was tall and lean and scythe-shaped overall. Around his shoulders he wore a black, fur-hooded mantle, and on top of his head was a great shock of black hair which spilled down over his white brow to his eyes. He stood for a time in silence, his chin resting on his chest, so that he looked like a rook about to gather himself for sleep. When he began to speak he did so slowly, in cautious, slightly faltering Norman French, introducing himself as Morice Regan, an Irishman and therefore, he said, a foreigner in Britain like his Norman audience. He came to them as a representative of Dermot MacMurrough, the rightful King of Leinster, who had in recent times been unfairly deposed in a clan war with his neighbours. Far and wide since their exile he and his master had heard tales celebrating the Normans' lust for battle, their bravery and chivalry, their genius for diplomatic and martial organisation, and he now wished to present them with a proposition. If they would sail with him to Ireland and put the King's enemies to flight – and what Celtic cattle-drover, armed only with stones and battle-axe, could stand up to the renowned Norman bowmen and glittering knights on horseback? – there would be lands and treasures enough in the vacated territory to make them all the equals of barons. The land in Leinster, he said, was then as it had always been, unscarred by roads and untrammelled by the crude geometry of agriculture, a rolling green land wound round with silver sweetwater streams, where otters whistled across the lakes and stags belled in the impassable forests, where the greatest pleasure was not to work and the greatest wealth was liberty – a life there of the open air, of hunts over the heathery hills, games of chess in the long afternoons, jugglers in the evening, white-necked women and vats of mead brewed from hazelnuts. 'If you as a race,' he said, 'could become Scots in the Lothians and Sicilians in Palermo, then could you not be Irish in such enchanting environs, where body and soul move with the dextrous speed and spontaneity of quicksilver?' He reminded them then that history is like a mill-wheel, and while they had been steadily ascending in England during the hundred years since their victory at Hastings, the epoch was now sated with them and they could now expect to descend through the long arch towards darkness. As he spoke about these things his hands waved excitedly before him like wings and his words took flight, entrancing the burly men ranged out before him in the room.

He rooted then among the folds of his cloak and pulled from it a large gold necklace, which he held aloft and let fall on his wrist, rotating it about so that it gleamed in the candlelight. Hervey went up on his toes again to get a better look and as he did he saw among the sea of corrugated pates and dun-coloured locks a head of white-gold, catching the light like the necklace and matching its luminosity. Up on the dais Morice Regan continued to speak but Hervey could no longer hear him. He concentrated only on keeping the golden head in his view and, when the speaker's voice was replaced by the murmur of agitated interest from the crowd around him he stepped forward and was buoyed along in the great press of men. He struggled and kicked among their heavy shoulders, inching his way through them like a drowning man moving through water towards a floating plank of wood. His heart was pounding in his ears. When he neared the golden-haired man he reached out and touched him on the shoulder. The man turned. And it was he. It was Milo, his brother. The two of them fell upon each other then in a rapturous embrace, the surging men buffeting them about like a leaf in an eddy of wind, and as he held

Milo tightly to his breast, the tears falling from his eyes, Hervey felt his long-standing burden fly from him as though through an open door. They moved forward together to the head of the room, where Morice Regan was inscribing names on a long sheet of parchment, and added theirs to the list. That night they talked the dark hours away in the hold of the boat where Milo had been working, each telling of their dismal year of exile from the other, of Bertrand de Paor, the strange and benevolent baron, and of life on the high seas, and they slept finally on some straw under cover of an old jib. When Hervey awoke the next morning he looked into a glass and saw there a face with the perfect smoothness and roseate glow of a peach.

Hervey presented himself to his master a few hours later to tell him of his plans, a broad winning grin traversing his clear face and his chest puffed out like a pigeon's. Bertrand, it happens, had somewhat anticipated him. His sprawling English estate had been assembled over the middle years of the century through the keenest, most opportunistic dealing, and when he had learned of Morice Regan's movements along the coast he had moved quickly to buy the largest boat in the Bristol docks that he could find, leasing it out to the desperate and spendthrift Irishman immediately upon his arrival in the city, the inflated fee for the single crossing to Ireland's south-east corner more than doubling the purchase price. He seemed to accomplish these financial coups with the effortlessness of a flame consuming a dry twig. After Hervey had made his announcement and Bertrand had in turn told him the coincidental tale of the boat – which, even then, was being loaded with the equipment of war – the old baron stood for a long while in silent thought, tapping his front tooth with the nail of his index finger. Hervey waited before him at attention, a new alertness in his manner. There was, too, something like love in his eyes. 'I think I will come with you,' Bertrand said at last. Perhaps, considering the revived aspect of his pupil, he was not yet ready to abandon his pedagogic experiment.

And so it was that they sailed for Ireland in the springtime of that year aboard Bertrand's boat, the *Pythagoras*, one of three expeditionary ships containing a voluble throng of Flemish mercenaries, Welsh bowmen, Norman knights and horsemen in coats of mail and a contingent of religious zealots intent on the task of bringing the anarchic Irish church into line with Rome. The vessel had acquired its distinctive name in honour of Bertrand's favourite pastime, that singular delight he took in numbers and above all in the strange fusion of mysticism and the science of mathematics executed by the first and, so Bertrand thought, the most entertaining among the philosophers, and the man he therefore felt compelled to honour in some small way. Milo was the ship's carpenter and Hervey attended to Bertrand's personal needs, and all through the journey they composed an excitable little trio, quite light-headed with the adventure of fresh territory. They kept watch for the green corner of the new land from the bow of the boat, the *Pythagoras* rolling languorously in the long waves, Bertrand standing with his arms around the two brothers in the fresh salt spray and the sea breeze, his grey beard wagging furiously as he poured into their ears his enthusiasm for the unknown.

The three ships landed at Bannow in Wexford on Mayday, and there the passengers pitched camp and awaited the arrival of Dermot, who had been summoned from his headquarters in Ferns. Hervey walked about in the twilight on the spongy earth in a state of wonder, his step delicate, as though he were treading on someone's skin. Afterwards, the warriors had a riotous night under the open sky, dining on pigs and mead which they had commandeered locally, their babel of chatter and battle songs rising into the dark air for many hours. At first light, when they could see the royal retinue approaching in the distance, this party of adventurers ranged themselves out across the landscape in a ceremonial line of three hundred men, a perfect stillness among them save for the white trace of their breath on the morning air. Dermot passed solemnly along the line, kissing each in turn on the cheek. He then led them northwards, into battle.

Bertrand de Paor and his small party followed along in the eery quiet of their wake, examining the countryside for a suitable site for settlement. Some two days' march inland from Bannow, not far from Bertrand's open-air establishment at Ferns, they came upon a fine hill, topped with a flat grassy meadow which overlooked from its pinnacle of safety the dark solitude of a wood, and they settled in there to build concentric circles of stone walls around a high wooden tower. Milo, whose skill at carpentry had progressed steadily into a capacity for design, conceived the plan and supervised the construction. It was an ambitious project, rising from a narrow base to what was then, in Ireland, an unprecedented height, and from its highest room Milo could gaze across the verdant miles upon the sea which he loved so well.

At this point in the unfolding of Hervey's story, as I spoke his words turn and turn about, I saw in the words and through the gaps between them a sudden and unexpected picture of this man, some eight and a half centuries old as I write these words, but then, in his story and in my picture, only seventeen. I saw him stride with purpose from the wooden tower set high on the flat-topped mound overlooking the undulating landscape. About him there were short stout men in leggings and subfusc tunics, carrying on their shoulders heavy logs that had been cut away from the edge of the forest below. His mouth opened to each of them in buoyant greeting and he continued on over a footbridge which spanned a ditch and then through a bailey where weapons were stacked – heavy mailcoats, bows and javelins in racks. His face was active and harmonious in the morning light. The outer gate led him to the top of a newly cut road which wound down the mound, through a pasture and finally to a river, where a group of men were building a bridge with stone. They were different from the men carrying the logs within the enclosure. Their cloaks, floating on the surface of the rushing water as they laboured with their stones, were brightly coloured and their hair was red or yellow or green, like the feathers of my mother's tropical birds, and the river, as it turned here by the bridge, was violet or olive or pink according to the way the early morning light struck it between the trees.

Hervey strode on down the road and broke off to cross over a field to an enclosed pasture, where beasts were grazing. He picked a wooden pail from the wall and bent down to milk a cow, pulling vigorously at the udders, his head thrown back in happy abandon. He stood up then with his feet planted well apart and raised the pail to his lips, letting the golden milk run in streams down the corners of his mouth and into the hair growing in thick clusters on his chest. He looked for some time then towards the river, at the men in their labours who seemed now to be singing, smiling a little and fingering the while something which he held within the folds of his tunic. He let the pail fall and headed back towards the tower across a ploughed field, the rich black earth squeezing up between his toes and the delicate green sprigs of the crops receiving the sun on this fine day. He met the road as it entered the gate, but instead of following it up to the tower he moved along within the outer wall to a ridge set into the curve of the hill beneath its flat summit. Here he dropped to his knees. Bending low he scooped out a little hole in the black earth and then took from a pocket within his tunic a simple gold band. This he placed carefully into the centre of the hole. He covered the hole then and gathered the loose earth which remained into his cupped hands, breathing deeply to take in its aromas. His lips moved rapidly and formed a short sequence of words, but I could not hear them, and when they stopped he placed the earth into his mouth and began to eat. I could see the clumps of earth breaking over his white teeth and turning to mud in his saliva, and when I looked past his mouth I could see that the bridge builders, whom I knew to be natives of the district, had formed a ring around him and were looking on in quiet appreciation like the group of people in evening dress whom I had seen gathered around my mother when she danced on the lawn tennis court with the old man.

I tried hard to hold on to this picture as it began to decompose, but found that I could not, and when my eyes focussed again on the things around me they alighted on the monkey, who was seated on the table looking at me with some concern. I thought it best to pause then, for his sake more than mine, for it was clear that the expression on my face, so savagely contorted through its efforts at concentration, had distressed him. We went into the kitchen and fetched some water and fruit, which we took together in the sitting room while listening to a programme of show tunes and gentle ballads on the wireless. The monkey liked to listen to the wireless while I was at my labours and had by now learned to turn it on for himself. I knew this particular programme very well, as it had always occupied a regular position in my mother's and my week. It occurred to me then that it must be a Wednesday evening, and so long had it been since I had taken any notice of the days of the week that the very word 'Wednesday' amused me and caused me to laugh aloud. The monkey joined in the spirit of things by running chattering around the room and performing some superbly executed somersaults along the bars of his trapeze set. I wondered had he ever entertained my mother in this manner. We each had a bonbon then and, carrying the picture of Hervey Synnott and the grounds in which he lived which I had developed in my mind, I returned to the table in the bedroom and resumed my labours.

Taking up where I had left off, and chanting again the short sequences of words from the list which I had compiled, I found that the vigour of Bertrand de Paor's curiosity was now being expressed in a series of exploratory tours of the district which surrounded his famous tower. He was accompanied always on these excursions by a smartly turned-out guard of a dozen armed men and Hervey, his young pupil, who looked forward to the outings with an almost tremulous eagerness. They were impromptu affairs, organised quickly at the whim of the master, and the little group moved along at a carefree, lolloping pace, their destination unknown so that Bertrand might scrutinise the phenomena of the natural world as they were there displayed and come upon its human settlements as chance presented them. These observations formed the basis of a series of lectures spontaneously composed around whatever topics they suggested to Bertrand, and Hervey, his mind quickened by the challenges of the new land and his spirit freed from the tyranny of its despair now that he had been reunited with Milo, was coming into his own as a student.

One fine afternoon in autumn, on their way home after a looping northward journey, they paused by a small lake to examine some berries that grew close to the ground.

'I have never seen such berries before, have you, Hervey?' said Bertrand at length. He placed a handful in his mouth and chewed, letting the red juice spill into his beard. 'Most rare and succulent.'

He positioned himself then on a stone and readied himself for a discourse. His head was held high and the low afternoon sun at his back shot through his hair and beard so that his face was wreathed in light. Between his thumb and forefinger he held the red berry which he would use to illustrate his talk. Hervey sat on the grass below him and the soldiers went off to the lake to bathe.

71

'We are fortunate, you know Hervey,' began the old man, 'to be here in Ireland, a country brimming over with prodigies of nature which I believe to be peculiar to itself. I have been thinking about this since not long after our arrival here, and I have come to the conclusion that such unusual manifestations as these' – and here he held the berry aloft – 'are the consequences of being here in the Western extremity, well away from the world's centre whence we came. When I was about your age I had occasion to travel to the East as part of a commercial expedition. Here too can be found a portion of natural wonders – such things as silk worms and gems and aromatic spices, flowering plants with the most eccentric foliage, beasts the size of a house, and herbs which can cure warts and others which can make you dream, even when you are awake. It is as though Nature too has her golden mean, which finds itself at the geographical centre, but when moved to remoter parts she relaxes and indulges herself in the creation of rare and secret freaks. Consider for a moment just a few of the things, quite undreamed of where we come from, which have been reported to me as being contained in this country. An island where no one dies. A well that can turn a man's hair grey. A wolf that could speak and a woman kept by the King of Limerick with a long beard and a mane of hair down her spine. In Ulster, it has been said, a great fish appeared on the shore with three gold teeth. There is also the uniqueness of absence. Have you ever seen a frog or any species of poisonous reptile since our arrival?'

Hervey assented that he had not, but so dazzlingly did Bertrand move his fingers before him in the light, and so mellifluous was his voice, that Hervey believed that he could conjure up any of these apparitions out of the air.

'I am given to understand that they are banned from this land. A merchant of my acquaintance, a sober man, not the least credulous, once told me that when some labourers of his were unloading their cargo in an Irish port they found a gathering of frogs in the bottom of the hold. They threw them out onto the shore but immediately they touched land they turned their bellies up, burst in the middle and died. Can you credit that? But the most astonishing thing of all that I heard was of an illuminated book that composed itself spontaneously in a cave. I would suggest, Hervey, that here in Ireland we are inhabiting the world's margins, as it were, as in such illuminated books where the phantasmagorical figures painted in the scriptoria with such daemonic intricacy suddenly reveal with their outlandish poetry a truth that is approached more prosaically in the text itself.'

Bertrand paused here for a moment to savour this formulation.

'But it would be unwise of you to become captivated merely by the bizarre – however seductive,' he resumed, a pained look passing briefly over his features, like a sudden breeze rippling a pond. 'In any case all that I have said is merely hearsay. These things have been no more verified than the monstrous figures with multiple heads and bestial shapes carved into the doorways of churches and said by our priests to inhabit the "Unknown World". This is the sort of paradox in which they deal – if it is unknown, how is it that they know of it? Now the point for you to bear in mind, Hervey, is that you must always and everywhere endeavour to keep your senses open, for there is no living thing, however ordinary, that does not carry a pleasure and a meaning unique to itself, but which might, nevertheless, sometimes bear comparison with our human world and thereby illuminate a truth about it. This process of comparison is called metaphor, often used by artists. Aristotle called it "the perception of the similarity of differences".

'Look,' he said then, 'look.' Bertrand dismounted from the stone and bent low by some reeds, pointing to a flock of cranes that were arranged on the opposite shore of the lake. 'See the cranes? Nothing in the least freakish about them, is there? They are well known in England. Now, do you see the solitary one set apart from the others? What is he clutching?'

The bird was standing on one leg clutching something in his free claw which Hervey could not identify.

'My eyes are better than yours even though I am four times your age. Or perhaps it is my ability to observe that is better. The thing which the crane is clutching in his claw is a stone. Now that the light of the day is failing and the flock wishes to sleep, one of their number is posted as sentry to keep watch against predators. The sentry approaches his duty with the utmost seriousness, so much so that he clutches a stone so that if he chances to drop off to sleep while on guard the stone will fall from his grasp and awaken him. Remarkable, isn't it? Now this practice reminds me very much of the rule of life in monastic communities. There the monks train their thoughts with such single-minded intensity on their Scriptural devotions that if for a minute they become distracted from them, the mind, missing the thought it has grown accustomed to, will become alerted as to its absence and resume its holy task. Both activities, that of the crane and that of the monk, are defensive, sometimes fearful and, though based on observation, are concerned not with the expansion of knowledge but with the preservation of the status quo. And so it is that the metaphor of the crane allows us to see the monk in a new way.

'Now if the crane and the monk, to take the argument to another stage, do share these characteristics, then perhaps, as Pythagoras believed, there is such a thing as the transmigration of souls, where a single essence passes through numerous physical forms, both animal and human, taking some of the flavour of one form on to the next. Perhaps this is the fundamental basis of all metaphors about animals and humans. Did you know, by the way, that Pythagoras preached to animals as well as to humans? Well, he did. Now look closely at me. See the sturdy build, the overall greyness of aspect, the square face within the round, compact head, and above all the fine hooked nose? We have already mentioned my keen sight. Now what do these things put you in mind of?'

Hervey pondered for a moment and then suggested some sort of bird, perhaps a bird of prey.

'Well done, my boy! But not the eagle, proud and magnificent and soaring to impossible heights. The nature of the eagle allows him to look squarely into the sun, but his magnificent aspirations sometimes bring him so close to it that his wings are burned and he crashes to the ground. Or so at least fable has it. I am more like the falcon, I think, a creature of caution and abundant guile – the qualities that made me rich, Hervey. I am proud to note that my features and the features of the falcon coincide with the classic features of our race, and also that the Irish sky is crowded with these wonderful birds. Perhaps this bodes well for our future here.

'Now the trouble with advancing the argument about metaphor too far is that the two elements being compared lose their distinctness and the comparison itself assumes a life of its own. This is how religions are born. The senses experience diversity but the mind is attracted to perfect shapes, to symmetries and unities and hierarchies. I myself, as you know, enjoy numbers for this reason, particularly Euclidean formulae. But I enjoy them merely as a game of skill, an entertainment like any other, and because there is a certain beauty in their operation. Certainly not because they represent a truth. Algebraic identities are, after all, a species of tautology. But to return to the point, the mind, being so disposed, conceives a theory whereby not only are the senses derogated as purveyors of truth, but the whole sensible world to which they relate comes to be regarded as illusory and base, and altogether inferior to the perfect and eternal and uncomplicated world as conceived by the mind. This theoretical world, which, remember, has no basis other than the mind's attraction to its shape, is thus used absurdly to explain the sensible world. This is how poor and unsubtle metaphors come to be made. I once endured a sermon by a Welsh churchman in which he compared the swan's habit of singing at the point of death with the soul joyously celebrating its release from the world and its imminent union with God. What rubbish! What can he know about souls and God and life beyond the grave, or for that matter about the simple happiness of the body and its perceptions? In our comparison between the sentry crane and the meditating monk at least both the elements in the comparison retained their individual integrity and are observable to all as aspects of behaviour or thought. You and I are sensible men, Hervey, who know that the world actively celebrates irregularities and cannot therefore be made to accommodate itself to the shapes which please the vanities of our minds. The churchmen, the system-makers, are different. They proceed from the idea rather than the evidence, discount everything which does not fit into the pattern of the idea, and thereby go blind about. *How I loathe them!'* wailed Bertrand. 'They are the bane of our age. Not content with being blind themselves, they must perforce make others blind also. Have you seen the look of insensible smugness on their faces? The world is choked with them now, with this great proliferation of sects all claiming that their ridiculous cosmologies and rituals reflect the true interpretation of the Word. What is this Word, I ask you? Whatever it is it appears to have gone into the ascendant over the thing or things to which it refers.'

Bertrand placed the berry in his mouth in an attempt to quiet his agitation.

'The falcon sees,' he said, 'and with his sight he carefully surveys the whole land before making one economical move. I am preparing myself to make my move.'

He then took up another of the berries and displayed it as before.

'You will be glad to know, Hervey, that I am now entering into that part of the lesson known in the science of rhetoric as the peroration, and that you will therefore not be required to stay seated much longer in the dampening grass and the vanishing light. Now, you will remember that I began with these berries. I passed on from there to the abundant natural curiosities said to be present in this country, and thence to a discussion of metaphor, the method of bringing into comparison disparate elements in the observable world so that one might illuminate the other. I then extended the idea of metaphor by speculating on the connection between the appearance of the natural world and what we understand as character, or perhaps soul, citing Pythagoras' theories. This in turn provoked an attack on the folly of allowing the idea inherent in the act of comparison to supersede the things being compared – of thinking, that is, always by means of general principles. Principles, if there are such things, must be firmly based in the observable and very beautiful world around us, and must therefore account for its magnificent diversity. I do not believe that it is possible, Hervey, to think in this blind and debilitated manner if you truly love the world. The churchmen have arrogantly elevated con- tempt for it into a fundament of their theology. Those soldiers over there trying to keep warm by the side of the lake cannot afford to love the world because otherwise they would be unable to do their jobs. The ultimate expression of this sensibility is in the tyrant, particularly the tyrant with a religious or political mission, because he will be inclined to annihilate everything that does not conform to his ideal. But all of us are prey to lapses in apprehension due to the governance of our rigid minds. These matters form the essence of what I have been trying to teach you since I came upon you that morning in the forest.

'Now where I am leading you to in all this, Hervey, and what I want
to put to you is my belief, following upon my observations of this new
country during the tours we have been making, that we are fortunately
placed here in Ireland to attempt an intriguing experiment based upon
the ideas which I have been expounding on this afternoon. The
experiment is essentially an attempt to strike a harmonious balance
between the characteristics of our race and those of our hosts, which I
perceive at present to be diametrically opposed. We are town builders;
they are pastoral. We can generalise; they see everything in the
particular. We tend to be even-handed and restrained; they celebrate
the final realisation of the passions. Likewise, while we are sanguine
they are fatalistic. They are strongly bonded culturally but politically
disparate; we are the inverse – we do not care about racial memory, but
we thrive on the building of societies. I could go on. Such sets of
opposites are replicated through all the aspects of living. I do not think
it takes a seer to predict with confidence that we are merely the first in a
long line of our race that will come to these shores in search of
opportunity, and that therefore these sets of opposites will become so
prominent that the way in which they are handled by their representa-
tives will determine how life is to be lived here for many centuries to
come. When such opposites are placed side by side they may conflict or
they may decline to have any relation whatever with one another,
though I think this latter is the least favourable of all courses, as
isolation is inevitably followed by degeneration. If there is conflict,
one side may annihilate the other, or, as Heraclitus has suggested, the
two may be suspended in a perpetual war, a finely tuned strife where
each lives from the death of the other. Here you have neither harmony
nor balance, and certainly not progress – but only stasis, or regress.
There is, however, another course to take with respect to opposites,
and here I return to the fundamental need to keep your senses open. If
you are governed and therefore blinded by principle, you will see that
which is opposed to you only in so far as it differs from you, and you
will therefore wish either to destroy it or to flee from it. If, however,
you can truly *see*, you will comprehend that that which is your
opposite is in possession of something which you lack, which may in

fact be your complement. And this is how I have come to understand our relation to the Irish.

'The fundamental act is the act of perception. From that all else follows. Now I believe that our ability to organise has been developed at the expense of our ability to perceive. For the Irish, on the other hand, perception is everything, and in many ways their thinking stops there. I have never met a people so hostile to intellectual systems. They abhor religion just as much as they abhor money-making and towns. Unlike you, I have taken the trouble to learn their language and I was therefore able to follow the lines of the poet who recited during our visit to the O'Rourke household last month. His verses cursed, they lamented, they satirised and they celebrated, but they did not attempt to elaborate these sentiments into a system of belief. When he spoke of the taste of the wild bees' honey or the scent of the wolf-packs in winter or the sound of dogs running home in the wind along the strand, he did so with awe and wonder, and not because they glorified the wisdom of God. I put it to you, Hervey, that the Irish perceive each particular thing in the world for its own value, and not according to how it fits into a system, whether a system of expediency, like agriculture, or a system of belief, like religion. The proof of this is in the great number of names they have for things and places. Where you see merely a stretch of land they see an intricate complexity of individual details, each with its own history and meaning and purpose. This is what they can teach us, and through them, perhaps, we may recapture what we have lost.

'The problem with this manner of living is that it is no longer compatible with the deployment of force in the world. We are privileged to observe it merely because the Romans never came here to supplant it with something else. But now we are here, Hervey. Our systems – systems of roads and ports and towns, of law and commerce and religion, and above all of war – are the means by which we have survived and prospered. Against them the Irish can put up no defence whatever. You were proud when you told me of how Morice Regan praised our soldiers, those barbarians there by the lake. But if they are allowed to pursue the course that has been set for them they will not only slaughter our hosts but take away our *eyes*.

'I come now finally to the experiment. My intention is to bring together on our lands a group comprised of one hundred people, fifty each of the Irish and of us, and to see whether the idea of the complementariness of opposites is demonstrable in fact. Now I understand, as you will have gathered from my talk with you this afternoon, that societies, like languages, do not come into being in an instant according to design, but rather take their shape through usage. I will therefore encumber our small society with the least possible number of precepts. Firstly, its members will be recruited and distributed as to age and sex and occupation according to the proportions normally to be found in both our regions of the world, and secondly, where the pairs of opposites are mutually exclusive, we will endeavour to find a third way. Such is the case in the matter of the administration of land, where there is no mingling possible between our baronial and Irish clan systems. Here I propose common ownership, where there will be neither king nor baron but where each member in exchange for his labours will receive an equal share of the yield. There will be neither clerics nor monks, unless they are willing to convey their learning in a secular manner; no soldiers, and no money, lest the disproportionate accumulation of it disturb the balance. From our people will come the craftsmen – the nailmakers, the tanners, the wheelwrights, the joiners, the tinsmiths, the coopers and so on, as well as men capable of the management of large farms. Milo can assemble a small crew and sail the *Pythagoras* back to Bristol to gather them up. The Irish will manage the beasts – the cows and oxen and sheep – for they have built their lives around these creatures, and will also provide the poets, the musicians, the men of law and of learning. Most significantly represented of all will be the men and women of your generation so that they might commingle across the boundaries of race and bring forth, for in their issue may best be determined the success or failure of the venture. Previously such speculative ventures as the settlement of Sparta or the theories of Plato and Plotinus were confounded by their dull assumption of uniformity. We, on the other hand, shall celebrate diversity. Think of it, Hervey! The men of craft will teach us their skills and the scholars their learning. The poets will teach us to look, the musicians will teach us to listen and the women will teach us to love. You do not yet know woman, do you Hervey? I have known many. You know I lay with O'Rourke's young niece after the revelries there last month and I tell you I do not think I have ever met before such unaffected vigour in a woman. Here, have a berry.'

Bertrand de Paor picked one of the succulent fruits for his young protégé and then mounted his horse. The soldiers followed suit. They rode homewards then through the darkening twilight, accompanied the while by the autumnal smell of turfsmoke from unseen settlements and the night noises of animals. They rode along the edges of woodlands that held a low, milky mist around the bases of the trees, over hilltops where stones had been heaped into strange patterns of stacks and rings, and through streams, where the black water rushed around the mossy rocks. Hervey took it in with a new acuity.

Bertrand spoke only twice in the course of the journey. On the first occasion he said: 'The falcon's qualities of cunning and ruthlessness are formed when he is a fledgling. A Latin monk called Cassiodorus wrote many hundreds of years ago that these birds expose their young to the exigencies of nature by expelling them early from the nest, beating them with their wings and compelling them to fly and sentencing them forever to exile from their families. In ancient Sparta they pursued a similar policy with their young, drowning those of a weak disposition and exposing the others to extremes of discipline and elemental discomfort. The result was a nation of killers. This, in a way, is what my father did to me when he placed me on the trade routes, alone. I learned, I suppose, through fear to manoeuvre my way through the world, and thereby accumulated my fortune. I have been trying ever since to rid myself of the resulting single-mindedness of purpose. It is because I expect treachery at every turn, you see? Now I am looking for something entirely different in the evolution of our little society. Instead of being like falcons, who have been orphaned as fledglings, I would like our young to be more like the creatures called elephants which I saw at Jaipur, for whom every cow in the herd acts as mother, until a certain ripeness is attained. You are not ripe yet, Hervey.'

Bertrand did not speak again until the clouds had parted and let through the diffused white light of the risen moon. It gave all the land around a cool blue-green look, even the low-lying mist that hung over the grass, and Hervey watched it ripple and stir as the horses trotted through it. He was startled then when Bertrand let out a sudden exclamation.

'Ha! Hervey, look!' he said, pointing to a squat, pulsating form on a stone. The moonlight shone along its green back and its bulging eyes gleamed blackly. 'It's a frog!'

The creature sprang from its position then, its legs splayed as it sailed through the air, and it neatly entered the foaming mist without a splash.

'Another theory demolished by the splendour of living evidence,' said Bertrand, and his resonating laughter filled completely the bowl in the landscape through which they were passing.

V

The season, I discovered, had turned. The light, as I walked on through the cooling air, was murky, suggestive of dusk. The last time I had been abroad in the streets in light such as this they had been thronged with people moving hither and thither, speeding homewards from their work places with their newspapers and satchels tucked under their arms, the noise and fumes of the city rising into the atmosphere like steam from a boiling pot. Now the population was sparser, and the pace more leisurely. The neon over the arcades along the wide boulevard in the City Centre glowed faintly in the last light of the day, and the burble of electronic noises from the machines within quickened in pace. The temperature too seemed a little warmer. I concluded that we were approaching the near edge of the summer.

I turned left at the bridge and proceeded along Bachelor's Walk towards the Antiquarian's whose name I had found on my mother's receipts. I had been drinking rum through the afternoon in a public house in Anne Street and with the greatness of my dimensions amplified by my uncertain swaying across the pavement I scattered pedestrians all about me as I advanced. The Antiquarian was still there at his counter, a small reedy man, quite alone and unprotected in the normal manner by a chain-link grille. The monkey and I came in and bore down upon him, brandishing like a warrant the wad of receipts. My beard was now long and copious, my hair fell over my shoulders and my eyes were ringed darkly as though bruised. My teeth were domed along the top row with a green moss-like substance. Though I meant the man no harm at all I had, since my mother's disappearance, lost track of the common manners of polite discourse. I believe he was quite unnerved. He stood very still, but he moved his thumb persistently in a circular pattern over his index finger, as though he was rolling a wad of paper into a ball.

I pointed to the item marked 'Antique volume' on the receipt and described the elaborate panelling.

The man cleared his throat.

'Yes, I do remember the book, sir, of course I do,' he said. 'A most unforgettable production, a masterwork of its kind –'

He enthused nervously at some length until I interrupted him.

'Where did you get it?'

The monkey had been gambolling among the hatboxes and lamp-shades along the shop's dusty upper shelves and was now installed in a glass case by the till, trying on rings. Wherever we went he behaved vandalously, scattering chocolates in the newsagent's, throwing ashtrays in the pub. The man looked down at him, his brow furrowed, and spoke more slowly.

'He did tell me some months ago that I might expect you. Each week he comes in to see if you have called. He said I would know you by the monkey, same as she had with her the day she bought the book.'

He raised his pale eyes to mine.

'Do you know her, sir? She used to trade here often, one of the regulars I would say. But it is so long since I last saw her. Is she all right, do you think?'

I winced. Never was my mother so emphatically around me as in her absences.

'Just tell me, please. Where did you get the book?'

'It's all a little mysterious, this. A Mr Declan Synnott gave it me. Do you know him at all? No? You see, he wanted very much for the woman to have the book as a gift, but he did not want her to realise it. He wanted her to think she had come upon it by chance, that she had discovered it, so to speak. He knew that she traded here and he brought it into me on the understanding that only she was to have it. The idea was that when she came in we would talk business for a while, exchange a few knick-knacks in the usual way, and then I would contrive to draw her attention to Mr Synnott's book, perhaps feigning interest in some of the baubles she carried around in her pouch. We

83

would haggle a bit, and then I would offer her the book for an unrefusable price. And that's how it happened, one pound on the receipt as you can see, along with a few worthless rings. I remember her eyes grew big as moons when they first fell on that book.'

Who was this man Declan Synnott? I had never heard my mother utter this name, never came upon it at all until I saw it inscribed across the cover of the book. I attempted to speculate on the meaning of what I had been told, but I felt a little vertiginous and my mind moved lugubriously, like a pearl sinking through syrup. The little man behind the counter, however, had found his form.

'Mind you, I hated parting with it,' he said. 'A collector comes to recognise the unique instinctively, you see, and that book most certainly had it. The cover, so rich and symmetrical, gave it a classical weight, as though you were holding time in your hands, but when you opened it, it was strange, all those diverse hands and languages, it was like the powerful discordance of a symphony orchestra tuning up . . .'

He pursued this course for some time, and as he spoke I felt a little movement within me, as of a small gear finding its cog. The process came briefly to life. I began to nurture in my mind a picture of the engineer of this transaction, this Mr Synnott, and when he drew into focus I found the image had a ghastly familiarity. I interrupted the man to demand a description, and item by item the features fell into accord – the long Irish face, fresh as a baby's, the moist pouting lips, the voice from beyond the grave. 'He has magnificent, unforgettable hair, white and fine,' said the Antiquarian, stroking the breast feathers of a stuffed duck on the shelf behind him, 'and at the back it is lightly suffused with gold. He wears black in all weathers and he never goes anywhere without his little poodle. A most memorable man,' he concluded. He seemed more a diabolical genius to me then. I shivered at the scope and exactitude of his efforts. He had placed his ancestors' secrets in my mother's hands and thence into mine with the deftness of a conjuror. He seemed capable of opening the folds of my mind and peering into them, like a botanist examining the petals of a flower. He had stirred within me an appetite such as I had never known before and then laid down bait in a subtle and beguiling path to his door. *What had he in mind for me?* His design was at that time inscrutable to me, but I sensed its severe presence all around me nevertheless. It seemed to me then a thing of vast dimensions and gravity, like a great machine being driven remorselessly by some secret force, with me as one of its instruments pitching about helplessly within it among the whirling gears.

I made my way across the road and looked down into the dead waters of the river. I thought briefly of jumping in. I had in my hand a map drawn by the Antiquarian which described a route to the home of Declan Synnott. He had, I felt, some responsibility in the matter of my mother's disappearance and may therefore have known something of her whereabouts. It was imperative that I see him and I should, indeed, have proceeded there immediately. But there was, too, the insistent lure of Hervey's voice, that voice which conjured a distant world as my hand moved across the pages, that voice which, along with the monkey, had been my companion during those weeks of composition. I had never known such wonder and exhilaration as when in its company. I wanted to be there again, to live in its cadences and dramas, to learn of the fates of Hervey and Milo and of the coming to fruition of Bertrand's social experiment.

I returned then instead to my mother's room and took up again the incantatory chanting of Hervey's words. Following on from Bertrand's ringing laughter, which brought to an end the first of Hervey's entries, were a further fifty-three reports, one for each of the remaining years of his life and all of them considerably shorter than the first. By the time I reached the entry dated 9 July 1215, the year in which Hervey died, my beard was resting upon my chest and the great expanse of my girth had been visibly reduced owing to the light vegetarian diet that I shared with the monkey.

Hervey's entry for 14 August 1172 records that the experimental community which Bertrand had outlined to him that late autumnal afternoon by the lake had duly opened a fortnight earlier, on the first day of the month, the Irish feast of Cugnasad. Timpanists and harpists played intricate music of, in Hervey's words, 'a delicacy and a beauty unknown'. Rent rolls from the district were ceremonially burned and, before they applied themselves to the feast, the entire company assembled themselves into a ring around the great tower and pledged themselves to the project on which they were about to embark.

It was an auspicious ceremony, but, with the great tidal changes of history taking place around and about it, it was not an auspicious era for political experiments in miniature. Out beyond their territory the Normans who had landed along with them were spreading about that south-eastern quarter of Ireland as quickly and indelibly as a dye moving through cloth. Everywhere they went they transformed the land, arranging the wild hills and woodlands into alien shapes with their fine husbandry of straight ditches, their tilled fields boxed in by hedges and their polygonal orchards and kitchen gardens. They stained the land too with blood and wasted it with fire. To the east they were building England into a powerful and centralised monarchy with imperial ambitions, so that within fifty years of the landing at Bannow the English Crown, through the obeisance of the Norman lords, controlled two-thirds of the country, the impenetrable fastness of Ulster the only territory of size that they did not breach. The monk and travel writer Gerald Cambrensis, a contemporary of Hervey's from the same county in Wales, wrote of our country that, due to the great saturation from the immoderate rain, 'What is born and comes forth in the spring and is nourished in the summer and advanced, can scarcely be reaped in the harvest.' And so it was with this little hilltop community in Wexford. In its springtime years the fields gave forth and the beasts multiplied. The ingeniousness of Irish design met with the meticulousness of Norman craft, and the artefacts thus produced were transported by Milo around the country and over the sea to England, bringing in return an abundance of wealth. The loyalties struck at the opening ceremony held and were reaffirmed each year on the feast day of Cugnasad, and Bertrand harnessed the childlike curiosity of his fellow citizens and conducted extensive enquiries into the habits of the fish and the birds and the movements of the stars.

But war and lust for land were, like the rain, general all over Ireland in those years, and their autumn followed quickly. Some distance up the River Slaney a newly arrived knight named Raymond FitzHenry had established himself and was casting his eyes at the land that lay beyond his perimeter. In his employ was an archer who had come to

Ireland on the *Pythagoras* and had served Bertrand until the beginning of his experiment. The archer told the knight what he knew of the community's foolish aspirations, their diminished defences and their surprising wealth. Raymond FitzHenry issued a notice to Bertrand de Paor informing him that, due to the distressing irreligiosity of his community and the immoral practices being carried out there, he was annexing his lands in the name of God and that he would expect thereafter quarterly payments of rent. He knew Bertrand by reputation and was confident of his refusal.

According to Hervey's records, the attack came after sunset on a November evening in the year 1178. They had made such preparations as they could, but there were no longer any professional soldiers among their number and they had altogether ignored the science of war. Hervey and Bertrand climbed to the top of the tower when it had been reported that movement had been heard in the distance. They peered together into the thickening darkness. 'I can't see anything,' complained Hervey. Then a row of hedges seemed to move forward to the base of the hill. As they continued to watch, shrubs and other manner of foliage crept nearer to them in the darkness, coming, it seemed, from all directions except the dense forest to the west.

'This is very clever,' said Bertrand. 'It is the type of warfare which we might have developed here had we been so disposed. But it is cleverness expended towards the worst possible end. Come.' Bertrand gathered everyone together then and gave instructions for the javelins to be stuck upright into the earth placed for that purpose along the walkway of the second encircling wall, thereby giving the illusion of attending soldiers. The greenery stayed still as FitzHenry's men braced themselves for a conventional charge or encircling movement. Meanwhile, through a hole in the earth which reached nearly to the woodland, there silently passed a single file of women in dark hooded cloaks, carrying tools of craft, written records, children and other valuables into the safety of the trees, whose pattern they knew intimately. Others quickly followed. Hervey ran along with Milo, silently weeping, the documents which I now hold before me bound to his chest with twine. By the time that Raymond FitzHenry finally made his move and breached the succession of walls, all the inhabitants and portable goods of the settlement had been removed into the woods. There they looked sadly on through the narrow gaps in the trees at the soldiers, now hideously metallic in their chainmail coats since they had cast off their leaves. They were swarming over the hilltop beneath the tower, frantically and aimlessly, like ants who have lost the door to their home.

I traced the movements of the wandering community on a map from the place names and landscape descriptions which occasionally appeared in Hervey's subsequent entries. Due to the great confiscations and settlements of land taking place around them, they could not establish themselves in any single place for longer than two seasons out of a year, and in consequence they never again collected a harvest from the earth. For food, they became wholly reliant on trading the products of their craft, stopping from time to time outside the walls of monasteries and towns before heading off again across the plains and through woodlands. It is clear from Hervey's reports that when they travelled they did so randomly, without destination, so that their path around the island was full of irregular loops and zig-zags and doublings back, like that of a beetle moving about in a field of stones. For Hervey, the only home throughout the thirty-seven years left to him after their expulsion from the hilltop by Raymond FitzHenry was the growing sheaf of papers which he carried about with him bound to his body.

Bertrand de Paor was no longer of an age where he could withstand with resilience such onslaughts to his mind as the collapse of his experiment. He had turned eighty in 1181, and in his entry dated 9 October of that year Hervey takes some trouble to recount the occasion of his birthday and to describe the condition of his old teacher at that stage of his life. His age and the years of travelling had made him gaunt, wearing away his flesh as time and weather wear away stone, so that the bones of his skull stood out in his face and his eyes now had a hollow, otherworldly look. He had lost the old solidity and fierceness of the falcon. He now wore a cloak of brightly coloured fragments of cloth and black woollen trousers that extended to his feet and served also as shoes. His hair, falling in long wisps about his shoulders, was no longer brown and grey, but had been bleached with lye after the manner of the Celts, and his fingernails, due to a superstition which he had unaccountably developed during his travels, had grown as long as the fingers themselves, so that he was unable to handle objects with ease. On Fridays in Lent he flogged himself to the point of drawing blood and for long periods he ate nothing but fish or those creatures whose nature and habits at all resembled those of fish – eels, frogs and oysters. He would walk to another county in order to buy anchovies. He spoke only in Irish and in numerical formulae. With age too had come the most painful disability of all: the diminution of his sight, the cornerstone of his philosophy. The world which he had looked upon with such sharp hunger had now become a blur of colour, and whenever he travelled he had to be carried along in a wooden cart. 'My encroaching blindness,' he said one day, 'is a punishment, just as Eochy MacDonlevy was blinded to punish the wrongdoings of his father, Dermot MacMurrough, the man who drew us to this country. I am being punished for my vanity.'

The eightieth birthday celebrations took place near the source of the River Shannon, somewhere, I imagine, in the present county of Leitrim. The company settled in along its placid banks just before sunset, and Bertrand was placed at their head in a large chair, designed by Milo and carved in oak. Water vessels made into the shapes of otters and vixen and badgers were placed around the tables for the washing of hands. There was Spanish wine and pancakes and larks made into pies and afterwards an aquamarine cake made of almond paste which Milo's wife had fashioned into a model of the *Pythagoras*. When Bertrand had finished he settled back into the depths of the chair to listen to a programme of music which had been devised in his honour, now and again anointing himself behind his ears with scents which he had distilled from herbs growing along the sides of the roads. Hervey, though he had heard the musicians on many occasions since the inaugural day of the community, marvels at their skill in his report. He writes of the great rapidity and nimbleness of their fingers moving over the instruments, of the flights and dives of the notes as they were borne away on the air, and of how, for all its speed and variety and long quivering measures, the music never once lost its charm, its sweetness and its overriding sense of proportion. 'Our musicians,' he writes, 'can show us the way, for it is their gift to achieve concord out of elements discordant.'

After the music, a procession was formed to bring Bertrand his gifts. Catherine Burke brought him a pillow covered in velvet and gold lace; Milo brought him a mathematical puzzle made of moving planes of wood whose overall shape was a cube; Diarmuid MacDiarmuid, the jeweller, brought him his daughter Emer, a girl of eighteen summers with light golden hair and delicate bones, for him to lie with through the night. He received many other fine things that evening, but there was no doubt that the most wonderful and original gift of all was the one presented by Hervey, brought forward with some ceremony in a specially carved oblong wooden box. It was a small object, but it represented the culmination of many years of intermittent research. When Hervey was a young boy in Wales, his father, possibly to relieve the tedium of the apprenticeship, had demonstrated to him the remarkable magnifying properties of water-filled glass spheres. Hervey had taken great pleasure in looking through them at the lines in his fingers and the veins running through leaves. Years later, when the community had been established and he had resumed his glass-blowing, he performed the same trick for Maurice Coady, the glazier with whom he shared a workshop. Coady speculated that the magnification was directly attributable to the curvature in the glass's surface, and also mentioned that some years before in Bristol he had heard from a trader that an Arabic scientist called Alhazen had produced the same effect with small disks of glass. These were called 'lens', said Maurice, after the Latin for lentil because of their shape, and they were superior to the spheres because they produced greatly less distortion. Hervey and Maurice Coady then set to work with Eamonn Dan, their assistant, in order that they might rediscover this invention. They heated and shaped and polished countless blanks of glass, striving for a purity in composition and a variety in surface curvatures. There were many failures, but they were left in no doubt that the glass could greatly enlarge objects brought near to it.

Then, in June 1181, just two months before Bertrand's eightieth birthday, Hervey made his splendid discovery. Looking through a section of a damaged disk of glass on which they had been experimenting, he found that where the surface curved inwards rather than outwards, where it was concave, that is, rather than convex, it was capable of clarifying the definition of objects standing at a distance from the glass without altering their proportions. In a fever of excitement he had cast for himself a small, dome-shaped iron mould, cut two clear slabs of glass into matching circles with his slitting disk, heated them in his furnace and then carefully worked one each of their surfaces with his mould. He brushed them over then with emery, polished them with wax, and had them mounted on a contrivance made by Milo out of flexible reeds. And so it was that Hervey produced Ireland's first spectacles.

'*Mirabile dictu*,' said Bertrand, as he had them fitted round his head. 'I can see again.'

The renewal of vigour experienced by Bertrand following the restoration of his sight lasted a little over a year. Hervey, in his entry dated 24 January 1183, indicated that the relapse occurred in the period running up to Christmas, when they had been camped on a plain in the Midlands. Early one morning they were awakened by a persistent, unbroken noise, as of stony earth passing through a sieve, and when they looked out from the hides they had piled over themselves to keep warm they could see that its source was a long straggling line of men marching across the frosty plain at some distance from them, guarded, it seemed, by soldiers. Hervey had not seen so many men assembled in one place since the passengers of the *Pythagoras* ranged themselves out along the coastline to greet Dermot MacMurrough. These men too had white clouds of breath issuing from their mouths, but their heads were bowed, and they moved with a shuffle.

'Who are they?' he whispered.

Bertrand had by now stood up and was peering through his spectacles.

'Men do not come together in such quantity and in such remote places except to join in battle. Those dispirited-looking men in saffron tunics and breeches are Irish. Some of them have sustained wounds. Can you see? They are being driven by some of our own race to a destination where, no doubt, their fate is to be decided. Let us follow and see.'

The column was moving eastwards, into the pale wintry sun, and Hervey and Bertrand kept up the pace at a distance behind them through the day, marching overland for nearly thirty miles without stopping before arriving just after nightfall at an open-air encampment bordering on a grove of trees. All the while the grass was brittle and white beneath their feet and the sharp cold stung their flesh. They sat down then among the trees and watched as the prisoners were herded into an enclosure bounded by a circular stone wall. This was accompanied by a great deal of furious movement and shouting, and at one point a tall, angular boy with flaxen hair and a large nose ran forward with a pail of water and threw it over one of the wounded prisoners, upon which there was an explosion of brutal laughter from the assembled company. There was a large swelling the size of a turnip in the boy's neck.

Seated on a long bench amid a soft bed of ferns was a group of men who appeared to be overseeing the proceedings. On one side were three Norman knights leaning on their broadswords and an archer dressed entirely in black, and on the other was a trio of Irish warriors. In front of them, lying in a barrow packed with straw, was a bald man with thick red eyebrows and a red beard which fell in wide curls upon his chest. He had a fierce and intimidating aspect, and he wore a long fur-trimmed cape held in place by a golden brooch. At the sight of one of the prisoners filing into the enclosure he became very agitated, so much so that his short, thick arm shot out from the folds of his cape and he began pointing and shrieking wildly. He did not cease until the prisoner, dressed in rich raiment like himself, was separated from the others and placed kneeling under his own guard on the frost-encrusted earth.

Hervey leaned over to Bertrand and repeated the question he had put forward that morning: 'Who are they?'

Here and there around the encampment large fires were blazing, and Hervey could see their orange light dappling over Bertrand's skin and glinting on his spectacles as it reached him through the trees.

'Those men sitting on the bench are the leaders of the victors in a battle which took place somewhere near the plain on which we have been camped,' he said. 'You can see that they consist in equal number of Normans and Irish. The man lying on the bed of straw I take to be a king, and the prisoner lying on the ground the leader of the vanquished forces. The archer I recognise because he was with Raymond FitzHenry the night we were driven from our home. I would say he is Welsh. All in all, the group you see before you is similar in size and composition to our own community, but its members have come together for reasons very different from anything we ever conceived. Perhaps we shall see how their experiment has fared.'

The bald man with the red beard then shouted in the direction of a small tent to his right, and from it one of the attending guards led a young woman, dressed in a grey hessian sack bound at the waist with rope. Hervey had never before seen such a wild-looking creature. She walked with a stoop and her long dark hair was knotted at the ends. Her blue eyes, bloodshot from weeping, darted frantically about and her lips curled and trembled in rage. Hervey could see that along the inside of her arms there were long red tracks from where she had been clawing at herself.

There was a silence then while the woman stood in the midst of the company, turning slowly about on her bare feet, and then a sudden chaos of activity as the prisoners were dragged from the enclosure and placed kneeling before a block of wood. When there was order again Hervey could see that the woman was holding an axe, and that it shone with a brilliance unequalled by anything around it. The woman lifted the axe then in a great sweeping arc and brought it down on the neck of the prisoner kneeling before her. It made a dull, heavy sound, as though it had struck dead, waterlogged wood, and this was compounded by the grinding and splintering of bone. One by one the prisoners were brought to her, some of them cringing and weeping in terror, others vomiting biliously, and she beheaded them, shrieking all the while, her strength daemonic, fierce and concentrated, like a wounded creature fighting for its life. With each blow she called the name 'Eoin!', her lover and, it transpired, the King's nephew, who had been slaughtered that day in battle. Before her hysteria finally overcame her and she was led away back to her tent, she had taken the heads of two dozen men, and, where the frost had hardened the disturbed earth into craters and furrows and pits, red blood was now flowing and steaming.

When at last the enclosure had been emptied of its final prisoner and all their heads had been rolled down the hill which sloped away from the encampment, their leader, who had been segregated from them when they arrived, was brought forward to the wooden block. The King then gathered himself up from his barrow, snatched a broadsword away from a knight who was seated on the bench, and brought it down swiftly on the man's neck. A little cloud of straw dust rose from his shoulders as the sword buried itself in the wood and the man's head and body fell away from each other. He picked the head up then from the ground and danced wildly around the fire with it, followed trippingly by the gangly boy with the swollen neck, and when he had circled the fire three times he stopped, roared mightily and tore away his enemy's nose and lips with great, gouging bites. The crowd had by now encircled him and were looking on in amazement as he picked the head up by the hair, swung it around his body and sent it flying over the ring they had formed. It spun freely, the open wounds leaving fine circles of blood in the air before dripping to the earth, and it landed on a sharp stone just short of the tree line where Hervey and Bertrand still crouched. Hervey was sick and fearful and he looked over at Bertrand, but the old man's head was turned half-away and he was gazing over the treetops towards the open sky. Large tears were coursing from his eyes down around the bottom of his spectacles, spilling over the bones in his cheeks and accelerating through the hollows until they ended finally in the complexity of his grey beard. Hervey wrung his hands helplessly.

Later, when they were back on the plain with the others, Hervey was awakened one night by an unusual noise. It was Bertrand. He was standing by a large stone, grinding the spectacles into a fine powder.

The old man lived on for another three years, into the spring of 1186, cared for in turn by Hervey and the young woman Emer, the jeweller's daughter. Both were profoundly devoted to him, but they could do nothing to alleviate the distress of his mind. He spent much of his time sitting in the branches of trees, fidgeting with his fingers and murmuring, like a nun at prayer. He took a great interest in funerals, crossing alone to distant parishes upon hearing of a death and conducting strange, mute rituals for the absent dead of the community. Two months before he died he gathered everyone together for his own obsequies, dressing them in black and setting up a dismal wailing among them as he prayed beside his own empty coffin. From the time he smashed his spectacles no one was ever to understand a word he spoke, though the flow of his speech was nearly unbroken. On 29 April 1185, Hervey records, perhaps in the hope that the words might come to have some meaning to future generations, the only complete sentence that Bertrand was heard to speak in those years. It occurred one evening in the midst of the company dinner, when he jerked his head up suddenly from his plate, looked at them all with a fierce expression, and shouted, 'God is addicted to numbers, you know!'

His death took place a year later, when they were camped by the sea in the north-east. It was evening time and the sun was low, but very bright, on the horizon. When, as was his custom, he began slowly to climb a tree, he put his foot out halfway through his ascent and, instead of there being a branch, as he believed, there was merely a long thin shadow created by the setting sun. He fell from the tree onto the stony earth, breaking the brittle bones in his hips and severely concussing his skull. He died before the sun rose again upon the following day.

Three days later, directly after the ritual of burial had been enacted, Hervey learned that he was to become a man of very great wealth. He writes, on 28 June 1186, that he was seated on a stone by the sea bathing his feet in the water when Eunan O'Murchu, a man of law, came up behind him and touched him gently on the elbow. Bertrand, he said, had lodged papers in Bristol to the effect that, in consideration of the ingenious gift of sight which he had bestowed upon him and the unchanging filial love which he had displayed throughout their years together, he, Hervey, was to be the sole heir of the de Paor estate. This estate, though it was encumbered with certain debts owing to the extravagance of Bertrand's investments in his Irish adventure, comprised nevertheless a considerable quantity of gold, the lands around

Bristol, five trading vessels and large stakes in the companies that operated them. The discharge of any debts presently attached to the estate could not materially affect the virtual impossibility of Hervey spending his way through even a quarter of this fortune within his lifetime. He was, perhaps, the richest man in Ireland.

Hervey remembered the admonition put forward by Bertrand by the side of the lake some seventeen years earlier concerning the divisiveness of money, and he did what he could to ignore the presence of his new wealth. The community which had been invented that day continued to roam about the island for a further twenty-two years, growing smaller and weaker and stranger with the passing of time. It appropriated the native religious belief that the act of wandering confers upon those who practise it the status of martyrhood, and it compounded this by deliberately exposing itself to attacks by bands of lawless men and renegade soldiers. Great penances were taken up with enthusiasm. Milo's son Flann condemned himself never to scratch. Hervey's old friend Maurice Coady passed an entire winter seated on the backbone of a whale. An elderly woman kept a large beetle in her bed with her, eating away at her sides. The more they suffered, the sweeter they felt. But new births could not compensate for the losses inflicted upon them through death and desertion along the way, so that finally, by the year 1208, the little group had been fully absorbed into the land. It had had a life of thirty-six years – comparable, I suppose, to the average lifespan of a man of that era.

Milo was with Hervey still at the end, a startling silver like trout-scales now shining through his white hair where once the gold had run. There was too a young man of twenty, Hervey's son. He was called Hugh, and had been born in 1188 during a commercial tour of the Shannon basin and the coastline to the north of Limerick. When he was fifteen, by virtue of his ability to read and transcribe, as well as his particular affinity for literary artefacts, he was appointed the community librarian, as Hervey was its historian. He set about his job with great industry, so that over the five years left to the little wandering community after taking up the job he had obtained or produced copies of such classics as the *Aeneid*, the *Odyssey*, the romances of Guy of Warwick and Bevis of Hampton, the story of the Grail, the legend of the Minotaur and the Works of the Philosophers; he had assembled a collection of Provençal love poetry; and he had devised a method of leather binding which protected such works from the elements as he transported them about the land. His particular speciality was Irish letters – the sagas, the tales of wizards and heroic penitents, *The Book of Invasions*, works by such freedom-loving heresiarchs as Pelagius and John Scotus Eriugena, and above all the verses that he took down from the poets they met on the roads. It is perhaps for this reason that, when his father became afflicted with a painful nostalgia for the legendary hilltop tower in Wexford, he sought for a remedy in the pages of books, finding a passage from his library and bringing it to Hervey, who was seated under a tree in an attitude of torpid gloom. It was from a tale entitled 'The Wooing of Emer', and it described the wondrous royal residence of Conchobar, a chieftain of Ulster. Hervey's eyes watered and he moaned as though being stirred from sleep at the memory invoked by the mention of the name Emer – a memory I shall relate presently. The passage read as follows:

Nine compartments were in it from the fire to the wall. Thirty feet was the height of each bronze partition of the house. Carvings of red yew therein. A wooden floor beneath the roofings of tiles above. The compartment of Conchobar was in the front of the house, with a ceiling of silver, with pillars of bronze. Their head-pieces glittered with gold and were set with carbuncles so that day and night were equally light therein. There was a gong of silver above the king, hung from the roof-tree of the royal house. Whenever Conchobar struck the gong with his royal rod all the men of Ulster were silent. The twelve cubicles of the twelve chariot-chiefs were around about the king's compartment. All the valiant warriors of the men of Ulster found space in that king's house at the time of drinking and yet no man of them could crowd the other. In it were held great and numerous gatherings of every kind and wonderful pastimes. Games and music and singing there, heroes

performing their feats, poets singing, harpers and
players on the timpan striking up their sounds.

Hugh's proposal was to rebuild this palace as a diversion for his father, and indeed the rendering of the passage into wood and precious metals was still engaging a team of labourers and craftsmen seven years later, when Hervey died. I was to learn from Hugh's records that Milo had ceased to supervise the construction when he suffered a mortal injury falling from a horse during a hunt, and that Hervey followed him two months later after the severe rupturing of an internal organ. The pain was located on his left side just above the waist, near the spot where Milo bled to death from a wound opened when he fell. The great glittering house had done nothing to alleviate his misery.

I come now to that page in the book marked by my mother with the photograph from my birthday celebrations, and to the previous entry, a section of four pages, dated 17 July 1187, just over a year after Bertrand's death. The word list which she made out to accompany these pages was more detailed and complete than the others, so that I had little trouble with the mechanics of translation. The earlier entry describes an incident which occurred when the community had stopped by the sea in the distant north-west, in the present county of Donegal. There, on the warm, moonlit night of 16 July – for he wrote his account of it the following day – he was lying under the open sky on a heathery hillside preparing to go to sleep when he was approached by Emer, the girl who had helped to attend to Bertrand. Others in the company were sleeping some distance away at the base of the hill under the shelter of rocks and shrubs. Emer sat down beside him and held her knees to her chest in the bow of her arms. She was wrapped in a red blanket, a vivid crimson red, and her fair hair fell in waves over her right eye. She had been walking, she said, and liked the way the land was in this place, swarming in purple heather and gathered up as though by a giant's hands into hillocks and ravines and conical mountains. Large bleached stones and islands disturbed the surface of the earth and the water everywhere. Bertrand would have liked it too, she said, because it was so unruly. She stretched her legs out then into the heather and lay on her side, so that her face was held above his and very close. He thought that her soft brown eyes and the smooth dome of her brow were very beautiful and he could see the lines in her body through the fall of the blanket. Beneath it, halfway down her thigh, her legs were bare and browned from the sun.

Hervey lay very still but things had begun to move within him. Through his legs and trunk and head and over the whole surface of his skin a current was running. He too lay on his side then, propping himself up on his elbow. Emer looked at him in silence for some time, then leaned forward and kissed him, very softly, her lips parted, so that it felt to him as though a gentle gust of warm air had passed across his face. 'Will I lie here with you for the night, Hervey?' she said, her voice deeper, more resonant, than before. He longed like he had never longed before to draw her to him and hold her, but he kept his place, very still, and looked at her in wonder. 'I'm here for you,' she said. Hervey reached over to draw the blanket over them both and when it fell from her he could see that she was naked. Her skin was smooth and faintly orange, like some of the fruits he had seen brought from Spain in the holds of boats, and her smell too was fresh and sweet. 'You take your clothes off too,' she said, and she helped him draw his tunic over his head and untie the papers that were bound about his body with twine. When they lay down they faced each other along the length of their bodies and she kissed him again, this time with the fullness of her open mouth, and then she placed her hand on his thigh and pulled him over so that he lay on top of her. She touched the side of his face then and began to move beneath him. His body was drawn taut as a bow and he could feel her small fine bones beneath her skin and the places where heat seemed to be gathering along the slopes and curves of her body. Her eyes were half-closed and looking into his. She reached down then and took the hard shaft of his penis gently in her hand, moving the top of it along the entrance to her body. His mind blazed and within him there was the riot and anarchy of an electrical storm. Emer closed her eyes and moaned a little. She placed her smooth hands around his buttocks and pulled him towards her, then heaved powerfully forward herself with her hips so that he entered her fully and at once, feeling the surface of his skin melt away where it was pressed to hers and losing himself entirely within her.

When I reached this part of the narrative I left off reading and began to assemble the picture for myself. I placed a fine galaxy of stars in the sky and a long jagged path of moonlight along the surface of the sea, broken only by the islands and the waves and ending finally in the gold line of the strand beyond the base of the hill. I saw Hervey and Emer from a long way off at first, as though from the sky, just the bright red spot of the blanket among the purple of the heather. I moved closer then and saw that the blanket had fallen away and that they were naked in the open air, Emer's legs entwined around Hervey's and his back and round white buttocks rippling rhythmically as he made love to her on the hillside. Closer still I could see that Emer's cheeks and lips were now flushed with red and that as she rolled her head back and forth on the heather fine strands of her golden hair were trailing across her face. It was the most beautiful face I had ever seen. I moved around then to look at Hervey, but found that the face there was not that of the man I had watched burying the gold ring and eating the black earth in Wexford. Instead of those sharp handsome features there were the familiar round, weighted jaw, the full gleamingly red lips and the heavily browed eyes beneath the pointed crown. It was my face, the face in my birthday photograph, like Coleridge, only animated now with passion. I felt my body too seeping into Hervey's, filling it up and spilling out beyond the limits of his compact muscular frame, so that it was now I who was astride Emer on the hillside and taking the wondrous pleasure of her body. And I took and I gave what I could until it ended, as these things do, in explosion and release and a cry in the night. Thus it was that, in my middle years, I finally came to lose my virginity.

The records show that Hervey and Emer remained together for the best part of the coming year. Between his entry for 17 July 1187 and the next one dated 21 June 1188 he has inserted some verses praising her beauty and celebrating the land they travelled through together. It is clear from their passion that through those months his senses had burst open and that he was living with a buoyancy and a rapture unknown to him either before or since.

Writing at the age of thirty-six on 21 June 1188, Hervey describes in a terse note of five lines, the shortest of all his entries, three occurrences of the greatest moment. Two of them pertain primarily to Hervey and the third pertains to me. The first of these is the announcement that on 8 May of that year a son, Hugh, was born to Emer somewhere in the centre of the province of Ulster, and the second is that the mother died two days later of massive internal bleeding. The last is a single sentence describing Hugh's condition at birth, and it affected me no less than the thunderous explosion I felt in my mind that night on the hillside with Emer. It said that this baby boy, the first in a long line of Synnotts to be born in Ireland, this future librarian and chronicler and builder of a mythical palace, had come into the world with a fine transparent webbing stretched between his tiny fingers.

V̱I

I turned right off the wide City Centre boulevard by the illuminated bride and groom towering in metal over the ring shop and passed then into the empty quarter of dereliction to the east, following the route marked out on the Antiquarian's map. There was a severe silence over the whole of this district, the hulks of cars rusting by the broken pavements, the evacuated tenements as imposing as tombs. Twisted sheets of corrugated metal filled many of the windows and doorways, and here and there on their surfaces I could still see traces of gold and white paint. This dated from 1979, when the municipal authorities had covered the vacated areas of the city with it in order to herald the Papal visit of that year. The paint was peeling now and blackened with soot, but I remember that it had shone brightly then in the sunshine of that fine summer day. My mother and I had watched it all – the ground-kissing at the airport, the ceremony at the park, the triumphal progress through the city – on a small telly we had rented in for the occasion, and in the evening we strolled down to College Green, where we were told the Pope would pass after his ecclesiastical dinner. There were scenes there of exaltation such as I had never known before. Tiny gold and white flags rippled busily among the tumultuous ranks, and behind us a small band of young people danced with tambourines in a ring beneath the high vaulted windows of the bank. The air rang with prayers and shouts and evocations of the events of the day.

After a long wait we all heard the rumble of the Papal motorcade gathering in the distance, and gradually the crowd began to still itself. The police motorcycles came first, then the long black cars brought out on occasions of state and finally, with the silence now general over the spectators, the Pope himself, gold and white like a flame, his broad peasant's jaw clenched but smiling, the fine white wisps of his hair quivering in the night breeze as his slicing hand described in the air the shape of the Cross. There was an awesome power in his narrow eyes. He stood out in the open atop a platform built over the cab of a truck which pulled behind it an electrically illuminated perspex carriage containing the chief bishops and cardinals of the land. Arrayed in purple and crimson, their faces pink and happy, they were like an arrangement of flowers in a floating globe of glass. I gripped my mother's hand as an awful surge of current moved about in my body at the sight of this spectacle, but found that it was clammy and limp. I looked over at her. A light smile was flickering about her lips, but her eyes seemed to be turned inside-out, as they were that afternoon in the Judge's kitchen when the carving knife had fallen from her hand and I had first heard her talk about lenses. The arrangement of hair on top of her head had slid down to the side and curled about her neck. She was leaning slightly forward and swaying gently as though to some unheard tune, and the forefinger of her free hand rocked back and forth in accordance with the same measure. Then she spoke, or rather sang, her voice weirdly light and high-pitched:

> Willy, Willy, Harry, Stee,
> Harry, Dick, John, Harry Three,
> One, Two, Three Ned, Richard Two,
> Henry Four, Five, Six – then who?
> Ned the Fourth and Dick the Bad,
> Harry's Twain and Ned the Lad,
> Mary, Bessie, James the Vain,
> Charley, Charley, James Again,
> William and Mary, Anna Gloria,
> Four Georges, William and Victoria,
> Edward the Seventh and then –
> George the Fifth in 1910.

'And that's our kings and queens, right back to the beginning,' she said. 'Can you say them for me, Tommy, can you?' She stopped then and cocked her head to one side, smiling more broadly, as though she was awaiting some reply, and looking beyond her I could see, as the crowd stirred once again into agitated movement, a small baby held aloft in his grandmother's bony hands, the only still thing remaining now, bar myself. He was wearing a new tee-shirt with the Pope's disembodied head stencilled across it and was staring out in front of himself at the spot where the motorcade had just passed, his chin glistening with spittle, his round blue eyes blinking in the lamplight. I took my mother by the arm and guided her through the crowd, laughing and gesturing meaninglessly so that we might escape detection. She walked with an eery stiffness, her face grey and quite terrorised, but she kept on nevertheless and somehow or other I got her down into the side streets and eventually into bed. All that, however, was very long ago.

I pressed on away now from the City Centre, the cavernous buildings around me ringing here and there with unfathomable sounds, and soon passed into regions unknown to me. The day was now beginning to darken more rapidly. I heard a whooping, jackal-like call and wondered was the Animal Gang on the prowl. The proportions of the map which the Antiquarian had drawn for me were by no means accurate, and it was difficult for me to tell at any given point how far I was from my objective. This made the journey to Declan Synnott's house seem endless to me. I pressed the map close to my face. The paper on which it had been drawn was stained with some manner of cleaning oil which the Antiquarian used in his trade, and the smell of it made me ill, so that I vomited painfully and copiously into the gutter. I felt thoroughly awful. Following the completion of my work on Hervey's manuscripts some days before, I had fallen into a colossal depression, the wonder of the story and the finely-tuned equanimity I had experienced in producing it all dropping away from me in heavy clots. This voice which had been so long within me, when I had turned again to address it I found only a vacancy and I plunged with remorseless purpose into a three-day bender. There was a small public house hidden away in the tangle of mewses and laneways which lay to the south behind our street, and I sat there in a darkened corner by the old coal fireplace drinking steadily through each session until the final bell, all manner of drinks – spirits and beers and sweet wines – and laying down in the intervals beneath a staircase in a forgotten house nearby. When eventually I returned to our quarters the monkey was beside himself. I could hear his mad screeching as I climbed the stairs, and when I opened the door he was there on the carpet before me, jumping up and down amid a debris of foam cubes from a pillow he had torn to pieces, his red mouth opened to its full extent and his eyes bulging with wound and rage. I attempted to bawl at him to shut up, but speech had become impossible for me and all that came from my mouth was a long, plangent roar, like the call of an elephant. I lunged forward to tackle him round the legs, but he was too nimble for me and in three bounds he had cleared my encircling arms and attained the bars of his trapeze, whence he maintained his shrill and abusive chatter. It was ear-splitting, but I could do nothing to stop him, for I found I could not rise from the floor. I slept there finally by the entrance to the sitting-room, waking again at first light with the monkey's tiny fists rapping me in the back of the head, my entire system in rebellious uproar. Worse still, I discovered that I had fouled my trousers.

I made my way now past the grey slumbering stadium, girdled in iron, and the old cemetery with its congestion of mossy stones. At the canal bridge my way was blocked by a group of young louts leaning against the wall and drinking from bright green and gold aluminium cans. I advanced with trepidation, but they let me pass. I don't believe they even noticed me. I entered then the mouth of a long treeless street flanked on either side by unbroken rows of artisans' cottages, their curtains billowing a little in the evening breeze, the blue-grey light of their television sets filling their meek windows. The street ended in a T-junction, and on the opposite side facing me was a fenced-in area described by the Antiquarian on the map as an 'Industrial Estate'. I had read in a newspaper article of a factory in this part of the city which still produced bicycle tyres, but here weeds grew liberally around the entrance gate and I could see no sign of activity. I turned left here and followed the fence around, the houses now beginning to diminish in concentration, until I was guided by the map to the foot of a grass verge. It rose steeply before me and beyond its crest there was a glow, a white halo like moonlight but more intense. This was the 'Shopping Precinct'. The monkey and I made our way across the empty, floodlit expanse of tarmac, the low-running arrangement of retail shops closed and silent for the night, apart from the lonely barking of a guard dog. The monkey, I think, had forgiven me my transgressions because he was holding me gently by the hand and looking around him good-naturedly. A small driveway led away through a series of purposeless curves from the far end of the car park and joined up with a main road, lit in a strident yellow from overhead lamps. Declan Synnott's residence, it said on the map, lay just around a bend some five hundred yards along this road from where I stood. Despite my enfeebled condition, I accelerated a little in anticipation of at last reaching my objective, and when I arrived at the bend I could see the estate spread out before me on a large treeless field, thick with weeds and grass that grew to the level of the knee. It was entered by a pavement that passed beneath a high arched gateway, made of green marble and garlanded in dust-covered ivy, its keystone bearing the fierce visage of a Druid and the date 1782 and the two supporting pillars surmounted by stone pineapples. Pineapples, I later learned, are symbols of prosperity. The rows of flats began just beyond. They were newly built and white-painted and they were set at odd angles and distances from one another, as though they had been dropped from the sky, their doorways short and narrow and their windows tiny slits, like the unfeeling eyes of insects.

Just above the unit number on the old man's door there was a thin strip of metal on which a legend of some sort had been engraved. I could not immediately decipher it because of the glare from the floodlamps which protruded from the rooftops, but as I stood on my toes and shaded the plate this way and that with my hand the inscription became clear. 'PYTHAGORAS' RETREAT', it spelt out in squat block capitals. I slumped on the doorstep. Another grim joke at my expense, I thought, and as I thought it I heard the slow, grating laughter of the old man, that same laughter I had heard before, like the night-cawing of a scavenger bird. His white hair and broad pink brow were just visible through the gauze netting drawn across a window to my right. He put his head out.

'Ah, my dilatory friend. At last,' he said. 'We've been expecting you.'

He disappeared and was quickly round to the door, his little dog squatted down at his feet in quivering attendance, its blackened gums bared in a menacing smile. I felt the monkey warily tighten his grip on my hand.

'Come in, come in, come in,' he said. 'The kettle is on the hob, as they say.' He led me down a short dark corridor then, through two right turns past a sitting-room and into the kitchen. The walls were barren throughout.

'Make yourself at home,' he said with ceremonial expansiveness and, positioning me by a table, he butted the back of my knees with the sharp edge of a chair until I was forced to collapse into it. It was made of a hard, moulded plastic material and was dismally uncomfortable. He moved lithely around the kitchen, singing what I took to be a grave aria in German and preparing a pot of tea. When he was ready he sat opposite me and lit his pipe.

'Now,' he said, 'tell me how you finally found us. Did you follow me that night after we parted outside the cafe?'

His light exuberance propelled me deeper into my gloom.

'No,' I replied.

'Did you trace Atma through the Canine Registry?'

'Not that either.'

'It was the special character of the book's binding, wasn't it. You took one look at the cover and you said to yourself, "Unmistakably the work of Rivière." And of course you were right. Antiquarianism is after all one of your specialities. You were London-trained, were you not?' He spoke this last sentence very slowly, and when he had completed it his right eyelid dropped in a slow collusive wink. 'You confirmed your assessment by checking the binder's signature at the base of the doublure and you were thereby led to the discovery, through records held in England, that Rivière had been commissioned by my grandfather, Joshua Synnott, in 1892. Manifestly a man of wealth and taste, you thought, and therefore not difficult to trace. It was thereafter an easy matter for you to locate me through a mere two generations of birth and death records, property deeds and the like . . . Was that it?'

I looked on in dejection at the steam wafting about on the surface of my tea.

'Was it the sign on my door . . . ? No . . . ? The telephone directory?'

I held precariously to my silence.

'Am I to interpret this as continuing denial?'

There was a tightening in my lungs so that I reverted briefly to my old habit of blowing in short gusts through my lips.

'You know very well how I found you,' I said rapidly. 'I found the receipts you left that day and the Antiquarian gave me your address. Just like you told him to do.'

'Simple and direct,' he said, 'if a little banal. Mind you, it took you two-and-a-half months to complete the journey. Did it tax you? Are you tired?'

I raised my eyes to his. He was gazing upon me with equanimity. I remembered sitting with him in the little square the last time we had met and watching my mother's face compose itself out of those same unlined features and float away across the gravel path until her body formed beneath it, arrayed in a bridal gown. I could only think of her now, a bodiless head, floating out over the city and unknown fields and hills to the sea, beyond the pull of the earth, beyond even the pull of my love. No matter where the face floated I could see it still, its bones as light and fine as porcelain, its lips serene, its eyes so tender. But touch it I could not. In some cavernous depths within me there began a rumbling. It increased in force so that my body filled with heat and began to quake and tears brimmed from my eyes. I raised my two fists above my head and brought them crashing down in front of me. The teacups shuddered across the table to the edge and the monkey dived into a cupboard beneath the sink. I could hear the saucepans rattling from his fear.

'*Where is my mother?*' I bellowed.

I was on my feet now and swaying over the old man, my éyes bulging and my face blazing red beneath my beard. He looked back at me benignly, with some amusement, as though he was watching a circus elephant attempting to perform a waltz. After a time I lowered myself into my seat.

'Don't you know where she is?' I petitioned. 'She was reading your book, she was studying it and making notes, and then she suddenly disappeared. Do you think she found something there?'

He made no effort to reply.

'You don't understand. She could be in terrible danger. She trusts people too much, and sometimes when she goes away she doesn't know where she is. She *needs* me.'

He was leaning back in his chair, drawing languidly on his pipe. 'Is it not perhaps the other way around?' he replied. I noticed then that he could raise his eyebrows independently of one another, and it provoked me to another attack.

'Well, you mightn't like it so well either,' I said. 'To lose someone like my mother. She was so kind and elegant and lovely. We can't all be like you, with just a little dog for company. My mother and I are different. We have a great love for one another. It's high and noble and pure, and people like you . . . I know you're very cute, but people like you just don't understand. We were complete together, you see. It was all the little things – the way she kept me tidy and peaceful, the way she sang to me when I had a bad night. She used to clean between my toes for me because I couldn't reach them. It's so hard for me to be away from her. Just look at me. I'm like an ape. I've hardly spoken with another human being for months and whenever I do a kind of growl comes out before the words. My clothes are stiff as slates. *Everything reminds me of her!*' I was beginning to wail. 'I passed a little shop today and in the window the mannequin was wearing a dress just like my mother used to have. It was made up of irregularly shaped panels of red and black and white like a stained-glass window and it clung tightly to her body. I used not to like her to wear it because men would leer at her. The sight of this dress made me weep in the street and I had to hide in a doorway until it was over. If I see a woman inclining her head to one side like my mother used to do, or who has eyes like hers, or if I see mothers and sons together I feel a powerful searing pain strike me in the chest so that it is hard for me to keep my feet. Even the sweet smell on the breeze now that summer is here makes me think of her. *I don't think I can bear another day of it!*'

The old man's pipesmoke had gathered in the warm, still air and stood before his face like a bank of cloud. When he spoke it eddied and swirled and I could only just see the trace of his moving lips.

'Your pain is a small thing,' he said. 'It is merely self-pity. Dissolve it in a greater thought.'

I knew I hadn't the strength to perform any such feat. Indeed I was by no means certain what a greater thought was. But the idea of it compelled me.

'What sort of greater thought?' I asked him. I saw the monkey put his head out the cupboard door.

'Thought is perhaps the wrong term,' he said. 'I mean, rather, a greater operation of mind.'

'Greater than . . . what, exactly?' I asked.

'Greater than that wretched whining which you have substituted for thought. I mean something with greater complexity, with range and amplitude and diversity, where the numerous activities of the mind can be made to come together in a harmonious movement. There is an equivalent in sound for what happens inside your head. I can hear it now and it is not pleasant. It is radio static.'

'That's not fair!' I erupted. 'It's not fair. You can't hear what happens inside me.'

He waved his hand in a leisurely fashion, as though he was clearing the air around him of a slow-moving fly. 'Your mother is missing. You may go as you are, or you may focus your thoughts and attempt to discover where she has gone. If you embark on the latter course you will perhaps come to understand what I mean by a greater operation of mind.'

I contemplated myself briefly. All through my life I had always gone wherever I had been led or pushed, my mind empty of any design whatever, and while it had been remarked by the Judge and a few others that I could absorb information with ease, it was abundantly clear to me that my utter fecklessness prevented me from distilling it and assembling it into a system that was in any way useful as a means of inquiry or belief. I resembled in this sense Hervey Synnott when he emerged from the forest and began his tutelage under Bertrand de Paor. I was now faced with the exacting problem of trying to locate my mother. She had disappeared in an instant some months previously, and such slender evidence as she had left behind seemed to me impossibly random and weird. It had been put to me that in order to complete my task it would be necessary for me to attain a rarefied state of mind such as might still remain elusive even after years of disciplined meditation. I slumped like a sodden hayrick into the plastic chair.

'Can't you help me?' I begged him.

He had allowed the pipesmoke to collect again in the air and had retired disconcertingly behind it.

'Perhaps we can help each other,' he said.

I looked at him expectantly.

'You have a gift.' His words drifted oracularly through the smokecloud.

'What?' He had caught me entirely unawares. 'I? What sort of gift? How can I help you?'

'I know more about you than you think,' he said. 'I know that since you were a child of nine years you have been visited from time to time by an unusual mental phenomenon. In times of agitation pictures of people you love enter into your mind and you embellish them into stories. The process soothes you, but you are unable entirely to control it. I find it interesting that you first came into receipt of this gift upon the removal from your life of the only man you ever looked up to as a father, the old American Judge in Kilkenny.'

'*What?*' I said. I leaned forward over the table, my jaw slung low in stupefaction, my webbed hands opening and shutting, as though to clutch at his astonishing words. The thought of it flailed about in my mind, like a fly trapped in honey. 'What do you mean about the Judge?'

'When you were informed of his death in St Louis you received into your mind a picture of the death scene. Very exotic it was, with lush foliage, colourful robes and a marching band. It entertained you and you felt ashamed, because you believed you should have been feeling grief.'

'*But how can you know this?*'

'That is a small matter. Will you accept my offer of help to find your absent mother? All you need do is to tell me your visions.'

'Visions? But they're just games I play. Entertainments. What use could they be to you?'

'I too am searching for something,' he said. 'You may be the only person capable of finding it for me.'

The monkey had by now remounted my lap and was looking at the old man and leaning his tiny head back against my chest. It felt warm, and light as a quail's egg.

'How far did you reach in your translations?' he asked me.

I told him that I had attained the entirety of Hervey's narrative.

'At that rate it will take you approximately six years to arrive at the twentieth century. Perhaps I can paraphrase a little for you.

'Proceeding from Hervey's last entry you will see that his son Hugh makes only a series of brief notes in the book. These are very much in the style of newspaper announcements: the deaths of Hervey and Milo in 1215, the completion of the castle three years later, his marriage, the births of his nine children – that sort of thing. Had you read them you may have thought to yourself that this was odd for a man who in his youth had displayed such a sense of history and love of learning. You would have been right, for Hugh wrote steadily throughout his long life – but not autobiographically, like his father. It seems that he did not believe that his life was eventful enough, and he devoted himself instead to scholarly commentary, work which he bound and stored in his library.

'After Hugh's final entry in 1252 there follow eight years of silence until his eldest daughter Anna comes on the scene to resume the family story. She is thirty-three at the time, single, and living as a recluse in Hugh's castle. Her father has been dead for five years, all her brothers and sisters have moved away, and the man she had loved in her youth had married his own cousin. She was utterly alone, and fallen upon hard times. The seemingly infinite supply of money which had been available to Hervey and Hugh had become severely restricted when the English Crown seized Bertrand de Paor's holdings across the sea. The fields, in consequence, wasted away and the bronze pillars lost their lustre. For fifty years Anna strolled in the grounds or sat out the winters in the long hall, embroidering wall hangings made of silk.

There are some dismally low moments in the records. In late February some time in the 1280s she writes merely two lines: "Nothing new since the onset of winter. Four trees down in storms. Days passed as usual — alone and stupid." Memories of her lover plagued her throughout her life. Even at the age of seventy-one she complains of the wind whipping down towards her from his home in the hills, mixed with the music of his voice and the laughter of his foul brood and bringing upon her a violent fit of screeching and psalm singing that lasted through the night. "Unremitting despondency of mind followed through the month of October," she writes. Poor Anna.

'Most of her writings, though, are reminiscences provoked by seasons or smells or places, happy memories in the main. There is one in particular that concerns you and me.'

He had already, it seemed, formed us into an alliance.

'On 19 October 1298 she sits on a fallen tree with her feet in the dust of an old flowerbed and remembers a sports-night held near there one summer evening when she was a girl of seventeen. The majority of her memories take place in the summer. On this occasion her hair was scented and she wore a dress of lilac-coloured velvet and white lace. There was a feast of roast pig and leeks, and there were barrels of mead and sweet wines from Spain. Men came from all around the district to throw heavy stones and compete in foot races. Afterwards, before the music began, Hugh entertained the company with his skills at clair-voyance. This was demonstrated in the following way. Anna was despatched to the library to select a book at random from the shelves. When she returned she positioned herself with her back to a chestnut tree – the same tree on which she sat many years later – and opened the book in front of her. Hugh took up his place with his back to the other side of the tree. Then, to the wonder of all around, he began rapidly to read, with Anna turning the pages for him, until the exercise was repeated with objects brought forward to Anna from the company – knives, valuable stones, a lock of a baby's hair – Hugh identifying even the colour! Anna writes at the conclusion of this entry that Hugh had been performing such tricks for her for as long as she could remember, and that throughout his life he had worked at developing his skills.

When he was an old man he was able to tell visitors what animals they had passed while on their way to see him, or what they had eaten for their breakfasts.

'Anna notes only one occasion on which Hugh predicted the future. About seven months before he died he looked at her in a melancholy way and said, "The house will be razed by barbarians." This eventually came to pass fifty-five years later, in 1315, during the course of the Scottish invasion under Edward Bruce. Bruce's hordes swarmed over the castle and reduced it to a pile of splinters and ash – an event which is presented by Anna in her final composition. She describes it all in a splendid language of apocalypse, writing unflinchingly of blood dripping from her silk wall hangings, of the smokeblacking of the bronze pillars, of the devouring by flame of Hugh's massive library. When Anna saw them coming she made her way immediately to the old nursery. It was there that Hervey's and Hugh's manuscripts were stored, hidden away in a primitive wall safe which Milo had designed over a hundred years before. In the last year of his life, a matter of weeks after he had foreseen the sacking of his house, Hugh had taken her down to demonstrate to her the workings of the safe and to enjoin her to guard the manuscripts with her life. This was what was on her mind when, at the age of eighty-three, she hobbled along the complexity of corridors some way in advance of Bruce's men. The safe was operated by pulling in a particular sequence a series of variously coloured cords that hung down behind a false wall in one of the closets and Anna was in the midst of this activity when a Scottish giant entered the room and began to prowl around. Anna peered back at him in terror through a crack in the door. She records that a large scarlet birthmark disfigured the right-hand side of his face. The nursery had been disused for over seventy years and in consequence there was nothing of value for the giant to loot. This seemed to anger him, for Anna writes that he roared out a curse and swept to the ground a row of fishes and frogs and forest creatures which, a century earlier, Hervey had fashioned for Hugh from pieces of delicately blown coloured glass. He crushed them then beneath his huge feet. But isn't that marvellous? Hervey must have been a devoted father to his only son. I can almost see those tiny figures.'

I wondered if I too, with the force of concentration, might see Hugh's childhood toys.

'After the giant had departed, Anna climbed out a window and quickly took cover among some low-hanging trees, taking with her a small collection of personal jewellery along with the family records. She then set out on a long overland march of some twenty miles to the home of her brother, Fingal. Bruce's men were at large about the countryside and it must have been a harrowing journey for a woman of her age. There she composed the story of the ravishing of her home, her final appearance in the book, and then passed on the entire collection of manuscripts to her favourite nephew, Ronan, a bright boy apparently, with an aptitude for law. Let us hope she enjoyed a peaceful death.

'So that is the story of Anna,' said the old man. 'Except for one thing – a postscript to her final entry, a note on the text she was passing on, possibly added at a later date as the ink appears different. It is of the greatest moment with respect to our task.'

He lowered his head here and looked up at me solemnly from beneath his brow. I believed that he wanted to emphasise the gravity of my responsibilities.

'Anna writes that when her father took her to the nursery to demonstrate the wall safe and show her the manuscripts they laid them out on the floor and counted the pages. They were, she said, loose pages collected in a soft leather folder. There were the eighty-seven pages written by Hervey in Norman French which you have collected in the book and some *twenty-nine* pages written by Hugh in Irish. If you were to look in the book now you would find that Hugh's section comprises only seventeen pages, the same number which Anna passed on to young Ronan. Anna says that she believes the missing pages to be the final twelve because she remembers there being a long unbroken section of prose at the end, and all that remained when she collected them were the short dated entries which we still have. This memory is operating in old age and across fifty-five years, but I trust its accuracy because Anna was particularly skilful at memory. She had little else with which to occupy herself. The missing pages are a complete mystery to Anna and she does not attempt to speculate about them, except to say that she does not believe them to be stolen as her father had told her that she was the only other living person to know of their existence. I, however, think that we may hazard an intelligent guess.

'The last of Hugh's entries which we possess is dated 17 April 1252, and it records the passing away of his wife Blanaid. That was three years before his own death. Now remember that throughout his life Hugh was developing his extrasensory powers so that at the end he was able to display to Anna an example of divination. It was a disturbing prophecy – the insensible annihilation of his home – and it pained him to contemplate it, let alone utter it, but he felt compelled to do so nevertheless. I believe that Hugh was a man of considerable intellectual honesty. What do you suppose he wrote about in those twelve pages? I think we may assume that it was something personal, or familial, because he deemed it more appropriate for storage in the wall safe than with his scholarly works in the library. The timing of the composition I believe could suggest something about its contents. There is nothing in the whole of Anna's considerable body of reminiscences of life with her father that indicates anything of significance happening in the family in those three years between the death of her mother and the death of her father – except the evolution of Hugh's psychic powers to the point where he could foretell the future. There was her sister Laoise's wedding, but an event such as this, were he to note it at all, Hugh would have despatched in a few lines. Now remember that those twelve pages were written during that time and they were present in the wall safe when Hugh showed them to Anna about six months before he died. Anna vows that she never opened the safe herself until the day of the house's destruction, and if she was the only person other than her father who could operate its complex mechanisms then it must have been Hugh who removed the manuscript. The likeliest reason for his doing so is that it contained something which he did not wish to form part of his literary legacy – something which was perhaps deeply disturbing. He was, after all, consistently presented by Anna as a devoted husband and father who took great pains to isolate his family from distress. Given that, what might he have done with his manuscript? There is nothing in what we know of his life to suggest that he would have given it away. He simply had no intimates beyond the family circle, and Anna was the only one within it with whom he would discuss such matters. Nor do I believe that he would have destroyed it. Hugh was a scholar and a librarian, and to perform such an act would have been antithetical to his character. I believe rather that he hid it. Interestingly, Anna remarks in passing in the course of an entry dated 1289 that her father went on a journey for four days on his own in the autumn of 1255 and when he returned he refused to divulge where he had gone. The entry is mainly taken up with happy memories of Laoise's wedding celebrations, which Hugh very nearly missed due to his uncharacteristically mysterious absence. He was weakened at the time through illness and he died at the onset of winter.

'Taking all these factors into account I would postulate that towards the end of his life Hugh was visited by a lengthy and powerful prophetic vision. Just as he had felt compelled to inform Anna of the coming destruction of their home, so he now felt compelled to commit what he had seen to prose. Initially he placed his manuscript with the others in the wall safe, but as he came near to death he worried about the effect it might have upon future generations. He therefore removed it and, I believe, took it away with him on his final unexplained journey. Where did he hide it? Here I have found it impossible to discover a basis upon which to speculate intelligently. That is why I have sought your help.'

He looked upon me with his watery blue eyes, round and unblinking. Atma his poodle was beside him, his hind legs balanced upon the seat of a chair and his front paws, with their black pellet-like nails, resting on the table in front of me. Both were completely still. They looked serene yet quietly expectant, like two pensioners awaiting their tea.

'I take it you want me to find this manuscript for you,' I said.

'That is correct,' he replied.

'But why?'

'An excruciating curiosity,' he said. 'In addition to which, the book is not whole without it.'

'And if I find it then you will tell me where my mother is.'

'Oh no,' he said. 'I couldn't do that. I could give you a broad geographical area towards which she may well have travelled, but, as to where she is at present, well, no, I couldn't tell you that.'

'*What am I doing here?*' I screeched, looking down beseechingly at the monkey. 'And anyway, this manuscript,' I said then to the old man. 'Even if it was hidden as you say, how do you expect it to have survived over seven centuries of Irish weather? Answer me that.'

'If the suppositions which I have made so far about Hugh are correct – that the instincts and practices of a lifetime forbade him to destroy a written work – then I believe that it is reasonable to assume further that he would have taken such precautions as were available to him to ensure the preservation of the manuscript. Remember that he was a binder as well as a librarian.'

'And what am I supposed to do, excavate the whole island with my fingers?'

'To bury the pages randomly would be the same as to destroy them. It follows that Hugh would have hidden them in a place where they might eventually be found – by the right person.'

'And you seriously believe me to be that person.'

'Yes.'

'You're even lighter in the head than I thought,' I said. 'Do you know to whom you are speaking? My mother wouldn't even let me into the City Centre on my own until I was twenty. Accidents would befall me. The rudimentary logic of the electric plug defeats me. Do you know that there are over thirty thousand square miles of land on this island? Your missing pages probably amount to no more than one square foot. Can you please tell me how I am to go about locating them?'

'I know precisely what you are,' he said curtly. 'You are slovenly and fat and you have the mental discipline of a slug. But like Hugh you were granted a capacity which is normally denied to others – a kind of second sight. Perhaps that is the meaning of your both being born with those amphibious hands, the sign of a double life. Of course Hugh trained himself like an athlete while you are simply idle. Nevertheless, I am relying on the development of your gift to enable me to discover Hugh's secret.'

'But you said that Hugh could see things that were blocked from his view, and even into the past and future. I'm afraid I can't do anything like that.'

'Perhaps you are abler than you think. When I learned what you had seen of the Judge's death I conducted a small investigation. I discovered that while some of the elements of your vision were either representational of other things or else simply meaningless, a good deal of the naturalistic detail was accurate. The car, for instance, was red, just as you saw it. The date of the accident was 4 July, the American festival of Independence, which would account for the marching band and the profusion of flags. And the Judge's sister did walk with the aid of a blackthorn stick. When I learned these things I knew that you too had the gift.'

I felt a sudden and powerful sensation of self-importance. It was a kind of giddiness, and was accompanied by a furious urge to laugh, as though I was being gently tickled on the soles of my feet.

'But why should I help you then?' I said. 'If I concentrate and use my powers I should be able to find my mother without your help.'

'Regrettably, you do not possess the means by which to go about it. You are like an electronic machine lacking a source of power. Your only hope in this matter is to give yourself over to my tutelage, for you will not be able to find your mother without first learning how to look. When I spoke to you earlier about "a greater operation of mind" I was referring to three distinct mental processes: the acts of memory, of logical thought, and of imagination. They must all act from time to time and as the need arises fully and separately, in consort and harmoniously. It is an extremely difficult business, one involving painful efforts of concentration and control. I would say that the effect in the end of its successful application is to make the unconscious gradually more conscious.

'Now in your case there is a fourth element – that of clairvoyance. You cannot realise this power through effort alone, but rather by attaining a state of constant alertness, so that, as in remembering a dream, you do not chase the image but rather allow it to present itself and then ensnare it. In this respect it is very like hunting.

'I do not believe that it is possible for a person of such abject helplessness as yourself to achieve in a void a development such as I am describing, as the activity of the mind contemplating itself merely is not verifiable. It is necessary to have some puzzle or project upon which to exercise and to perceive the consequences of your work. That is the function of looking for Hugh's manuscript. You must apprentice yourself to the task.'

He rose and stood smiling for a moment in the centre of the room, his lips and teeth sparkling with a diamantine brilliance beneath the overhead bulb. He moved off into the darkened corridor, briefly laying his hand on my matted hair as he passed. Atma grinned at me across the table like a victorious junior barrister and then trotted off after his master. The monkey and I were alone. We listened for a while to the sound of cheerful whistling and of running water before following it to its source as it seemed we were being bid to do. We found the old man on his knees beside the bath, gently stirring an aromatic powder into the steaming water and being watched from the toilet seat by Atma. Borne on the steam was the smell of mint, which seemed to seep gently into my bones. The old man looked up.

'Ah,' he said. 'I thought I would draw you a bath. There are a few preparations which it is advisable to make before embarking on a journey. Bathing is one of them. You may remember our little conversations about the meaning of water when we buried your tortoise. Apart from that you smell like a cesspit.' He was shouting a little to be heard over the running water, though without diminishing the deep and spectral sonorousness of his voice.

He ordered me to undress, which I did as though hypnotised and then stepped into the steaming foam. When I had lowered myself completely I so filled the bath that the water flooded profusely over the sides, drenching the old man's trousers.

'A miscalculation,' he said. 'Mind you it is difficult to estimate displacement at such scale.'

He lowered the water level and tipped me forward, so that I was hunched over with my arms around my knees. I could see heavy rolls of white fat from my gut spreading out over the curve of my thighs. The old man began then to lather my back gently with a loofah, moving his hand in wide languid circles until he turned his attention to my neck and ears, cleaning with a fastidiousness that reminded me of the monkey. When he had finished I leaned back into the enveloping warmth of the water, the little prismatic bubbles of foam popping about my ears and the mint-scented steam seeming to drift through the chambers of my head. I felt thoroughly relaxed, as though made of liquid, and though I had no urge to sleep I seemed to be on the precipice of dreaming, my mind too spilling from its confines. I rolled my head over and looked at the old man. His own head was interposed between me and the burning bulb that hung down from the ceiling, so that its light gathered luminously in the steam around him before falling away to shade, giving him the appearance of owning a halo.

'Who are you?' I asked him.

He did not answer me, but merely gazed back, his head inclined forward, his face smooth and radiantly serene.

'How do you know so much about me?'

'I've been watching you for a long time,' he said.

'Me? – But how?'

'Do you remember the landlord from the flat in Herbert Place? He came sometimes to fix the taps or the window sashes and he would bounce you on his knee.'

I pondered for a moment. I remembered the frayed grey carpet that ran along the darkened corridor and the little fold-out bed I slept on in the corner of my mother's room. Above all I remembered the view of the canal barges from our sitting-room window. But try as I might I could form no picture of the landlord.

'No,' I said. 'I was very little then.'

'What about Blake, the Judge's gardener?'

'Oh yes,' I said. 'I remember him.'

'And Curran the grain dealer who came to Skinner's farm?'

'Yes.'

'The actor with the walking-stick whom you encountered on O'Connell Bridge when you arrived in Dublin?'

'Yes, I remember. He helped me to escape from the beggar. But I cannot see any of them clearly.'

'Behold them now,' he said, his smiling face glowing and appearing to float among the tiny particles of water which glistened in the air. 'I was all of them.'

'Ah,' I said. My sense of incredulity seemed to have deserted me. 'Do you suppose you could wash between my toes? I still can't seem to reach them.'

The old man applied himself assiduously to this task, burnishing my nails with a hard brush and pumicing the callouses while I absently lathered the expanse of my torso. He returned then to my top end and began to root busily through my hair with his fingers.

'Mercy,' he said. 'I thought I detected movement. You've nits.'

He padded over then to a small wooden cabinet and returned with a number of articles, which he laid out along the edge of the bath.

'Hasn't the monkey been looking after you?' he asked.

'We had a row,' I explained.

The monkey had in fact moved progressively closer and was now hanging by his tail from the curtain rail and looking at the old man through very narrow eyes. I believe that he was jealous. The old man paid him no attention whatever. He carefully cut a cube of amber gelatinous substance from a brick and vigorously washed my hair with it. It had a deep mossy smell, as of the forest, lightly sweetened by something like honeysuckle. I allowed my eyes to close so that I could take it in. The old man doused the back of my head with a few mugfuls of water and then began to snip away at the hair that hung down over my neck. Next I felt him draw a line with his thumb from ear to ear across the dome of my head through the lather that was still gathered there, and then a series of short scraping motions about the lower part of my face and over the front of my skull with something cool and fine. I opened my eyes and saw only a field of intense white light. After a while I could discern a bone-handled straight razor held delicately in his pink fingers, flashing like a signal mirror as he turned it this way and that beneath the overhead bulb. He had shaved my beard and was now at work on the front of my head.

'What are you doing to me?' I murmured.

'An old rite,' he said. 'Celtic tonsure. The monks here followed this pattern until they were forced in the seventh century to adopt the Roman fringe by the Council of Whitby.'

'What does it mean?'

'The Greeks and the Semites offered their hair to their deities as a sign of dedication. Gautama Buddha sliced off his locks with his sword when he renounced the luxury of his home to take up the life of the spirit. The monks use it to signal their leave-taking of the world of the senses. It is to remind you of the worthiness of your path. There, do you like it?'

He held up a small mirror before my face and I regarded the wonder of my skull, perfectly smooth and white up until the starting line of thick black hair which bisected the crown halfway back. It reminded me of a stone washed in the flowing waters of a stream, a thick crop of moss clinging to its side. I passed my hand experimentally over its surface. It moved easily, as though over oiled metal, the skin pulled taut across the smooth crest of hard bone. I could feel the humid air resting upon it as lightly as my mother's hands. Further down, my brows were as thick as gorse and beneath them my eyes glowered into the mirror with an unfamiliar power.

'I like it very well,' I said.

He sprang nimbly to his feet but the creaking in his joints betrayed his advanced years. The sound was as of a single slow step over a pile of dry twigs. I felt the waters swelling within me and tasted faintly a surge of brine rising in my throat as I was moved by the splendour of this aged man. It was as though that small involuntary sound in his knees revealed the entirety of him in an instant – the extremes of life he had seen and felt, the fineness of his aspirations and their battering by the world, his long progress from infancy to old age, where the enormous mechanism of his mind struggled with the infirmities of his body – and the sight of it brought tears to my eyes. That a man such as he should in the closing stages of his life look to me for the fulfilment of his dreams! The sentiment was altogether new to me and I revelled in its sumptuousness and breadth, the tepid water of the bath lapping gently under my chin. I looked over at him. He was just visible through the bubbles of soap foam that lay along the length of my arm. I could see that he had in his hands a long wooden mop handle and that he was bent over and gripping it like a turfdigger's loy. When he straightened up again the heap of clothes which I had left lying on the tiles was hanging from the far end, the trouser legs stiff as a dead man and the entirety spotted with oily grime. He passed slowly from the room then with his contrivance held out in front of him. There was a slow solemnity in his movement, like an altar boy ascending the steps with his cruets.

As I watched him the blue and pink and orange of the soap bubbles were slowly obliterated by two walls of darkness which moved to the centre from the corners of my vision. This was accompanied by a kind of music heard as if from a great distance, a mournful dirge-like whine. I could tell from the sensation of co-ordinated movement within me that a picture was about to appear, and I was interested to note the new addition of sound. When at last my eyes had adjusted to the darkness I could see a number of figures moving slowly against a background of green and grey. It was a dark and sombre picture – the figures mostly clad in black, the green the deep shade of moss and grass at twilight, the grey from the massive rain-washed tables of slate breaking everywhere through the ground. There was a mist in the air which, unlike the lightly wafting steam in the bathroom, was dense and inert. The figures were moving in a straggling procession along a stony path from right to left across my field of vision and were innumerable, for as long as the picture held they continued to appear, singly and in clusters, from the darkness to the right. The women were small and crouched under their shawls and seemed as stones moving, while the men were mostly slight and spindly and walked crookedly, as though dazed. A few, however, proceeded with a military bearing. One of these was at the head of the procession, a tall man wearing a three-cornered hat and carrying a wooden pole, just as the old man had done. Hanging from the end was a green flag, faded almost to white in places and frayed along the edge. Behind him there marched a piper, the startling pink of the buckyrose in his hatband the only exception among the shades of green and grey. I had lost the sound by this time, but I could see the way he played nevertheless, his enormous bony fingers plunging and sliding over the holes in his chanter, his whole body clenching as if shot as he squeezed the bag. His head was inclined so far forward in concentration that I was unable to see his face, and when he pressed a note his finger went white to the knuckle. There then followed a formation of six men, three to each side of a stretcher fashioned out of dark canvas, which they bore along on their shoulders by means of long wooden poles. Lying upon it were two corpses, side by side, wrapped in a green flag of the same design as headed the procession. The flag was very large and of the bodies I could see only two heads of hair splayed out on the canvas. As the men underneath moved along the bodies rolled listlessly on the stretcher, but the hair rippled as though in itself alive.

When again I resumed a wider view I could see that the group was advancing upon a small, low-lying field protected semi-circularly by a cliff which rose some two hundred feet above it. Here the atmosphere was very still and the grass a shade lighter, more like jade than emerald. In the centre was a sharply cut rectangular hole, bordered on two sides by piles of black earth. The path wound down now through a slope all the way to the field, and along its near edge and facing away from me I had added a number of massive figures surmounting plinths and cut from pale stone. Some were archangels with great wings folded in upon their sides and others were Virgins and saints with long robes flowing away from their shoulders. Crouched hugely over the pitiable line of mourners they seemed somehow to contain life within them, like crows ranged out along a wall and awaiting some event. I wondered would they and the corpses move before the picture finally broke up and went away, and I suddenly felt the exhilaration of fear.

The head of the group had by now reached a stretch of flat ground near the edge of the field and I hastened around to a position near the open hole to watch their final advance. I was placed in such a way that I could see only the flag-bearer and behind him a swelling snake-like line of black, pulsating irregularly as the mourners made their way over the stones. It was some time before I could distinguish the flag-bearer's features, his head swinging back and forth in a pendulous arc as he made his way towards me through the mist, but when I did I found that they composed unmistakably the face of Hervey Synnott, that same young and vigorous face which I had seen when he buried the ring, but fixed and serious now under the burden of his solemn duty. It struck me then with staggering force that here was the progenitor of a long familial line that through the centuries had painstakingly transcribed the events of their lives for those that would follow, that he was the forebear of the elderly gentleman who had just finished bathing me, that they were separated from each other by a great expanse of time but were equally alive and vivid in my mind, and too that the weight of the ages could be compressed within the pages of a book and held gently in the hands. I began then to see more faces. I looked out over Hervey's head, past the corpses and along the great black line to the row of statues ascending the slope by the side of the path. The nearest to me was an archangel, his expression heroic, his eyes without pupils and his features those of Declan Synnott. Hervey in the meanwhile had moved away to my left, leaving me a clear view of the piper. I had not previously been able to see his face, but now he was looking straight out ahead of him as he marched resolutely towards me, his long feet seeming to crash like falling trees upon the soft ground. Upon his shoulders was the head of a falcon, large as a human's but with delicate grey feathers, black darting eyes and a fearsome beak. His mouth hung open and was flaming pink, like the flower in his hatband. He too passed me by, following the route taken by Hervey. I was next confronted with the corpses and team of stretcher-bearers, who now appeared to comprise an additional member, a solitary mourner who walked along at the back with his hand reaching up somewhere near the head of the corpse nearest me.

Of him I could at first see only the legs, but then the entire assemblage passed in front of me to follow the flag-bearer and pipes, revealing him for the first time. I saw his hand next, for I was looking up at the corpses and he was gently stroking the brow of the one nearest me. He paused then briefly to work the little ringlets of hair around his fingers. It was a very odd head, with islands of hair scattered about the stretch of smooth pink skin. There was, though, something in the texture of the hair, something too in the angle of the ear on the side of the head that I had seen before and that I knew well. My eyes travelled down the length of the arm until they came to rest upon the most surprising and familiar face of all, my own, a good deal leaner than I had ever seen it, certainly more serene and unafraid, the cast of the mouth knowing yet forgiving, the eyes altogether at home with all that they saw. All at once then I heard the piercing screech of the pipes and the sound of water crashing down upon heaped rocks, until the darkness tumbled in from the sides and I could see and hear nothing at all.

I reclined for some time in a kind of humming silence, as though I was at the bottom of the sea.

Then I heard the old man speak.

'Have you been on another of your excursions?' he was saying.

I looked at him.

'Dear boy,' he said solicitously, 'you look quite wild-eyed. Where *have* you been?'

'A funeral.'

'A fine Irish image,' he said. 'We've never strayed far from the funeral this last millennium. Anyone I know there?'

'Well,' I said deliberately, 'I was there, but not so fat, and you were there too, but you had wings and were made of stone. There was a creature with a falcon's head and a man's body who played the pipes. There were hundreds of others in a great long procession that I couldn't see the end of. Some had faces I seemed to know well but somehow I couldn't place them.'

'What about the corpse?' he asked.

'There were two,' I said. 'I couldn't see them very well. Only the heads. One of them had a small body and a head that was very strange, mainly bald with clumps of long curling hair on it. I couldn't see either of the faces. Their bodies were covered over with a flag.'

'Ha!' he barked aridly. 'Even better. A funeral *and* a flag. You have your finger right on the national pulse. Now then, look. I've brought you this.'

He held up an enormous rectangle of heavy white material.

'This is your own gown. I could find nothing in my wardrobe large enough to encompass you, so I made this up out of a bolt of material left by the previous tenant of this dwelling. It's sailcloth. He told me that he had long intended to navigate the seas of the world, but that he had had to abandon the project when he realised that he had become too old and too poor. You want to see the length of it! I got it all in exchange for a smoking jacket, made of Chinese silk. It's still brilliantly white and ready for travel. Appropriate, don't you think, for one so newly cleansed as yourself?'

His right brow raised slowly, as though pulled from the ceiling by string.

'I'll be cold,' I said.

'You'll have a thermal vest and drawers and long woollen socks that can be pulled up over your knees. And I've a brown cowled cloak of the first quality, purchased from a very wealthy religious order. You'll feel no pain. Now get up.'

I rose like something dredged from the sea. Water poured around the hollows and crevices and great lumps of my misshapen body and I felt so heavy that I wondered would my legs be able to hold me up. I looked down upon myself in deep shame, at the terraces of dimpled white flesh ranged along the slope of my gut, at the sagging fat hanging down over my elbows and hips. Would I ever move at speed, I wondered, would I ever see my own fine anatomy of sinew and bone? The old man threw me a towel and I patted myself dry. I then dutifully put on vest, drawers and socks, and held my arms up high above my head so that he could slip on my penitential sack. I stood uncertainly in the clearing air.

'You look quite the little cherub,' he said, stepping back. He wore an expression of officious cheerfulness, like a field guide.

Though I was, by now, more or less resigned to anything that would come to pass, and altogether too numb to gather the things that had been said to me into a coherent picture, there was one point which I was able to seize upon and which agitated me greatly. It had, I knew, serious implications with respect to my relationship with my mother. I let out a few brief gusts of air and attempted to steady myself.

'I'll do whatever you ask me to do and go wherever you say,' I said. 'I'll try very hard to see Hugh's missing pages so that you can put them back in the book. But I need to know something first. Do you mind?'

'My dear boy,' he said, '*of course*. Ask away.' His eyes looked as innocent as bluebells.

'Well, you see, I –'

I halted, my silent round mouth like a shellhole in a wall. Unusually, however, I was able to draw my breath and force upon myself a degree of composure.

'When my mother and I lived together,' I began again, 'there were just the two of us, alone, and then there was the rest of the world outside, more or less undifferentiated. We were very private, and this world intruded upon us only minimally. The only exception was the Judge, but as you know yourself that was freely and happily undertaken by my mother and me and was in any case tragically brief. I never knew my father. My mother used to entertain me as a child with stories of his impossible adventures, but when I was old enough to put a little order into my thinking I realised that the stories were mutually contradictory and that the man as he was variously presented to me didn't really exist. I was happy enough to dispense with him because it meant that he would never reappear and disturb our peace. We had, in short, no intimates apart from each other. My mother, of course, had a succession of lovers who from time to time displaced me from our bed, but while this tortured me with jealousy I knew in my heart that she gave nothing of her *self* to these men. Her self she reserved for me. That, at any rate, is how I have always imagined it to be.

'If, however, I were to discover after all these years that there had long been something essentially counterfeit in my mother's relations with me, if, while she was leading me to believe that I was everything to her, she was in the meanwhile exchanging clandestine confidences with someone else – with *you*, for instance – then that world which I had thought we had built and nurtured and lived in together would cease to exist. My past would become a wasteland. So I am sure you can see that it is a matter of crucial importance for me to know the exact parameters of your relationship with my mother. From what you have told me this evening, it is clear that, in your various guises, you have known her for a minimum of thirty-five years and that you have been with her during some of her most vulnerable moments. Unless you are a clairvoyant – and you deny that you are – the only way that you could have known about the picture I had seen of the Judge's death was if my mother told you about it. She therefore thought enough of you to speak with you about my most private thoughts, and you thought enough of her to give her the thing you value most in the world, your book of family manuscripts. So what I really need to know, before I go on . . . is whether my mother . . .' I found it painfully difficult to form my mouth around the words, so I released them abruptly in a single breath, with a sickening shock passing across my chest and tears stinging in my eyes, '. . . if my mother betrayed me.'

'Still the cossetted little boy, aren't you?' he said with cold certainty, as though from a High Court bench. 'Well, you needn't worry. Your mother and I could not have exchanged intimacies because she knew next to nothing about me and no doubt cared even less. To her I was merely gardener, landlord, actor, *et alia*, and she never troubled to notice the similarity between them all. It was chance that I learned of your vision. I came upon her one evening in a state of distraction on a bench in the orchard not long after the Judge died. I sat down beside her and gave her a drink from my flask of tea. She told me then how deeply affected you had been by the old boy's death, how you had been overtaken upon receipt of the news and had seen in your mind the lethal accident in excruciating detail, and how this was undoubtedly a consequence of your having been robbed so unfairly of the only man who might have been a father to you. A pale moon had arisen and a few stars had begun to appear, and she told me all of this with her head inclined upwards, as though addressing them as much as me. I could have been anybody.'

'I see . . .' I looked downwards in an effort to control my happiness. I could never tire of hearing of my mother's love for me. 'But then,' I began slowly, 'if you don't really *know* each other, why did you want to be near her so much? Why did you follow us about the country and wear disguises?'

He moved so close to me that I was forced to look into his eyes and feel the living heat of his body.

'I've been watching you,' he said, 'ever since you were born. Just like I watched your mother.'

It was as though the words had come from the walls around me and the sky outside.

'But who are you?'

Atma yelped sharply and the monkey arched his back. He seemed as unnerved as myself.

'Perhaps you already know,' he said. 'Try and think. Have you seen me someplace before?'

'You know very well when I've seen you. The day we buried

Hercules, today, and those other times when you pretended to be someone else.'

'I mean in another way entirely,' he said. 'Did you ever see me in your mind?'

He spoke very gently, like someone humouring a madman.

'Well, yes . . . I did. Twice. Today when I saw the funeral. And then one other time.'

'And when might that have been?'

'It was on that day I first met you, when we were sitting on the bench in the square. After the burial. You closed your eyes and became very silent. I saw you then.'

'Was I alone?'

'No. There were many people there, and I saw you last of all. I had been looking at your face, you see, and then I saw my mother in it. Her head floated away from yours and her body formed underneath it. She was very young and pretty and she was wearing a bridal gown. She walked out onto a kind of dancefloor which was surrounded by people watching her, and then you appeared. You had black shiny hair and you were wearing a tuxedo. The shirt had a wing collar, I remember.'

'So,' he said. 'Not only do you see things as they are and have been, but also as they *should* have been. What was I doing there?'

'You must have heard music from somewhere, because you began to dance.'

'How charming!' he said. 'I was a very keen dancer when I had black hair. When the Charleston was imported into this country I was named champion of all Ireland. Was I dancing the Charleston by any chance?'

'No. It was a waltz. It was like you were on ice.'

'I like a good waltz,' he said. 'And so did your mother.' He furrowed his brow to suggest a moment of nostalgia before moving on. 'Now then, here's a little problem of deduction for you. What do a bridal gown, an expectant crowd and a waltz suggest to you?'

'A wedding?' I ventured.

'Patently. Anything else?'

I was utterly at sea. 'I don't know,' I said.

131

'*The first dance*, you turnip. You're really going to have to think a little harder if we're to make any headway with our task. Now, who dances the first dance at a wedding?'

'Well, I've never been to a wedding,' I protested. I paused for a moment. 'One would be the bride, of course, and the other . . . the groom?'

I looked at him in sudden terror as I realised the implications. Had my errant father at last come from the gloom to claim me? It was a horrible, inconceivable idea.

'No,' he said. 'Not the groom. The bride's father gets the first dance.'

His arms reached out towards me like the encircling walls of a harbour.

'I am your grandfather, my darling boy.'

VII

O ur journey had at last begun. My grandfather had awakened
the monkey and me in time for the dawn to a breakfast of
nectarines and pears and paradise apples — 'the produce of a
native orchard', he had beamed – and a pot of pale herbal tea, and we
had set out while the sun was still low in the sky, carrying our
provisions and travelling items in canvas kit bags slung over our
shoulders. I walked silently and a little nervously in my grandfather's
wake, contemplating our curious and impossible journey – a journey
without a known endpoint or even a method by which to plot a course.
He had divested the monkey of his ornaments and placed them in a
pouch. 'Silence may at times be crucial to our movements,' he said. We
moved in a southeasterly direction along the route I had taken the
previous day, through the great low-lying rectangles of suburban
development and thence into that silent region of dilapidation where
nothing stirred. It was somewhere along the borderland between them
that I finally caught my grandfather up.

'Where will we go, Grandfather?' I asked him.

'We will wander the land until our destination makes itself
manifest,' he replied, his eyes trained on the road ahead of him.

'And how will that happen?'

'Your gift, my boy. You will find it for us.'

He slapped me heartily on the back.

'Hallucinations aren't normally among the tools of human
navigation,' I said morosely.

We moved on in silence past a terrace of derelict tenements, where
in a gap a white goat stood tethered to a railing, chewing on weeds, her
udder bountifully full and pink as the morning sky.

'How will I go about . . . you know, recognising it?' I asked.

'Empty your mind and take nothing for granted,' he said perfunctorily, like a policeman giving directions. He had a knack for drawing an exchange to a conclusion and I dropped back to my former position at his rear, little knowing the privations I was soon to suffer in pursuit of this goal.

We were soon within the familiar precincts of the City Centre. It was by then mid-morning, and as we made for the river my grandfather directed that we stop for tea at a mobile café parked on the pavement at the north end of O'Connell Bridge. It was made of smooth, brightly shining metal and had been festooned by its proprietor throughout its interior and around its serving hatch with authentic rodeo memorabilia from the state of Wyoming in America — silver spurs and a saddle and a lacquer-stiffened lasso. Inside was the proprietor, a man as large as myself with a sweat-drenched face and a red bandana around his neck, and when he moved the entire caravan swayed uncertainly on its springs. Of all the things that he had gathered, I remember in particular the enormous black head of a long-horned steer mounted on the wall above the steaming pots, its fur worn away and gleaming here and there with beads of water, like diamonds scattered in the grass.

My grandfather, with the animals at his feet, placed his order while I looked around me. It was altogether pandemonious. Motorists and cyclists were bunched thickly in the roadways and shoppers and promenaders thronged the pavements, a pack of gypsy boys slithering among them on roller-skates. Their wheels were spinning circles of phosphorescent colour, like hypnotists' tools. Looking westwards, the quay walls on either side of the river were occupied uninterruptedly by lines of men, talking with animation and smoking cigarettes. In the other direction, stretching away from the café eastwards and extending nearly to Tara Bridge was an assemblage of Performing Beggars, their pitches marked out in chalk. I presumed that we were in Saturday.

I made my way along the line. Progress was difficult among the dogs and jostling crowd and the noise was loud and cacophonous. I passed in succession a tap dancer, a talking dog, a letter writer, a harpist, a prayer-sayer, a freak, a bagpiper, a lamenter and a trampolinist. There was a budgerigar called Robespierre performing tricks with cards and salesmen with umbrellas and knives and religious pamphlets. At the end I came to two narrow boxes where side-by-side there stood a newsreader and a storyteller, each of them bawling out their wares at full voice. They were lean men with white shirts buttoned up to their necks, but I could see them only fleetingly as my view was blocked by a number of broad-backed women gathered with their shopping trolleys in front of me, and I could not with certainty disentangle what they were saying. Their voices rose above them like twin wisps of smoke, curling and plaiting about each other over the heads of the crowd to form a single indistinguishable column. I learned the results of the previous day's race meeting at Leopardstown, a report on the forest fires of Argentina, and the news that a Roscommon farmer was being flown to Rome following an account to a bishop of his descent into Hell, but which voice was responsible for which item I found it impossible to say.

I moved back along the line and found my travelling companions gathered by the quay railings just to the bridge side of the café. The heat of the day made ripples in the air. Atma and the monkey were close together and drinking from bowls of milk and my grandfather was looking out over the river through the steam wafting from his upheld mug of tea. He looked intensely contemplative, and I struggled to think of something interesting to say to him that would make him think well of me. Before anything came to me, though, there arose from the west and from the banks of the river the sound of oaths and exhortations and cheers, moving ponderously towards us like a long-breaking wave. After it had arrived at the other side of O'Connell Street from us, we saw emerging from under the viaduct of the bridge a grouping of thick-set men clothed in broad-striped bathing costumes and shiny, brightly coloured caps, cutting eastwards through the Liffey waters with impressive energy. It was the annual equinoctial race. My grandfather joined in the applause and I followed him. A silence then followed along behind the uproar, a brittle, unnatural silence like in-held breath, and I saw progressing eastwards along the opposite bank a convoy of three prison vans, their windows barred and darkened but filled with faces and palms pressed against the glass.

Two foot patrols of eight soldiers moved towards us along each of the river banks and I heard the faint slow sound of a nearly idling motor. They kept their eyes on the river as they walked along, their rifles cradled in their arms. When they reached us we saw the solitary figure of a fully clothed youth emerge from beneath the bridge, his long hair splayed out and buoyed on the green murky waters, his breathing laboured, his progress painfully slow. A small boat with an outboard engine and two armed soldiers as passengers followed close behind. All along the quay the crowd fell silent and the Beggars ceased performing while the figure in the water passed by. There was no sound save that of the traffic, the boat and the sudden bursts of noise which erupted from the radios fastened to the epaulettes of the soldiers. We held the silence as had those before us for an impossibly long time, a silence filled with discomfort, as though throughout it I had been standing on my toes. Finally then the little figure and his accompanying boat passed out of sight beneath Tara Bridge. In the mounting hubbub which ensued, my grandfather spoke.

'Do you like history, boy?' he asked.

I told him that I knew next to nothing about it.

'You should learn. History ripens your sense of the places on which your eye falls, or the ground on which you walk. It permits you to see in detail and in depth, like the spectacles which Hervey presented to Bertrand de Paor on his eightieth birthday. Do you see that bridge?'

I looked along the bulking concrete structure straddling the water, incalculably heavy in its denseness. It still bore the carved emblems of its imperial construction, corroded now and weather-blackened.

'Yes,' I said.

'That bridge bears the traces of its history ever since its completion in 1798. That was the year of the United Irishmen. When the uprising took place that May the authorities directed that the scaffolding around it should remain in place, rather than be dismantled. The protruding poles were to serve as impromptu gallows for the legions of the condemned. Now the bridge was then, as it is now, the most populous thoroughfare in the city. Can you picture the scene? The citizenry passing to and fro, the bodies swaying in the sea breeze. An edifying example, wouldn't you say?'

I looked anxiously at his profile and could see from his narrowing eyes that he was building remorselessly upon a theme.

'What had they done?' I asked quietly.

'What had they done? They were *rebels*, child. They had responded imaginatively to the alien presence. But, alas, unprofessionally. They became victims of what was, even then, a long-standing practice here of – shall we say, containment?'

He now turned upon me the fullness of his face. His eyes were bright and he appeared to be smiling, but his lower lip had been drawn down like a provoked dog's, so that I could see his small, even teeth. His arm chopped at the air in a southerly direction.

'If we were to cross over the bridge and turn right into College Green we would arrive eventually on the left-hand side at Dublin Castle, whence that directive had been issued. Here is another structure that bears the markings of history – markings invisible to the ignorant but redolent with meaning to those who have taken the trouble to search the past. There is an old picture of it, a sixteenth century engraving, showing the leave-taking from Ireland of the Lord Lieutenant Sir Henry Sidney. It is crowded with his men regarding him with expressions of sentiment, but above all the picture has that peculiarly Elizabethan look of righteousness and brash adventurism. If you look beyond this grouping you can see sticking point upwards along the walls around the entrance gate – and here is the real point of the illustration – a number of long sharpened poles. Each of them is surmounted by a decapitated Irish head, and, in contrast with the Englishmen, the looks on their faces are of pure Hadean terror. The engraver has appended a lyric to the bottom of his picture:

> *These trunckles heddes do playnly showe*
> *Each rebelles fatall end*
> *And what a haynous crime it is*
> *The Queen for to offend.*

What do you think of it?'

Sometimes I thought my grandfather should not be allowed out of doors, so angry did the world make him.

'I think it's foul,' I said. 'I think you are a repository of unpleasant facts.'

'I am an historian, dear boy,' he replied. 'And we have in this country an unresolved and blood-stained history. In consequence of my acquaintance with it I have in my mind a kind of map similar to one which is made available in shops to tourists who come here. This map depicts by means of a variety of small symbols the innumerable instances of blood-letting here since the twelfth century and the spectrum of their severity, ranging from assassinations and ambushes and sieges all the way to full-scale massacres and the wasting of towns. As I travel about I think of such a map and I can feel the warmth of the blood under my feet.'

'I think that's disgusting,' I said.

He looked into me, his blue eyes bright and hard like moonlit ice and his lips parted and wet. I stared back, but I could not outlast him.

'Why are you telling me these things, Grandfather?'

'By way of overture to your readings and to the stories I will tell you,' he said. 'So that you will know that here the present contains the past and that history can be felt as something tactile. I would like now to tell you the story of Ronan.'

'Ronan?' I said.

'The successor to Anna as keeper of the records.'

'Oh yes,' I said. 'I remember. You said he had . . . what was it? I know – "an aptitude for law".'

'He had, he had,' he said. 'And many other things too. He was tall and fair and good-looking and had lands of some extent. He had a number of children. And he wrote verse too, better than passably. Hard, imagistic – rather Japanese. He claims he composed them in his head while lying on his back like a bard on hard planks in a darkened room.

'But the great thing in Ronan's life was to formulate a new code of Irish law. He thought it a way to meet the English occupation. He used pass his winter months reading about the customs of the past and then adapting them to what he took to be the needs of the time. He wrote it all down in an enormous book. When he had completed it to his satisfaction he spent the month after each spring planting touring the land on horseback and seeking acknowledgement of his new laws. He paid particular attention to those districts where the Crown's writ was weakest.

'There then came into his area an Englishman named Samuel Cooper. Cooper had been granted a large tract of confiscated land on the understanding that he hold the district for the King. The man was an obnoxious bully. Ronan describes him as having an immovably square head, flat metallic hair, repellantly fleshy lips and narrow eyes and a complexion the colour of filleted salmon. A very *English* face you might say.

'Now it became Cooper's practice to tour the entirety of the area of his jurisdiction quarterly in company with fifty armed soldiers, collecting tributes along the way. Those who spoke Irish were invited at swordpoint to put forward the larger amounts. Ronan and Cooper loathed one another. So offensive was Ronan to Cooper's imperial temperament that whenever he set about his excursions, and whatever his ultimate destination, he routed himself directly across Ronan's land, trampling his crops and confiscating his beasts. Seven times Ronan suffered these humiliations. What could he do? He was without weapons and had only his young family.

'Finally, he conceived a retaliatory plan. It was spring, 1337. Cooper was next due to come his way on the summer solstice. Over the weeks leading up to this date Ronan spread the word that he was to commemorate the solstice that year by holding a bardic convention on his land. It would take place on the solstice itself and the two days surrounding it, and there was to be music and verse-saying and drinking and games. He had read about such events in his researches but so far as he knew none had taken place in the country for over a century. Well, in the end two and a half thousand showed up. People came from as far away as Clare and Antrim. Nothing like it had been seen there in living memory.

'Spirits were high by the time Cooper and his men arrived at the borders of Ronan's land on the evening of the second day. He attempted to advance, but so Anglophobic had the crowd become under the influence of the drink and the verse that they drove the mounted company off under a hail of missiles. Many horses had bolted from under their riders and been taken by the crowd. The whole thing was a disaster for Cooper, because all around the country was empty where the people had come to the festival and only the old were left to pay any tax. It was a write-off.

'Cooper regrouped in the village below Ronan's lands. When night fell he ordered a dozen of his men up to Ronan's house, where they took him from his bed and beat him nearly to senselessness. He was warned that unless his land was cleared by noon of the following day the empty villages and houses in the area would be wasted by fire. Then they did something strange and cruel. With his wife looking on, one of the soldiers held the tip of his sword to Ronan's left eye, twisted his wrist and gouged the eye whole from the socket. In the morning the people found him with his family sitting in the grass by his house, a gruesome, Cyclopean figure.

'A great surge of fury moved through the crowd. Hundreds took up stones and cudgels, and others with swords ran down the hill to the village where Cooper was bivouacked with his men. They set upon the whole of the fifty-strong guard and beat them all to death. Cooper was dragged out into the road and staked out naked by his hands and feet. All around him were the blood-oozing corpses. One by one then the whole of the dead men's one hundred eyeballs were dug out from their heads and gathered in a canvas sack. With a sword held at Cooper's gut and another at his scrotum, and large strong hands holding open his jaws, these were fed one by one down his gullet. Over and over he vomited them up, and when he could take no more they poured the remainder over his white body. He lay thus into the evening of that day.

'They had thought to drive him mad, but Cooper was hard. Through it all he held onto his wits. He covered himself in sacking and made his way to Dublin. There he raised an army and within a fortnight he had cleared the whole of his district of poets and musicians, brought them to the town where the slaughter had taken place and hanged them. Ronan's house and lands were burned and his family dispersed. He too was brought to the village, where his back was broken with heavy stones. As he lay dying Cooper cut him open with his sword and had him tied to a tree by means of his own intestines. No one dared move him through the whole of the summer.

'Poor Ronan, eh? A lawyer in an era of lawlessness. Couldn't read the pulse of his time. Wouldn't he put you in mind of Prometheus, bound up by an imperial god by his own gutstrings?'

With this my grandfather came to a halt, and in his silence there was to be heard a rising clamour of shouted beguilements, tinnily recorded calliope music and the murmurings of a crowd gathering at the perimeter of the first pitch beyond the café. I was still unsteady from the effects of my grandfather's tale but nevertheless moved forward as best as I could along with Atma and the monkey and gained a position by the café's side panels and amongst the front rows of the spectators. My grandfather hoisted Atma up to chest level and the monkey sat on my shoulders with his legs clamped around my neck and his tiny hands folded on my brow, so that in the end we all had a clear view of the performance area.

Here could be seen now the slow, heavy manoeuvres of an escapologist, an enormous man stripped to the waist and without shoes who was summoning the punters and gathering himself up for his entertainment. I took him to be a countryman. The skin of his torso was pink, and seemed unused to the light. He wore brown, grime-stained trousers that might have belonged to a suit and his sea-blue eyes looked sorrowful and shy. Russet-coloured hair grew neglectfully over his sunken face like reeds in a flooded, disused field. He had made three apparent concessions to showmanship: around his waist he wore a wide leather belt, its silver prizefighter's buckle recessed deeply into the flesh of his gut; his large heavy eyebrows had been tweaked into elongated points with moustache wax; and across his chest was tattooed in green letters the simple word 'FREEDOM'. I placed him as hailing from one of those forgotten, clay-heavy counties along the old border – Leitrim or Monaghan or Cavan.

The escapologist was moving rather morosely within the confines of his chalk box, bawling out at passers-by, 'Step forward, ladies and gentlemen, step forward! Come and tie me up! Tie me up for a fiver! Which of you can do it? A tenner for you if I can't get free! *Tie me up!*' His countenance grew more dour as he spoke, and there was an intensity to his delivery which I thought well exceeded the demands of this sort of fairground commerce. There was some jostling among a group of boys but no one actually penetrated the escapologist's territory until two men with broad Oriental features and wearing low-ranking military uniforms stepped forward from the back rows brandishing their notes. At their hips they wore stiff leather holsters containing powerful-looking guns. Some members of the audience applauded demurely. The soldiers then set about a lengthy and complicated procedure of binding which involved the neck, wrists and ankles and which resulted in the escapologist being supported by the palms of his hands and the soles of his feet, his head upside-down and perpendicular to the pavement, his back painfully arched and his navel pointed straight to the sky. The knots were strange and complex and may well have been Chinese. Frankly I could see no conceivable method by which he might extricate himself from them.

There was a pause then while the three men in the box regarded one another, and in it I distinctly noticed a brief rearrangement of the features of each, a common look, I thought, of grim and silent satisfaction. This progressed in the case of the Orientals into broad, gap-toothed grins, and they waved like victorious athletes at the crowd while the escapologist wriggled and squirmed and made his way backwards in a painful crab-like manner along the pavement until he disappeared beneath a canvas sheet suspended from a line and bisecting his box. It was painted white and bordered in small green shamrocks, and in red letters it announced his performance thus:

Ireland's Celebrated

MR TIE – ME – UP!

An Artist in Freedom

Between lines two and three there was a space in which glowered the crudely drawn, disembodied head of the escapologist himself, surmounted by a crown wound round with the thick hemp rope of his trade.

The sign began shortly to tremble and shake with his exertions, and there was a woeful row of gurgling and strangulated cries as he struggled to unbind himself. To my right I heard my grandfather grunt ruefully and murmur, 'His box, I would say, is more confining than his ropes.'

I sidled nearer to him. 'Grandfather,' I said.

'Hmmm?' He was concentrating on the escapologist's stage.

'I understand that Ronan wrote about his life as you told it me. But how did you learn about his death?' It occurred to me that I had no means of ascertaining the validity of anything he said, that he might have invented the entire episode, much as my mother had pleased herself with tales of my father.

'An historian's question. Very good. I learned it from Conal, Ronan's son. He was brought to the village to witness his father's death.'

'How horrible!' I said.

'Regrettably there is little known of him. He was hanged under the Statutes of Kilkenny while still in his twenties. His crime was riding a horse in the Irish manner, without stirrups. But he had a fearsomely detailed eye for the grotesque. You should read his account of the Black Death in the year 1348. It took Cooper and all his family, one by one, and Conal writes with great relish about the black suppurating boils disfiguring their legs and torsos and their hair-pulling madness derived from the pain shrieking inside their heads. It's like reading about the end of the world.'

The two Orientals had remained within the pitch and were regarding one another smugly, their stances wide, their arms folded across their broad, belted chests. The spectators around them stared out ahead of themselves with expressions of bovine patience. Mr Tie-Me-Up's cries still rose up from behind his sheet, and his lurid painted visage quavered fearsomely. I began to feel a little embarrassed, as though I had chanced upon a sad, solitary ritual being enacted in silhouette upon a drawn blind. The monkey, I think, felt similarly. He had bounded exuberantly from my shoulders and gained the metal roof of the café so as to have an unrestricted view of the escapologist at work, but after a moment or two looking beyond the curtain he averted his eyes and took up a new position on the quay railings, looking down at the murky waters of the Liffey as they flowed out to the sea.

Presently there was a loud burst of recorded trumpet fanfare which emerged from a small plastic speaker resting on the pavement, followed by a static-polluted rendering of 'The Soldier's Song' on a single metallic instrument, a xylophone or triangle – it was difficult to tell – and then finally the appearance of the escapologist himself stepping forth from behind his canvas sheet, his coiled rope raised triumphantly in one hand and extending forward in the other a small velvet pouch in which to collect his offerings. A kind of spiritless applause waved about me, joined rather sportingly, I thought, by the Oriental soldiers. The escapologist flexed and strutted his way around his box jangling his bag of coins, and as he did I noticed that through a twist in his mouth the expression on his face had progressed to one of consummate self-righteousness. But there was something else there too, a look of mirth in the eyes which I would not have thought attainable in one so forlorn. And then there were his trousers. These too were brown and stained heavily with black, oily grime, but they were also cuffed and marked out in feint, wide-gapped chalk stripes, where I was sure they had not been previously. There was something going on here, I was certain, and it began to make me quite agitated. The escapologist affected a wide and ungainly bow and moved about the box collecting his bits while I attempted to focus my thoughts. 'An old-fashioned nationalist,' I heard my grandfather declare obscurely. He threw some coins into the pitch and, before I could speak, bundled us all together and propelled us along the road at speed. We passed by the sprawled mendicants stretched along the bridge, landing down on the southern shore and turning left into Burgh Quay, the calls and clamour of the Performing Beggars widening and then receding into the clamorous marketplace babel. When we drew level with the mobile café on the opposite bank, glowing warmly now in the summer sun, I looked at the quay wall just along from it and discovered there leaning over the river, a burning cigarette dangling loosely from his lower lip, his free hand methodically massaging his shoulder, his neck and wrist still bound to each other by means of those devilishly intricate Far

Eastern knots, the self-same Mr Tie-Me-Up as originally presented to us.

'I knew it! *I knew it!*' I exclaimed, gesticulating wildly. 'Grandfather, look! *Look!* There were two of them all along. That's how they did it! I knew it — the trousers, that smirk. The eyes! What about that, Grandfather? Eh?'

'Commendable, my boy, commendable,' he said. 'Most observant.'

And that brought the subject to an end for the present time.

We continued to pursue our south-easterly course, keeping well to our right the congested area of Historic Sites and Public Monuments where the life of the city ebbed and flowed, and picked our way among the narrow streets and walkways that divided up the old warehouses and long strips of public housing in this district. My grandfather enjoyed the society of blocked-up windows, of brick walls burst through with trees, of weed-split tarmac, of narrow passageways made of smooth worn stone, dull-sheening with damp; he liked abandoned and forgotten places, ancient and modern, and he steered us through them whenever he might. He called them 'symbols of our forfeited citizenship'. We proceeded circuitously, it seemed, and I soon lost all bearings. We met almost no one along the way. At a silent crossroads, only a short distance from our point of entry, a frenzied man came out of a laneway to our left pushing an empty handcart at a great lick, its iron-rimmed wheels rattling over the cobbles, bawling out of him at full voice a long indecipherable complaint. His eyes were crazed and wisps of hair stood upright on his balding, capless head. He charged on without looking our way.

Through a further sequence of turnings we came upon the ruins of an old baths, its walls and fixtures lying in heaps of mortar and piping and painted tiles. A section of its front wall remained standing, its arched windows and porticoed doorway closed over with cinderblock. There emerged then over one of the piles of rubble a woman, and we paused to look at her. She carried with her a clawed hammer and hacksaw, and was collecting where she could whole tiles and nails and lengths of piping made of copper or brass. These she segregated into plastic carrier bags ranged out along a section of flat ground near the wall. Her stiff, wiry hair was orange, as in a certain strain of rust, and around the crown of her head was a circle of dark grey like a skullcap where the dye gave way to new growth. Her lips and cascading cheeks were likewise decorated a lurid orange. She wore cowboy boots over her bare, dust-caked legs, and a rawhide waistcoat and mini-skirt with tassled fringe. She was old, and the collapsed muscles of her thighs drooped like elephants' ears over her knees.

'Good to see the old styles making a comeback,' intoned my grandfather, like a priest saying a funeral prayer.

We pressed on through the emptiness, the sighs and odours and muted murmurings of the Bus Garage away behind us to our right. We came then after some time to a housing estate, where in a tarmacked forecourt a heap of cars burned moodily, attended by some dogs and very small children. These too, as with others I had passed that day, did not trouble to look up at us from their wild encircling leaps. This, I may say, surprised me very considerably, for ever since I had stepped out into the sunlight dressed in sack and sandals and entered the domain of the public I had been expecting all manner of unwelcome attentions. I feared children and youths most of all. This sensation of self-consciousness was so acute during the first few hours of our journey that whenever we came upon a group of any size I fell into a kind of flinching, abject crouch until they passed. But no one seemed to care a damn, and I soon forgot all about it. In those days there were, as it happened, all manner of zealots and novices abroad in the streets in pursuit of religious positions, and I might, I suppose, have been thought to be numbered among them.

Just a hundred or so yards further on from the housing estate we emerged into the wide thoroughfare of Pearse Street and cut quickly across to South Erne Street, up Holles Street past the hospital into Merrion Square, and then finally to the familiar stone steps rising to the residence which my mother and I had inhabited for so many years, coming at this point to a decisive halt. I looked uncertainly at my grandfather.

'You had better go up and get the book,' he said evenly.

My weight passed back and forth from one foot to the other, and I released into the atmosphere some puffs of air from my inflated cheeks.

'Go on,' he said.

I stayed where I was, my cheeks out like bladders. All that could be heard were my whistling gusts.

'What the devil are you doing?' he said. I could tell that I had made him cross.

'Nothing,' I said. A reddening heat was spreading upwards from my neck.

'I *demand* to know,' he said. 'This insufferable habit. You sound like a begging spaniel! Now tell me, why do you do it?'

I kept my eyes to the ground, and it was some while before I could gather myself to speak. 'I do it when I'm afraid,' I said then, my voice small.

'To what end?'

'It's like there's something nearby, a dark force, that wants to take things from me. I don't have very much and I'm afraid it will take everything. It's there almost all the time but sometimes it gets very close and when it does I feel I have to blow at it to keep it away. It's terrible. Mostly I'm afraid it's going to take my mother. It's been like this ever since she started taking her turns and going away. If I blow, you see, I don't think about it. I'm so *uncertain* of her.'

'We'll put an end to that,' he said. 'You need reorientation. "Spiritual unhealthiness and misfortunes can generally be traced to excessive love of something which is subject to many variations." That's Spinoza. You need to broaden your outlook, boy.'

At this he turned away. I did not understand him, and I still had no wish to go. I fretted about the unpredictable effects a visit to our old rooms might provoke in me now that we were under way, and the book was after all quite a heavy article to be carrying about on a pedestrian expedition of such uncertain duration, but I could see by my grandfather's stance – he was looking out ahead of himself over the road we were to travel along, the metal tip of his walking stick tapping rhythmically on the pavement as he whistled a light air – that he intended to brook no equivocation from me.

At this I took the monkey by his warm little fist and we climbed the stairs. As we rounded the landing at the second floor I thought I sensed cutting through the ponderous atmosphere of mildew a sharp and sweetened scent, as of whinbush. It was a woman's smell. My heart quickened. Had my mother at last come home to me? I bounded up the remaining stairs, leaving the monkey standing. At the top landing I found our door enticingly ajar, but the sharp smell had passed – it may never have been there – and when I entered I found the rooms to be as we had left them some twenty-four hours before. They were flooded now in bright summer sunshine which poured in through the skylight and windows and fell with gleaming vitality over our dust-covered piano and our failing plants. Here and there about the floor were the tightly balled pages of my translation notes and the remains of some of the meals the monkey and I had taken together. I looked in at the birds in their glass case. They seemed care-worn and elderly now, as though they had been standing long in the rain, their alarming tropical colours quietened by neglect, their glass eyes un-focussed and inert. I went about from room to room, coming finally to the bedroom. I looked at the tossed, sprawling bed, at the detritus of my long literary labour, at my mother's rail of dresses hanging limply on their hangers. The drawing she had made on the mirror had lost all definition and become a meaningless pattern of lines, the chalk having crumbled away here and there and lying now in dustheaps along the frame. It was all very odd. I had been gone no more than a day and already the rooms had taken on an aspect of long abandonment. They were like a bowl of fruit growing mould, a still thing ageing. What is more, they had ceased to bear any trace of my mother's living presence, or really of any life at all, and I found that they meant nothing whatever to me. The feeling thus engendered, I may say, was less one of loss than of release. I took up the book and a page or two of my mother's notes from the table in the bedroom and collected in addition the photograph of my mother and me taken by the Judge and the collapsible telescope with which we used to examine the constella-tions, still on its tripod by the window. I passed then into the hallway. There I found the monkey sitting poised like an owl at the top of the hatrack. I cast my eye about the place a final time and we made off down the stairs. All that remained behind us now could rot, so far as I was concerned, and indeed I never laid eyes on any of it again.

When we came out again onto the street we found Atma stretched out on the pavement taking the sunshine, but there was no immediate sign of my grandfather. I ran up and down the road and discovered him a little distance away, leaning in the shade of an old bus shelter. His face was distorted with pain and he was holding himself as though he had taken a blow to the stomach.

I hastened to his side.

'Grandfather,' I said. 'What's wrong? Are you all right?'

'I'm fine,' he said, but his jaw remained clenched.

'You're not,' I said. 'What's happened? Have you been attacked?'

'It's nothing, I said. Indigestion perhaps. Have you the book?'

I watched as he forcibly composed his features, seeming to drive the pain out of himself with the strength of his will.

'I have,' I said.

'We can move on then,' he replied.

'It's an impressive weight,' I said, holding my ground. I wanted to give him time to catch his breath.

'Three-quarters of a millennium, more or less,' he said. 'All detail.'

'Have I to read it all, would you say?'

'You will want to in the end, I should think. But sequentiality is not the issue. You can skip around. It has its longueurs, after all.'

I considered this.

'How far into the book does the account of Ronan come?'

He pointed to a spot not even a sixth of the way along from the front.

'My God,' I said. 'It will take years.'

'Well, I shall endeavour to find something more suitable for you then,' he said. 'The *Beano* and a packet of sweets perhaps. Would you like that?'

The pain had made him a bit more tetchy than usual, but this soon passed under the brightness of this fine summer's day. He packed the book away in his kit bag and we set off again, crossing over the canal and making our way through the leafy avenues of Ballsbridge until we reached the sea, and then hit off straight down the coast road towards the mountains, a topography according to my grandfather which has long been associated with the receiving of visions. The road and the sky opened out grandly as we reached the water, and the constraints and burdens of the city flew from me like a flock of birds rising from a strand. Out on the wide sands and in the shallow waters of the bay were clamdiggers and picnickers and children, scores and scores of children besporting themselves in the salty froth. It seemed to me then as we sauntered along, as it had seemed too to an Italian travel writer of long ago, that all nature wore an unusual smile. Overhead us, gulls turned in wide arcs, stunningly white against the blue sky, a light sea breeze clarifying the air. Everything gleamed with a hard, diamond-like purity – the chrome on the passing cars, the intense blueness of my grandfather's eyes, the light moving over the rippling water of the bay. I have never seen such natural clarity except in close proximity to the sea. With the sun warming the expanse of my back, my mind began gently to empty and I abandoned myself utterly to the leisurely momentum of the afternoon.

We suffered our first interruption near Booterstown. Here two rows of police, standing arms akimbo, had formed a thin conduit which traversed the coastal road and through which marched a column of young men and women. They were being channelled onto a gravel path which led down from the road and onto a broad wasteground on which a fenced-in compound containing long white structures of concrete had been newly built. Scattered randomly about the entrance gate were a number of jeeps crammed with lounging soldiers. Beyond them, and nearer the railway line which hugged the bay, there stood a white twin-humped camel, looking towards Howth, its hind leg tethered to a van. The van was from Fossett's Circus. I looked out past the line of police. The prisoners were being emitted from the back doors of three large vans, the same grey vans I had seen making their dark progress along the quays, the same prisoners I had seen with their faces and hands pressed to the glass. They were still emerging when those at the front of the column had reached the compound, anxious and meek-looking, like things new to captivity, and we were held in our positions until all of them had passed. I looked for the long-haired swimmer among them, but could not make him out, and while I looked I thought of the long, sad phalanx of saffron-tunicked warriors watched by Hervey and Bertrand as they were driven overland to their deaths.

'Who are they?' I whispered to my grandfather.

'Rioters,' he said. 'Two barracks and a tax office went up last night.'

We continued on our way then, keeping to the coast as we drove on through the sprawling conurbation that extends out along the bay from the city, and arriving at Bray in the wake of the returning commuters. Here we stayed a while among the long, low beams of warm yellow light that streaked the ground about us. My grandfather and I were still quite surprisingly fresh after the long tramp, but the animals were altogether done in. The monkey, whose physique was unsuited to long-distance travel overland, first showed signs of weakness at Blackrock and was visibly trembling at the knees by the time we had cleared Sandycove, so that I had to carry him the rest of the way, his long thin arm slung around my neck and his warm little head lolling back and forth on my shoulder, like a loose orange in the hold of a boat. Atma had been hobbling since just beyond Dalkey, where a golf ball had emerged over the brow of a hill, descended whistlingly past my right ear and struck him smartly on the hind quarters. He was left structurally sound, but had been badly bruised and shaken. We took some sandwiches and other provisions from the station café and sat out on the sea wall of the promenade, watching a pair of grey-haired ladies in ball gowns playing the slot machines in the arcade. After a while a man in a green tracksuit trotted past with his daughters. I placed a handful of raisins and nuts in front of the monkey, but his eyelids were flickering and his head was dropping, like an old man in the lounge of a seaside hotel. We thought it best to get out into the open countryside before putting in for the night, and with that in mind we made our way out past Bray Head along a small road that led up into the foothills. The evening was pleasant, and Atma stayed the course as best he could for above an hour or so, but he finally staggered off down a winding, weed-clotted flagstone path which led away from the road and disappeared behind a thick growth of trees and shrubs. He did not re-emerge. We paused in our progress then, the light softening now to blue, the sea having calmed almost to stillness, my grandfather filling the bowl of his long-stemmed pipe.

'Those two men you saw back at Eden Quay,' he said pleasantly. 'The Messrs Tie-Me-Up. How do you suppose they got away with it?'

'Well, they look very alike,' I said. '*Very* alike. But I spotted the difference!'

'You did. And what does their similarity suggest to you?'

'They must be brothers.'

'Twins, actually,' he said. 'They perform that act or a variation on it at that location on Saturday mornings and then again in the afternoon at Stephen's Green. They are called Synnott, cousins of yours, the last of a distant and unregenerate strain of our family who have long been living in reduced circumstances.'

I opened my eyes and mouth very wide in a kind of soundless exclamation, but immediately he finished he turned away and issued forth that strange warbling whistle with which he summoned animals. He then called out 'Atma!', the two short notes seeming to cling ringingly to the still evening air. Atma did not reply, so we made off in his direction, the path beyond the line of trees and shrubs winding down easily through a mossy incline to a stretch of land, the black fertile earth in the foreground giving way to sand and marram grass as it extended trapezoidally to the sea. In the distance was a large settlement of rabbits sitting in the hills above their warrens, most of them still and calm but a few others lumbering about like guests after a large dinner. Before us, within a shelter of trees, was a scavenged and rusted motorcar, its chassis sinking into the black earth, its windows outpouring with wild flowers, and upon its still sun-warmed bonnet was Atma, stretched out and inert, like a heap of bleached kelp pitched upon a strand. He was deeply and all but unrousably asleep.

'Valuable dogs in their way, poodles,' said my grandfather. 'But bred more for intelligence than endurance.'

He led us then across the field. I saw as we passed the car that it had recently been used as habitation, for in the rear seat were a hairbrush and a waterlogged baby's shoe, and scattered on the ground near the door were a number of empty food tins, soup and spaghetti and stew. At the far end of the field, we reached a sandy path which led through short overarching trees to the heavily bouldered shoreline, the rabbits scattering with our passing as though blown by a sudden wind.

Here we encamped for the night, at the sea end of the path, partly sheltered under the overhang of trees but with a fine view of water and sky.

It was grand to see the full reach of the sky, suffused with rose where the sun touched it from beyond the hills and everywhere else blue giving way finally to the tenderest shades of violet and purple where it darkened on the horizon. I had walked under the claustrophobic skies of Ireland, under the low boiling clouds, dank and murky like the ceiling of a cellar, but they had opened now onto the great vault, immense and impressive and suggesting the greater immensity beyond it. I felt free now in this floating world of blueness, as light and as blue as air itself. The stars began to come out then as I sat with my grandfather and the animals in the sand, the sky darkening around them until it reached finally the profoundest of all blues, a colour so cold and beautiful and uncompromising as to seem all intellect. I thought of the dome of my head and the dome of the sky and the enormity of the universe. The water was tranquil among the heavy rocks, and the sand cool on my throbbing feet. The rainforest smell of the monkey filled my nostrils. I felt the pull of these earthly things and the ineffable lightness of the sky. Could I drift there among the stars? I wondered then as I sat had I been there before in the silence and emptiness, watching the Judge die and my mother marry and Hervey bury the ring. Did the sky in its strength and size and change-lessness see and record all that happened beneath it and hold it in memory? Could I see it too if I 'emptied my mind and took nothing for granted'? Could I see Hugh's manuscript? *Could I see my mother?*

I looked around me. Atma was asleep at the base of a tree and my grandfather was stretched out in his bed-roll, his hands folded behind his head, looking up at the sky. I put out my own blankets and lay down beside him, feeling the sand shape itself around my back.

I addressed him then.

'Do you think is my mother watching the stars tonight, Grand-father?'

'I hope so,' he said. 'She likes a starry night, your mother.'

153

'I know. We used look at the stars on clear nights when we were in the big houses out the country. Here,' I said, remembering.

I drew the telescope out from my bag. Its brass fittings and green leathers were fine in the starlight, and I could see fleetingly the colours of the spectrum play on the surface of the glass. I buried the tripod deep in the ground so that my grandfather could put his eye to the lens.

'Look,' I said.

We manoeuvred our heads close together and lay there for a time, passing the telescope back and forth between us and tracing the constellar patterns in the sky – Orion, the Bear, the Seven Sisters, those oddly angled lines that contrived to make a flatness out of the firmament. We followed new patterns too of our own making, lines leading outward, of depth rather than containment, going from star to star, flecks of diminishing brightness, on and on neverendingly. My mind ran about like a dog in a field.

'My mother bought me this,' I said after a time. 'We had drawers full of things made of glass – spectacles and lorgnettes and binoculars. Anything with a lens. D'you know, she couldn't get enough of them.'

He considered this, a sudden rippling passing over his brow.

'I wasn't aware of this.'

'Is it significant?'

'Possibly . . . I don't know. When did she begin her collection?'

'When we were on the road,' I said. 'After the Judge died.'

There was a long silence then while my grandfather pondered, so long that I lost track of him. I lay on my back, the earth seeming to hurtle through the universe at terrible speed.

'Spinoza was a polisher of lenses,' he said finally. 'And he was the noblest of all the philosophers.' The muscles in his face were taut with exasperated concentration. Here was another facet of my mother to which he applied the full force of his mind, yet which he could not unriddle. '. . . Goethe wrote a treatise on optics!'

I shifted in the sand so that I lay on my side. All was still again.

'Will we ever find her, Grandfather?' I said. I spoke very quietly.

He put the telescope to the side and looked at me, his face an oval bowl, his eyes the blue of dusk.

'I don't know, my heart, I don't know,' he said. 'It's a long absence.'

'Yes,' I said. 'She was never gone so long as this. Three years ago, in the winter, she went out for a newspaper and she was gone for nearly a month. That was the longest before this. She turned up in a trawler in Donegal. She could get shot, some of those places she goes.'

'She's looking for something,' he said. 'She's been looking for years. I've seen her. She goes about in a trance.'

'But what could it be?' I asked him. 'We were happy, the two of us . . . most of the time.'

'Lord knows. Everyone with a brain is looking for something, until they learn to still the urge. With your mother it's different. There's no focus to it. She just gets to a place and wanders. She travels with evident purpose, yet when she arrives at her destination she is uncomprehending. I am still unable to fathom it.'

I sighed.

'If only I knew what it was I could find her,' I said.

'That, I should say, would take a rare mind indeed.'

'I think I like this, you know. I've never really looked for anything before.'

'It will grow wearisome.'

'But why?'

A fish leapt in a stiff, ungainly arc from the sea, the muted glow of pewter along its scales.

'It's the way of it. I have lived a long life and have learned one thing at least. That is that the exercise of will, particularly in the form of a quest, is both metaphysically necessary and ethically evil. It is without end and without rest and without point. It is described by an interminable cycle of thirst and frustration and satiety. Its issue is suffering and delusion.'

His meaning, as ever, was beyond my reach.

'But you're still looking. Aren't you?'

'Yes. You know that I am. All my life I have been looking for things, and I am still looking now because I cannot stop. But now I am only looking for one thing. I hope it will be the last.'

'Hugh's pages.'

'Yes.'

'I still don't really get it, you know. When I asked you before what was so important about those pages, you said that the book would not be whole without them. Why does it matter so much? Why does it mean you would stop looking for things?'

'I will tell you why.'

'Please.'

'The book, I think, is like the world. It is full of wounded and bored and awe-struck minds. None of them knew where they were going, only where they had been. It has no plot, no hindsight, no *selectivity*. No historian has come along with his censorious logic to assemble it all into a grand schema of cause and consequence which dispenses with the unassimilable and presents the resulting contrivance as manifesting God's or man's or a nation's destiny. The book is full of blind striving, all of it unassimilable. All of it, like life.

'Now I hold in common with a certain philosopher and parapsychologist from the city of Danzig the view that the separateness of things is illusory. It is our sense of ourselves as distinct that promotes the activity of the will. We may release ourselves from the imprisonment of will through an embracing flood of identification with all that is – an embrace whose quality is that of universal suffering. In the most profound and ineffable mystery of all Christian mythology, Christ mounted the Cross to take on the foibles and confusions and crimes of all the souls that ever were and thereby attained and re-opened the Kingdom of Heaven. It was an act of redemption through suffering, redemption not only for himself but for the whole world. Now as I said to you before, I have coveted out of painful curiosity the missing pages ever since I became aware of them. There is also an element of scholarly fastidiousness. But above all I want the book completed because I want to create a model of the world, a plenum of suffering, a suffering I can embrace with the totality of my being. It is a suffering both sweet and pure, I think. And when it comes to me I will perhaps want and suffer no more.'

I looked closely at my grandfather. There was something about his face that was most suited to the pale silver light of moon or stars. I could see that his eyes were moist, but he looked happy at the idea he had outlined. As always in those days when my grandfather gave forth his ideas I felt belittled by them, as though he knew things about the world both profound and particular that would always elude me. He would speak, and his thoughts would seem to move beguilingly like wraiths in the air beyond my fingers. That is long ago now, and since that virginal time I have seen and studied and experienced much. I can see now at least in part the great interconnecting rooms of his mind, majestic and fabulously detailed, of great dimensions and intricate workings and full of paradox like all minds but pervaded above all by this yearning for release. I can see it, I may say, but I wish it might have been otherwise, for as I look back now I think with some sadness as I write this of the great distance the thinking of my family had moved, from the robust empiricism and social experiment of Bertrand de Paor, as transcribed by Hervey, to my grandfather's weary, valetudenarian denial of the sensible world. I know, of course, that it was not always so with him. How must it have been to have known him in the vigour and passions of his best years! I had felt the ghosts of those passions and their presence still was awesome. It was, in part, age that had brought him to this, but it was also, in a sense, insanity. This great mind striving to deny its own knowledge of the world. He had, like no one I have known, gone out into the world and been wounded by it and had now arrived at the point where he wanted above all else to be free from the pain. In time I came to learn the source of this wound and to love him for it.

But then, as I say, these mystical ramblings merely belittled me, and with them the bestirrings of my mind, which had begun with the coming out of the stars, now arrived at their endpoint, like a spring mechanism that had worked through its sequence. I breathed in heavily and felt with some melancholy the great ponderousness of my weight, lessened now from what it had been but bound to the earth as surely as the stones. The burden of it wearied me.

'I want to go to sleep now, Grandfather,' I said.

'Yes.'

'Would you tell me a story first?'

'What would you like?'

'Something from the book. About who comes after Conal.'

'Rather a bad choice, I'm afraid.'

'Why?'

'Because here the longueurs which I spoke to you about are at their most fatiguing. A really dreary bunch they are. I could tell you instead about Thaddeus the builder or Peige who married her brother or Michael who went to Peru. Or there was my grandfather Joshua. Now he was a marvellous character. He wrote Gothic novels which he had privately printed, and on the ceiling of his drawing room were paintings depicting his favourite scenes. In the end he tired of excess and founded a cult based on plain speaking and nakedness. His wife made him wear a cowbell to warn the servants of his progress through the house. These are the better subjects for a bedtime story.'

'I have to take it in order, I think. I'd get lost otherwise. Go on, tell me what they were like. Please.'

'There is not a great deal to say. Conal had a son called Padraig, a farmer. Padraig had a son called Henry. He was a farmer too. They wrote in the book, lived quiet lives, as did those who came after them. Henry established himself in Kildare and they lived on there for a very long time. They're very dull. After Conal something seems to have gone out of them. I've often wondered if it was Conal's awesome portrait of his father's rotting corpse, sitting so heavily on their necks that they couldn't lift their heads. Perhaps it was this fear. There is a sense, you know, that they looked out from their little windows at the world as changeless, unknowable and uniformly hostile. They did very different things. Some were time-servers or settlers or pretend divines, others had those qualities which we associate with the small farmer of medieval England – industriousness and stupidity, obstinacy and superstition. But they were united in their lack of vigour and narrowness of outlook. The only thing I can think of that was remarkable about them – and it was all they really wanted – was that they *endured*. I cannot recommend you to read their accounts. They are full of grain yields, matchmaking, Royal gossip and low-level alchemy. There are sightings of flying hermits and lengthy comparisons of the properties of holy wells. All their names were taken from across the water, names like Tobias and Marmaduke and Lucius. Another thing I have wondered at in reading them is what they made of those who went before them. They couldn't have taken it in. They couldn't *allow* themselves to. I suppose they were like the ill-educated copyists with their learned texts, passing them on with great reverence and want of understanding. Ronan's death was really the turning point. In this sense Samuel Cooper was like the Roman soldier who put to death the mathematician and hydrostatician Archimedes at Syracuse, thus marking a symbolic end to the era of political liberty and original thought in Greece. Enervation, withdrawal. Such are the fruits of imperialism.'

Now as I lay there I felt in my bones the wonderful enormity of exhaustion from our long trek along the coast, but I tried to hold it at bay as he spoke. Sleep approached and withdrew, again and again, the sensation in its dizzying dips and surges like that of being on a small boat pitching about in a high sea. My grandfather seemed far away from me, his words ringing out high in the still night air like distant reports from a gun. They held me, more or less, but when I slid down beyond the borderline of wakefulness halfway towards sleep they mutated hazily into a life of their own, a life I knew that ran along beside my own, so that I saw those succeeding generations of medieval Synnotts, all got up in their belted, lustreless tunics, making their way awkwardly in a straggling line along a stony, rutted road. They were in a thick, congealing mist and appeared to be moving towards a destination somewhat against their will. I saw them only briefly and at intervals, as though the whole scene was lit by a swinging lantern, but I established at least that they numbered a dozen. They were all men and ten of them were identical, short and squat, with narrow eyes and bulbous cheekbones like small red apples. They had black drooping moustaches. Around their necks they wore black satin sashes, but they seemed more irritated than grieving. They did not seem capable of anything quite so large as grief. They bickered among themselves and shoved and elbowed each other as they stumbled along. In among them were two long spindly creatures, emaciated beyond the point which I would have thought capable of sustaining human life, their bodies curved like scythes. These two were quarrelsome, arguing it seemed about which of them had the longer beard. These beards were long and black and pointed and wagged agitatedly in the air above their chests as they argued. They too wore the black sashes. Where could they be going? I wanted badly to know, but I was very tired and I hadn't the strength to draw back from them to a distance where I could place them in any setting. I attempted to follow along beside them as they walked but lost sight of them in an instant or two behind an obstruction. It was white and curved and gleamed a little like granite. I gave it up then because my grandfather had ceased to speak and sleep was now so powerfully upon me that I could restrain it no longer. I fell towards it and in the sweet and embracing darkness I felt my grand-father kiss me lightly on the cheek and bid me goodnight.

VIII

'Brian O Linn had no breeches to wear,
So he got an old sheepskin to make him a pair.
With the fleshy side out and the woolly side in,
"They'll be pleasant and cool," says Brian O Linn.

Brian O Linn was hard up for a coat,
So he borrowed the skin of a neighbouring goat,
With the horns sticking out from his oxters, and then,
"Sure they'll take them for pistols," says Brian O
    Linn.

Brian O Linn had no brogues for his toes,
He hopped in two crabshells to serve him for those,
Then he split up two oysters that matched like a twin,
"Sure they'll shine out like buckles," says Brian O
    Linn.

Brian O Linn to his house had no door,
He'd the sky for a roof and the bog for a floor.
He'd a way to jump out and a way to swim in,
"'Tis a fine habitation," says Brian O Linn.'

The notes of my grandfather's song rebounded brightly among
the walls and rafters of the old abandoned chapel. His voice
was light and pure, a tenor in his youth I thought, and it put me
in mind of cold spring water, blue and silver as it turned and
glimmered among the rocks. We were still more or less a happy little
quartet some four months into our travels, my grandfather reclining
easily against the transept wall, and the monkey, Atma and myself

ranged out along a stone slab opposite him in respectful silence while he sang his song. Above us, the galaxy moved luminously across the wide holes in the chapel roof.

'The blind perseverance of optimism and resourcefulness in the face of adversity,' announced my grandfather as the air settled around the final, ringing notes. 'That must be our motto. There may be sore days ahead of us.'

I slapped my bared thigh with gusto.

'That was mighty!' I said. I had heard this expression given forth in a public house by a large bearded man in a sailor's cap upon the completion of a song.

'Go on, give us another one.'

My voice echoed back to me through the cavernous gloom. It had an awkward, jarring sound, like the braying of an ass. I had become quite drunk.

'Later,' he said.

He leaned forward into the pool of light that lay between us. His face was lightly suffused with pink and orange – the pink, I thought, from the claret we had been drinking and the orange from the little Primus stove over which he was frying us up a pair of eggs. It looked like the fading glow of a sunset on a calm, clear day. He rooted in his kit bag and extracted another bottle of wine.

'Here, open this,' he said, and then began delicately to baste our bubbling eggs with a small silver spoon.

We were now deeply into the autumn. We had made no provision for recording the passing of time when we had left the coastal road and headed towards our pilgrimage in the mountains, but the rowan branches were now thick with berries, the days were foreshortened and the air crisp, and the great broad leaves of the oaks were crimson and orange. I could not at first understand the mountains, their unforgiving endurance, their vast desolate shapes falling randomly in upon one another. They were surprisingly large. I found them wild and treacherous and deceptive, and here the categories as I had known them of perspective and distance and direction were suspended entirely. In time, though, I came to accept these uncertainties, and even to embrace them.

This was due entirely to my grandfather, to my abandonment to the pedagogic disciplines which he imposed. It was a time unlike any other in my life. I learned to walk soundlessly, to detect the smell of animals on the wind and, with great effort, to control at least in part the movements of my dreams. He ordered me from time to time to fast from sleep, for periods of above five days, so that I would be able to contend with hallucinations and the famine of rest. My hands grew darkened and calloused from the gathering of wood and foraging for food and my body too, from my nightly sprints about the agonising slopes, began to harden and to resemble more closely the human form. The monkey came into his own here, staying airborne for hours as he swung with dazzling energy and finesse among the branches of the chestnuts, the ash trees and the oaks. Throughout this period my grandfather pressed me hard on my vagaries of speech, the slovenliness of my attempts at definition. He said that to explain something is to know it and feel it, and the more you can explain the wiser you are. In the evening then, in the aftermath of our meals, we played games of memory and of logic – chess and labyrinths and puzzles – and with this exercise these qualities, like the muscles in my legs, began somewhat to prosper, though still my grandfather saw fit to shave my head and face and thus maintain me in the aspect of the novice.

One day then in the latter part of our stay there, not long before we came upon the chapel, we paused in a bogland high up in the mountains. Below us was a round blue lake held in the landscape as though in a pair of cupped hands, an area of utter desolation and majesty – like Tibet, thought my grandfather. Here we found a low, stone-built shepherd's hut. I was instructed by my grandfather to assume a position within it, my legs folded over one another and my back against the wall, and to remain thus until he told me otherwise. It was not unusual for him to initiate such exercises or experiments, whatever they may have been, and I expected thus to pass the afternoon, but, though he returned twice daily with water and a kind of tasteless gruel to sustain me and he allowed me to lay flat on the ground to sleep at night, it was a full seven days – I know because I counted them – before he allowed me to unravel and emerge from the little hut. The pain both physical and mental of this posture and deprivation and tedium I found at first to be unendurable, but then by the fifth day I discovered something strange, that with concentrated focus I could not suppress the pain but could at least move it around my body at will, into my nose or fingers or the crown of my head, just as though I was lifting it like a ball with my hand. So too with the river of debris that I was accustomed to find running without cease through my mind. This I could start and stop as I wished and examine the contents like beads on a string. It was, as I say, a strange and salient experience, issuing for a time in a sensation of wondrous mental purity. I still remember it, though rather distantly. My grandfather contrived on numerous occasions and in various ways to put me *in extremis* mentally, to see, I supposed, what it might produce, but I received no clear pictures in the mountains, not of Hugh's pages, nor of my mother either.

It was, then, on a cool autumn evening, just beyond Derralossary, that we came upon the little chapel where my grandfather sang the song about Brian O Linn. We were looking for a place to put in for the night and finally it was Atma who found it at the end of an overgrown path, obscured on its road side by an impossible tangle of trees and shrubs. It was stone-built and long abandoned, windowless along its flanks and gap-roofed above. I remember my grandfather taking up a position on the worn slab of stone at its entrance and looking on with pleasure at this old house of worship and its grounds, at the wild flowers running among the broken gravestones, at the vines and brambles climbing the walls and pouring through the window spaces, at the deep green moss obscuring the squat figures carved in stone on the pillared doorway – at all the wild fecundity of the earth reclaiming this once-blessed structure. He entered then and moved about among the long evening shadows for some time while the monkey and I lingered hand-in-hand on the path. Finally we were summoned in by his grave, echoing voice.

The pews and much of the statuary had been removed and the floor had been broken up into heaps of drifting brick, but my grandfather had found a level space near the Virgin's altar. Here he had spread a white tablecloth and had laid out our Primus stove, the cutlery and the various foods and implements with which he was to prepare our evening meal. Among them was a bottle of claret. I saw him then ahead of me, down on his haunches and running an appreciative and, I thought, knowledgeable hand over a length of altar rail which had been left leaning against a wall. It was marble and pink in colour.

'Tuscan,' I heard him murmur, as though to an intimate.

It seemed the shrewd and sensuous knowledge of the dealer in stone rather than that of the geologist.

Later then, after the song, I leaned back against a pillar, handsomely fed and warmly in wine. My grandfather was reclining opposite me along the length of his side, his arm bent at the elbow and propping up his head. He was reading by lamplight from a small leatherbound volume of Euripides. Out beyond the walls and rooftop the night had settled deeply into a dark and vast silence, the only light that of the stars throbbing in the heavens. It must, I guessed, have been past midnight. Just beyond my grandfather here in the chapel and within range of the glow of his flame was a plinth, upon which was perched the monkey, still and quizzical as a parrot as he digested his food, and from the plinth there arose a statue of Our Lady, her plaster extremities mutilated but her halo of phosphorous multi-coloured spheres intact and still glowing weakly where the lamplight gave way to the gloom. Between my grandfather and me was our wine-stained tablecloth and the scattered detritus of the meal we had shared. All was, it seemed, just as it should have been on this tranquil night and I was thinking of nothing at all until in an instant I was put in mind of picnics I had known in my youth, those torchlight barbecues with great hampers of food and wines laid on by the Judge in the distant reaches of his grounds. I was then led more latterly to the happy excursions my mother and I had taken together on fine-weathered bank holiday weekends after we had settled in Dublin. On these occasions we would take ourselves off to Skerries or Howth or some such seaside resort and pass the whole of the time there together, walking along the shore with our feet in the water until we found a place where no one would see us. Here we would spread our blanket, our flask of tea, our cream pastries and, now and again, an old wind-up gramophone which my mother had taken as part of a deal and upon which we played operatic highlights while we ate. Always we talked of the Judge, because it made both of us happy. These were grand times, some of the grandest I have known really, and I remember how on the train journeys home I would place my mother by the window and me on the bench beside her so that I could follow the lines of her eyes and see each thing that she saw, each cloud and stream and heap of stones. That way, I thought, there could be nothing which separated us and it would be as though we were one.

As I thought of these things there broke over me in a long and engulfing sweep a great tide of love for my mother. I saw her in a succession of faces that spanned the entirety of my memory of her over the four decades we had shared, a seeming infinity of faces that stretched in a line away from me until they were claimed by the darkness, faces laughing in the wind, faces twisted in grief or dementia, faces glowing warmly as though lit by a fading sun. I craved to see beyond them into her own life as she had lived it previous to me, to know in particular detail what she did and said and looked like back beyond the point of my birth, her youth and infancy and even that mysterious sequence of life that led back to the loins of my grandfather. I wanted the whole of it just as my grandfather wanted the whole of the book.

I sat then with these waves breaking around me, holding onto myself until they faded away. All was as it had been, Atma gathered into himself and asleep, the monkey staring impassively at the dark ruined wall. In the resumed stillness I let the time pass, thinking long and hard and elaborating in my mind an interrogative campaign on the subject of my mother which I would put to my grandfather. There was no other living being who could supply its answers.

'Grandfra –' I faltered at the outset. I had not taken a drink for several months, nor had I even spoken for the past hour or so, and the wine had undermined my capacity for speech.

'Grunfa –'

I performed a sequence of stringent facial exercises in order to focus my mind.

'*Grandfather!*' I blurted at last.

He continued with his Euripides, paying me no heed.

'Tell me about my mother when she was a little baby,' I began. 'Go on. From when you first saw her, just after she was born. Her hair, her eyes, her – Was she fat? Hmm? Did she cry? Was she – aaahhh . . . was she lovely?'

His brow rose speculatively and his eyes moved to meet mine, but they clouded mysteriously en route as though pained and he returned silently to his book. I pressed on.

'Well was she? Was she a lovely . . . lovely little baby?'

He held obstinately to his silence.

'Grandfather,' I said. 'This is important to me. It's only fair that you help, and I really thank, I mean think, that if we are to maintain our partnership it is necessary that our relations with one another be entirely open and – hic! – open and above board.'

When eventually he looked up I could see a dampness spread like dew across the expanse of his forehead and collected into a beaded row along his quivering upper lip.

'I did not know your mother as a baby,' he said. 'She was got upon a peasant in Galway when I was a boy of eighteen. The birth took place in December 1921, and I did not encounter her – and only then, as afterwards, under false pretences – until the summer of 1925.'

I jerked upright into an attitude of belligerence.

'What?! It's not possible . . .' I waved my head about uncomprehendingly. 'My excellent and lovely mother! *You abandoned her!*'

'I did not abandon her,' he countered. 'I did not. I was not afforded that opportunity. She was adopted within the first week of her life – by an elderly and childless couple from County Limerick. Most attentive they were, as I understand it. He was a shoe salesman and a Knight of Columbanus.'

'Adopted? *A shoe salesman?*'

'Nothing wrong with adoption,' he said rapidly. All of this clearly made him nervous. 'The raising of children by people other than their natural parents is an ancient and respectable practice, the central tenet as it happens of Celtic family life.'

'Ha!' I said. 'Some excuse. And what of this . . . this . . . *peasant?*

By God, you're a low, degenerate, debauched . . . *No wonder my mother was promiscuous!'*

'Oh, with what ease do the morally negligible become the morally superior,' he retorted tremulously, then snapped shut his mouth like a tortoise. In the silence the chapel seemed to fill with the pounding of our agitated hearts. I was on my knees with my fists balled up and my jaw jutting out. My grandfather looked at length and with concentration into the blue-flaming wick of his lantern. Ripples moved like an electrical storm about the muscles of his face. I had never before seen such suffering in restraint.

'It is right that you should know these things,' he said at last. 'I've long known it. Many times during our travels here in the mountains I have wondered how to tell you and now . . .' He looked up then like a man condemned. 'Tell me what you want to know and I will answer.'

'That's better,' I said. 'Now then, I want to know everything. From the beginning. Tell me about my grandmother.'

'Your grandmother,' he began. 'Strange to think of her like that, for she never knew of you. Honor Costello she was called. I wonder . . . I wonder is she living still. Same age as myself, a year younger maybe. I met her in 1921, late in January I think or maybe February. The whole country was at war with England. I was on a walking tour of the West before beginning my university studies later that autumn. I remember well my first sight of her house. I had come out of the great emptiness of the Connemara mountains and was making my way across the bogs when I saw it, a large two-storey structure set apart from a straggling little village down by the sea among some trees. Downstairs it had a small bar on one side of the hall and a dining room on the other. Guests stayed in the rooms upstairs. A widower called Michael Costello kept the place. He was short and wiry and was a great hurler in his day I was told. Costello is your great-grandfather.'

He allowed me to absorb this for a time while he lit his pipe.

'And Honor,' I said. 'What way was she?'

'Oh, she was beautiful,' he said. 'Really very stunning. So was her sister Orla. The two of them were famous for it, though there was no sign that they knew. Orla was red-lipped and dark and Honor was fine and fair, with hair the colour of cornsilk. They behaved towards me as a Dublin man with a most outlandish formality, calling me "sir" and expressing themselves in an elaborate syntax and curtseying even. But I had hopes of winning one of them, so I stayed on in the house. I used to lie for hours in my bed upstairs in the darkness in a state of painful delirium as I imagined the two of them coming to me in their shifts, their hair about their shoulders, one followed by the other . . .

'I soon found out that Orla was being courted by a schoolteacher, so I turned towards Honor. She was at her peak then, her blue eyes filled with brightness and hunger. She wanted to know all there was to know about the wide world and she thought that I could tell her. She used sit for hours opposite me across the white tablecloth after my breakfast, asking me questions. Sometimes I read to her in Italian and her body swayed a little with the words . . .

'When the weather brightened then in March with the onset of spring she came to me early one morning and suggested a walk. It was a very, very long walk up over a number of hills and along the shore to a place she had visited as a child. We held hands over the walls and ditches. It took *hours*. I remember the day was dry and gusty and the leaves that had lain through the winter blew into vortices and clattered on the stones. It sounded like tap-dancing!

'Anyway, we came to the place finally. It was a small green valley set among the brown hills and opening onto the sea. A small finger of grassy land extended from it into the water. It was a strange place, and very still. In it were a number of structures, a ringfort, some cairns and pillar stones, ancient shapes made of dark rock and scattered about. From above it looked like an upturned chessboard. Honor took off her shoes and ran around in the grass before coming to rest against the wall of the ringfoot. The way the light was her eyes were very blue and she looked up at me, her lips parted. I went to her and put my arms around her waist. I remember the feeling of it, her body warmed and heaving a little in breathlessness, light as filigree against the massiveness of the wall. I kissed her then and held her for a long time. I stayed as still as I could while a wild turmoil blew like a hurricane within me. It felt as if it would knock me from my feet. The next morning, with her father away at a horse market, she let me take her to my bed.'

I had been studying throughout this account my grandfather's face, a face, I thought, that, among other things, knew women, the way some faces know wine or diamonds or complex abstractions, and I felt with sudden and grievous weight an indignation at my pitiable state, my pointless and unwilling chastity, my terminal inexperience. Would I ever know women in fact as well as in mind? Had it all passed me by? My grandfather, it appeared, had been born to it while I knew as little of their ways and means as I did of ploughsharing.

'I won't hear any more of this!' I announced. 'Lurid and illicit carnality. This book I carry around for you – one long tale, I suppose, of debauchery and seduction, starting with that filthy old man Bertrand and then Hervey and Emer. God only knows what followed from them. And then of course there's you and my mother. I suppose neither of you would remember even half your conquests. It's a wonder I'm not in some madhouse with congenital syphilis! Did no one ever bother to tell any of you about the sanctity of wedlock?' I had become quite shrill and breathless and now made a large effort to contain myself. It was a difficult matter as we had continued drinking throughout and my emotions were very unruly. 'That poor girl,' I said. 'Corrupted by the likes of you . . .'

All of this lifted his melancholy spirits considerably.

'My boy!' he beamed. 'Innocent fellow. I may tell you that your grandmother was a great deal more experienced in all that ensued in my bed that morning than I was. I kept my silence, of course, in order to preserve myself from the knowledge of how and with whom she had acquired it. And anyway I caught up with her soon enough. What a riot we made of it through the month of March!'

He narrowed his eyes in pursuit of the memory.

'There's something, you know, about sex like that,' he said. 'When it's that good, and especially at the beginning, you'd go *anywhere* for it. It's absolutely the principal nourishment. You'd nearly *kill* for it.'

'All right, all right,' I said. 'Just get on with the damned story.'

'Oh, I will,' he said. He was laughing. He was doing so, as ever, in a grating, crow-like pitch, and it had the methodical rhythm of wood-sawing. 'But you'd do better to disguise your vulnerabilities. They're so *tempting* . . .

'Now then, where was I? Yes, I know. Honor had to leave Carraroe and go to Gort. There was an elderly Protestant vicar there name of Blanchard used pass some time at Costello's learning Irish, and Costello had promised him that Honor would look after him while his regular housekeeper was away. She'd been called home to the North to look after her sister. Something to do with a rather bad miscarriage, I think. Now I met Blanchard years later. He was tall with a short little English moustache and spectacles, and he smoked a pipe. He jabbed the air with the stem of it as he spoke. He was urbane and intelligent and gracious in the pre-War manner. Full of moral duty and enthusiasms. He knew all about clarets and sherries and how to fold a breastpocket handkerchief. He was very good to Honor. Anyway, I accompanied her to the outskirts of the town, and when we parted company she was carrying within her the foetus of your mother. I never laid eyes on her again.'

'You never . . . ?' I began. 'Oh yes, that's you all over. Love them and leave them. The hard man. The . . .'

He had struck a match and put it to the bowl of his pipe. Long, macabre shadows were cast upwards from his features, the white tobacco smoke writhing fitfully among them. His eyes glared like furnaces. I felt a tingling and then a stiffening in my jaw. Even as the invective continued within me I could not produce the words.

'I loved her,' he said then. 'Let you remember that. I loved her. And she loved me.

'. . . But it was not, I'm afraid, sustainable without stimulus. We wrote letters to each other, feverish letters, but by the autumn I was back in Dublin and taken up with my studies. For a long time I could not think of her without the most intense longing. But it passed. It became a comfort, the sweetness of nostalgia. It is a slow process but it is inexorable, like the evaporation of water.

'I heard nothing at all from Honor through the autumn and winter. Then one day in March when I was sitting alone in my rooms in the college I was handed a letter with an American stamp. Beneath it was my name and address written out in Honor's hand. It was from New York. She began, "Since last I wrote to you I have had our baby and given it away. I was not allowed to look at her. I suffered a terrible

171

illness when she was being born and we both nearly died, but we got through it all right, thank God, and now I live in New York." There was no return address on it and it was the last message I ever had from her, poor girl. I hope she hadn't a bad life. She might have felt she had a reason to be bitter, but instead she decided I'd a right to know. I'd never have known otherwise of course. The letter was very long and had been written in a changeable hand that now and again looked quite frantic. It told how she discovered herself to be pregnant in the summertime when she was still with Blanchard, just at the time when his housekeeper returned from the North. She thought there was nothing for it but to place herself at their mercy. Between them they found a doctor and old Blanchard arranged with a priest he knew from Limerick for the adoption of the baby. The housekeeper was called Miss McInnerney and Honor became very friendly with her. I met her myself the same time I met Blanchard. She was a fine-looking Protestant woman from somewhere out beyond Derry, very independent. Honor says in her letter that she drove a car, drank whiskey and ate nothing but vegetables. She kept a cockatoo in a cage in the sitting-room and she used put her ear to Honor's stomach and listen to the sounds of the baby.

'Then in November, a month before the birth, she took some very bad turns. Terrible pains and lightness in her head and her ankles swelled up like gourds. The contractions when they came were very heavy – grinding, unrelenting pains. She remembers lying in her room upstairs in the vicarage, trying to concentrate on the mustard-coloured walls, thinking she would die. Miss McInnerney was there. The doctor was unpacking his instruments. Blanchard was very nervous and moving about the room like a heron. Then she remembers nothing at all. She began to fit, it seems. When she woke the room was empty and very quiet. She felt her stomach. It was flatter but still distended, and she did not know whether she had given birth. She lifted her nightdress up and found a long red gash across her belly, stitched together with black thread, and an hour or so later she heard the cry of an infant.

'The following morning she heard a car come into the drive and she got to her feet for the first time and went to the window. She saw a rather elderly couple with rounded, humble shapes go through the front door. After a while they came out with Blanchard, the woman walking awkwardly and carrying a swaddled infant out in front of her with stiffened arms. Blanchard made his way along beside the man with his whole body inclined inwards and making gracious, sweeping gestures with his arm as he talked. When they reached the car the man lifted his fedora and revealed his parchment-like scalp, ringed with a narrow band of oily, dun-coloured hair. Then they were away. She called out for Miss McInnerney but Blanchard put his head around the door and said she had gone, another urgent errand to the North. What did she have, she asked him. Oh, a girl, he said, a very lovely girl. He was all around her then for a day or two, bringing out the crystal and silver for their meals, reading to her in the evenings, smiling sadly. Then he drove her home to Carraroe. She never did get to see our daughter's face . . .'

Some time in the course of my grandfather's narrative I lost sight of him entirely, my eyes rolling back in my head into darkness. I thought when it happened that it was the wine and that I would pass on into sleep, but I held onto my faculties, my hearing at any rate, and the darkness was soon overtaken by a soft yellow glow that filled everything around me. It gleamed more brightly in spots from time to time, like autumn sunlight entering a pond in shafts. I was sitting, or rather gently rolling, in an expanse of liquid, thicker than water and fine as a child's tear. My grandfather's words were very disturbing, but the place I was briefly inhabiting seemed to be one of immense peace, so that I had no wish whatever to leave it, as in like manner I would have no wish to leave the warm enclosure of my bed on a winter morning. There was too a sound that came from within this place, a sound something like the hoofbeats of a galloping horse on a bass drum, muffled and made distant as it came to me through the liquid. At first the sound seemed to project an echo, but when I listened more closely I discovered that the two sounds derived from distinct sources, running in parallel and discordantly, as though there were now two horses moving together on a distant plain.

Out beyond the perimeters of all this I could hear my grandfather crying quietly. It was a long while before he spoke. When he did so it was to describe how a civil war was under way in the country around the time he had received Honor's last letter, and how this had hindered him in the search for my mother. In the summer he was arrested on the top deck of a Dublin tram in possession of a small handgun and some pages concerned with the purchase of arms in Rotterdam, and he spent the next two years interned in a military camp on a plain in Meath. There he gave classes to his fellow prisoners in shorthand, Italian poetry and the playing of the violin, and he passed the remainder of his time thinking about his new daughter.

'They were strong men in there with me,' I heard him say, 'men who had long been living with death. But so fervently did I imagine her and the wonder of her birth that in the telling of it I could bring them to tears.

'The war spent itself finally and we were all let out. The land was ravaged. One day then I got myself up in a dog collar I rented from a theatrical costumiers and made my way over to the vicarage in Gort. Miss McInnerney came to the door. Gripping her around the knees with both arms was a tiny girl with a pale face and black ringlets. My heart jumped into my mouth when I saw her. I thought she was your mother. But Miss McInnerney told me she was her sister's child down from a place called Eglinton. She had a most lovely face, and a wonderfully round brow, Miss McInnerney. It looked as though it was carved from white oak. Anyway, she took me into the drawing room to Blanchard and gave us tea and scones. I told him I was a young seminarist on an ecumenical walking tour of the West, calling on men of the cloth of all creeds to discuss the way forward in the new Ireland. Such tosh it was, but he sat across from me with a tartan rug over his knees and the flames from his fire flickering on his spectacles, a look of saintly credulity on his face. Now and again he put his finger through the cage and ran it along the beak of Miss McInnerney's cockatoo. When I had finished, he questioned me closely on what I had learned and where I intended to go. In the end up we talked for hours, me as sincere as an actor's greasepaint, him as true as a bell. He was an amazing man, an anachronism in those bleak years. He could become rhapsodic about anything from Mozart to septic tanks. And he loved Ireland with an innocent sanguineness. I felt sullied by my lies, but by the time I left him I had what I wanted – the name and parish of the priest who had effected the adoption of your mother. It was not a difficult matter to find them, an elderly couple fussing over a small red-haired child . . .'

I could see that he was struggling under an intolerable burden. His breathing was laboured and he shifted about unrelentingly where he sat. He looked at me then with what I took to be a sudden loathing and malevolence. I know it now to be merely the overspilling of his pain. He took up his walking-stick then and hooked the crook of it onto the neck-hole of my sack, drawing me towards him so that my face was nearly over the flame from the little stove. I held on to my place within my enclosure, the serene liquid all about me, the pale yellow glow suffusing me, the syncopated beat of the two horses galloping in the distance.

'What do you suppose my life has been like then? Hmm? Do you suppose that in your dimness and timidity you can begin to comprehend it? Can you? Since the time I first saw your mother in Abbeyfeale, County Limerick I have never stopped watching her. Sometimes so closely that our noses nearly touched. I watched her grow up and get married and give birth. I watched her wander about the land losing the faculties of her mind. And through it all I could not claim her nor touch her nor guide her . . .

'I know what the love of a child is like. There is nothing so intimate in all the world. It is pure and intense and unequivocal. It simply shines from their faces. Now you have charged me with gross negligence. Do you suppose that had I the opportunity of receiving a love like this I would have forsaken it? To miss her struggles with movement and speech, her calls in the night? To have watched instead as she looked with affection and faith into the eyes of my usurper rather than into mine? *Do you suppose that I have lived this way through choice?*'

I watched distantly as a trickle of clear saliva spilled over my grandfather's lip and down his chin, gleaming blue and silver in the light from the lantern. The waters around me had grown turbulent and the sound of the hoofbeats tinny and elusive.

'I met on numerous occasions your presumptive grandfather,

175

Thomas Burke he was called, the purveyor of low-quality footwear, the Knight of Columbanus. You're fortunate never to have known him. The last time I saw him was on a railway platform during the War. He was with his wife and the two of them were saying goodbye to your mother. She was off to Dublin for her first job. Burke was there holding forth and as the train pulled in a fierce wind whipped along the track and blew the hat right off his head. It went bounding along the length of the platform on its rim straight into a hedge. He chased after it to ferret it out and your mother boarded the train. He was still thrashing about in the branches and never heard the station master's whistle. I was watching all this from a doorway on the train. The train pulled away and your mother waved and shouted, Burke's wife standing there on the platform like a heap of silage not knowing what to do and her husband still not hearing anything. The last your mother ever saw of the man she thought of as her father was his great broad shiny-trousered arse sticking out from a railway platform hedge. He died not long afterwards.

'A ridiculous life, eh? But he had nearly twenty years of your mother. The man was a fool. He told ridiculous jokes he had learned in the lounges of hotels for commercial travellers. When he spoke it was as though the shutters of a long-closed cellar had opened and released a cloud of foetid air. Your father, O'Banion, was another thing altogether. He seduced her at a party held in a cottage up in these mountains. He was a feckless and unprincipled cornerboy with enough talent for prose to get him a job as theatre critic for an evening paper. In the end he ran off with an American heiress to Kinsale. These have been the men in your mother's life, followed by you. She was my only child, the only other being in my life really, at least the only one that maintained my interest. In order to pursue my remote guardianship of her I have been compelled not only to ingratiate myself with these men, but to do so invisibly, to hide behind disguises, disguises so numerous and inventively detailed that I feared at times they would bring about the nullity of my personal self. That has been the course of my life, innocence gone, broken into fragments before I hit my stride. A multiplicity of lives . . . all of them ephemeral . . .

'My first sight of your mother was in the front garden of Burke's

176

house in Abbeyfeale. She was sitting among the flowers looking at a picture book. Her red hair was about her shoulders. What a curse it is to live in a country overloaded with red-haired children! What I felt then, young as I was, was a flood of wonder at my paternity followed instantaneously by the intense pain of being prevented from exercising it. Time has done nothing to diminish this. It has, if anything, merely tightened the screws. I cannot even look at fathers and daughters together! Such a simple, natural thing, denied me. For decades, more than I can remember, I have been beset by dreams. Excruciatingly vivid dreams, realer, *more tangible* than fact. They are all the same, or very nearly. Your mother is always three years old, sitting in Burke's garden as she was when I first saw her. I pass through the gate and when she hears me she looks up at me from her book. Her eyes are like great lakes of pity. She recognises me and throws her book into the flowers and runs to me. Her arms are around my neck and she is holding me very tightly. I sense the smoothness of her skin, her breath on my neck, her smell. I begin to weep helplessly. I always do. I can taste the brine and feel the tears between your mother's cheek and mine, then running down my neck. I *beg* her to forgive me. And always she tells me it's all right, we're together, she loves me. The dream runs this far and then I wake. I can hardly believe the emptiness. But of course that's all there is. I was beaten very young . . .'

He drank deeply from the wine and looked at me very evenly.

'What would you say to a lifetime of that, eh?' he said. 'A rich and rewarding life, would you say? Do you suppose it's been pleasant for a mind such as mine to be so transparent to itself? Listen. I have long been considering the lives in our blighted line robbed of their fruition – Hervey's and Anna's and Ronan's and Honor's and mine and your mother's and so many more. Answer me this. Do you intend to take your place in that line and number yourself among them, or will you find another way?'

He fixed me with his stare for long, dreadful moments, all the while holding me to him with the crook of his stick. I could not move and was beset by an encroaching sensation of claustrophobia. I was now out of the yellow-hued waters and more or less back in the chapel, but I nevertheless feared to open my mouth to speak lest the waters rush in and I drown. In any case, all that he had said was passing only dimly comprehended around the wine-sodden routes of my system, like a great bolus of undigested food, and I could not bring my mind to bear coherently on his final question. I looked back at him vacantly.

After a time he got uncertainly to his feet. His breathing was laboured and he swayed where he stood. He was, I am sure, as drunk as I was, though not so adversely affected. He shuffled away then out of the range of light and I lost sight of him, tracing him only by the rasping scrape of his shoes on the floor, a sound like that of sandpaper on stone. Finally he passed out of the door and there was silence. It occurred to me then that he had abandoned me there forever, but such was my state that I could not bestir myself to do anything about it. The monkey then leapt from Our Lady's plinth onto my shoulder and thence into my lap. His face was white and marked with innumerable fine lines and furrows, giving him an aged and dignified look. He gazed at me for some time with a grandmotherly concern. It was difficult for me at the time to think or feel anything with succinctness or clarity, but I sensed at least that I loved the monkey very much. I felt that had my grandfather gone on his way without us that we could nevertheless sleep the night there together and somehow or other make our way down out of the mountains. The monkey combed for a while with his slender fingers the long strands of hair that remained on the back of my head. More time passed, a very long time, it seemed. He went over then to my grandfather's bag and searched out some handfuls of nuts, which he cracked between his teeth and fed to me through my thick, yielding lips. Finally then we lay down together, side by side, my arm around his tiny waist, in much the same posture in which my mother and I passed our nights in her grand canopied bed.

Much later then, with me in that twilight world of nervous, uneasy sleep, I heard emerging from out of one of those deep pockets of gloom, unperturbed by the light of either the lantern or the stars, that high, clear, unmistakable sound, pure as springwater, the voice of my grandfather singing a song:

'I am a roving sporting blade, they call me Jack of All
   Trades,
I always placed my chief delight in courting pretty
   fair maids,
So when in Dublin I arrived to try for a situation
I always heard them say that it was the pride of all
   the nations.

I'm roving Jack of All Trades, of every trade of all
   trades,
And if you want to know my name, they call me Jack
   of All Trades.

On George's Quay I first began and there became a
   porter,
Me and my master soon fell out which cut my
   acquaintance shorter,
In Sackville Street a pastry cook – in James's Street
   a baker,
In Cork Street I did coffins make, in Eustace Street a
   preacher.

I'm roving Jack of All Trades, of every trade of all
   trades,
And if you wish to know my name, they call me Jack
   of All Trades.

In Baggott Street I drove a cab and there was well
   requited,
In Francis Street had lodging beds to entertain all
   strangers.
For Dublin is of high renown or I am much mistaken.
In Kevin Street I do declare sold butter, eggs and
   bacon.

I'm roving Jack of All Trades, of every trade of all
   trades,

And if you wish to know my name, they call me Jack
of All Trades.

In Golden Lane I sold old shoes – in Meath Street was
a grinder,
In Barrack Street I lost my wife – I'm glad I ne'er
could find her,
In Mary's Lane I've dyed old clothes of which I've
often boasted,
In that noted place Exchequer Street sold mutton
ready roasted.

I'm roving Jack of All Trades, of every trade of all
trades,
And if you wish to know my name they call me Jack of
All Trades.

In Liffey Street had furniture with fleas and bugs I
sold it,
And at the Bank a big placard I often stood to hold it.
In New Street I sold hay and straw and in
Spitalfields made bacon.
In Fishamble Street was at the grand old trade of
basket making.

I'm roving Jack of All Trades, of every trade of all
trades,
And if you wish to know my name they call me Jack of
All Trades.

In Summerhill a coachmaker, in Denzille Street a
gilder,
In Cork Street was a tanner – in Brunswick Street a
builder,
In High Street I sold hosiery, in Patrick Street sold all
blades,
So if you wish to know my name they call me Jack of
All Trades.'

When he had finished I heard the light step of his feet moving towards me and then discovered his white head coming out of the darkness at my side, a mirthful look now displayed over his rejuvenated features. On the crown of his head he wore a semi-circular garland of ivy leaves and in his right hand he held a light stick enspiralled in vines and wrapped at one end in cloth.

'*E uno plures*, eh?' he said. 'Out of the one, many – to invert a well-known national slogan. That's me. A whole galaxy of selves, and none to call my own. At least the versatile Jack had a sense of place to go on. At least he knew who he was, whatever that may have been at the time. I have had only the precariousness, the *uncertainty* of invention. I have walked on a piece of string over a void. Without a destination! Ha!'

It all seemed to amuse him a very great deal.

'I think you have been very brave, Grandfather,' I said reverently.

'You like music, don't you my boy? Hm? I think you do. You *should*! Now the very first time that I heard music so *physical*, so thoroughly and ecstatically infusing of the body and spirit as to make the concept of self and its wilful accoutrements an irrelevance entirely, was when Honor and one of her brothers took me down to an outdoor dance held on a great slab of limestone by the side of the road leading out of Carraroe. There was no light, only that of the moon. Everyone was sat around the edge on low benches and rocks, drinking from tin mugs. I was in between Honor and her cousin Mairead from Rosmuc. These country girls! Honor's hand was on my shoulder and her body was leaned into the side of my arm and Mairead was propped up along the length of my thigh, their noses not a foot apart. I could feel the warmth of Honor's body and the shape of her breast through her clothes. Lord! It was lovely. But that's the way of it with them. If you meet one of them on the road or alone in a room they're very demure, but in public they'll practise on you a physical intimacy unseen in towns and cities. Maybe you'll find out yourself someday . . .

'Anyway, after a little while a fiddler and a lilter came along and began to play. The lilter called the tune and led off with his mouth music. There was a great gathering then from all sides onto the flatness

of the stone and they began to dance. Well I'd never seen anything like
it. Spinning circles and crosses and converging lines! Honor was
there among them, her red skirt spinning up around her knees, the
yellow blur of her hair flying out behind her on the breeze of her dance.
I was sitting on the bench drinking when she took me up into it. I
couldn't make anything of it. I stumbled around among them like I'd
taken a blow to the head. All around me were throbbing temples and
reddened, sweat-gleaming faces, flashing past me in a blur. They
looked so happy, so radiant! Honor grabbed hold of me again and I
held desperately to her, following her steps and slides and spins. The
music raged on. Then on a sudden I just got it, you know, like learning
to whistle. I utterly amazed myself. She let go my hand then and I was
with them all in the dance, stepping it out. It seemed I was nothing
only movement. No thought, no past, no future. I was like a monkey
moving through the trees! A model of controlled abandon! Do you
remember?'

He lay his stick aside then and picked up the monkey, placing him
on his shoulders and beginning to shuffle about the chapel floor. Out
of his mouth there came softly the notes of a light meandering air,
accompanying his steps. These notes increased in volume and in pace
until they emerged brightly into a discernible tune, to which he
danced in and out of the fall of light with a buoyant fluidity. The
monkey's eyes were very wide and he was holding tightly to my
grandfather's ears. Before even he had finished his dance he had drawn
out of one of his pockets a long mouth-organ, into which he now began
to blow a wilder and faster tune than the one he had just completed,
and his feet moved so quickly that I was unable to disentangle them
and were ringingly loud as they scuffed and slapped over the floor. As
he spun about the monkey was projected spread-eagled through the air
and landed doubtfully on the altar steps. My grandfather danced
before me in tight little circles and then let out a fierce, joyous shriek
and pulled me up to join him. The music was moving through me and
I stepped it out.

'Yeeeeeooooowww!' he yelled.

'Oooooeeeeeehaaaa!' I replied, linking his arm and swinging him
wildly around, my head thrown back, a vortex forming out of the

hole in the roof above me. The stars were like luminous spinning wheels.

My grandfather broke off to pick up his garlanded stick, dipping its rag end into the burner until it blazed into an orange-red flame. He ran about then holding it high, still blowing his mad jig on the mouth-organ. The monkey had gathered himself up and was now jumping up and down in place as though he was on a trampoline. I could see my grandfather running about among the pillars and then on a sudden he stopped and let out a terrific whoop.

'Oooooooaaaaaa! Io, Io, Io! On, on!' he exclaimed.

'Run, dance delirious, possessed!
You, the beauty and grace of golden Tmolus,
Sing to the rattle of thunderous drums,
Sing for joy,
Praise Dionysus, god of joy!'

He planted his stick into the earth just outside the door and ran out into the darkness.

'Io, Io, Io!' I shouted after him.

I felt that my mind as I had known it was falling away from me as I danced, and I suffered no regrets at its passing. The monkey clapped his hands and shrieked. Atma was at the door barking savagely and without cease. I heard my grandfather's distant cries and exclamations on the plain outside and their resonating echo from the surrounding mountains. I drank deeply from a bottle of wine and ran back and forth excitedly in front of the altar.

Finally then my grandfather appeared again in the doorway. He was an entirely awesome spectacle, the flame from his stick lighting up his mad eyes and daemonic grin. In his right hand he held a long fierce-looking knife and his powerful bared arms encircled the girth of a fully grown sheep, its legs sticking out in front of it and frantically paddling the air.

'Whoooheeeee!' he screamed at full voice, a pattern of veins briefly rising up on his brow and neck.

I had always been greatly fearful of sheep. Their elliptically shaped eyes and the rapid, mechanical movements of their mouths gave them an aspect of stupidity so impenetrable and alien as to produce in me strong sensations of nausea and dread. I tried to avert my eyes but could not, so engrossing was the tableau. The sheep's head was waving back and forth, its horrible pink mouth opening and closing soundlessly. Broad clouds of white steam were forced upwards from their mouths by the heavy breathing of both the sheep and my grandfather. It seemed an abomination that their breaths should commingle thus in the air. The animals stopped their agitated movements and fell into an awed silence, and I too sensed the inexorable return of my commonplace self. I remembered my Euripides well enough to have some sense of my grandfather's plan. '. . . Our cattle were there, cropping the fresh grass. They tore them limb from limb; you'd see some ribs, or a cleft hoof, tossed high and low; and rags of flesh hung from pine branches, dripping blood . . .'

I saw my grandfather draw the knife point up to the sheep's neck. Soon he would have us tearing at its flesh with our teeth! The sheep too must have sensed its fate for it ceased its struggle, held itself still and urinated wildly over the floor. I could see the yellow foaming tributaries coursing among the stones. I had somehow to halt this terrible event. My grandfather stared at me with his infernal eyes, blazingly lit by the flaming stick, his knife drawing ever closer to the sheep's neck. Finally I lunged forward and propelled myself into a widely circling swoon about the chapel floor. My arms were out at both sides and I was like a plane falling from the sky. I collapsed then against a slope of rubble, issuing forth a long stream of tormented sound such as I thought might suggest the Pentecostal speech of tongues. I was silent then, my eyes rolled back to reveal white blanks.

I heard my grandfather drop the terrorised sheep and trot expectantly over to me. He leaned very close to investigate me, so close that I could feel the heat of his face on mine. The sheep slid and stumbled and finally galloped out the door.

'Can you see anything?' he enquired. '*The pages*. Can you see them?'

I wanted to hold this position so that eventually he would abandon his project and go off to his bed-roll and sleep, but I caught suddenly the smell of lanolin from the sheep's wool mingled with the smell of sweat and wine. It was all too much for me. My belly erupted and poured out the yellow of the eggyolk and the now episcopal purple of the claret onto the heap of stones on which I was reclining. I let out a low groan like an afflicted bull.

'Omadhaun!' he shouted. He paced up and down in agitation until finally he wore himself out and sat down on the floor some distance away from me. 'You're a waste of good claret,' he declared.

I rolled slowly and with caution onto my side, my head coming to rest listlessly upon a brick. 'Oh God,' I said. 'This is the worst ever.' I kept as still as I might as there was yet the threat of turbulence in my lower regions.

There was no sound, only that of my grandfather drawing rapidly on his pipe, the tobacco leaves crackling in the bright red glow.

'What was all that about anyway?' I asked him.

'Enthusiasm!' he replied. '*En theos*, etymologically, the entry of the godhead into the reveller. Divine intoxication! The Bacchic frenzy! Vision! The power to see, and to see beyond . . . I had hoped to awaken your fitfully somnolent inner eye so that it might survey the land and at last locate Hugh's manuscript.'

He looked over at my recumbent form bulked in the shadows across from him. My socks had collapsed around my ankles from the vigour of the dancing and my hand prowled around beneath my sack, twirling the hair around my navel into rings. He turned his head wearily up to the stars.

'A vain hope in your case, I should say,' he said. 'You haven't the means to rise to the occasion. You have governed your life according to the principle merely of avoiding disagreeable sensations. In this you are like an insect or an infant, though you have neither the industry of the one nor the charm of the other . . .'

'Oh lovely,' I said. 'A nice thing to be saying to your only grandson. A very nice thing indeed. *You're drunk!* Visions, ha! I never heard of anything so childish. Why don't we get a ouija board? Then maybe you could talk to Hugh directly. Anyway, I certainly wouldn't tell you if I saw anything, after all you've put me through. I can't just perform tricks on demand, you know, like that dog. You'd think I was something in a circus!'

'I very much doubt whether you would pass the audition.'

'Well a fat lot of good you've done with your . . . your parlour games! All I've got out of it is sore feet and a throbbing head. And sick on my sleeve!'

He thrust out his long prognathic jaw into an expression of wounded dignity.

'I am an historian, as I told you before. Not a medium,' he declared. 'This is not my area of expertise. I can only research the available practices and endeavour to implement them. It's for your own benefit too, you know. I would have thought that instead of this petulance you might care instead to show some appreciation for all that I have tried to do.'

I lay there for a time while he studied me over the bowl of his pipe.

'For my benefit?' I said.

'Yes, yes, of course,' he said. He manoeuvred his way rapidly across the floor towards me. 'Did you ever think, dear child, why a wise and adventurous man like Bertrand de Paor admired Pythagoras so much? You might have thought had you addressed yourself to the question that it was because of Pythagoras' contemplative society, where, like Bertrand's, men and women were equal and all property was held in common. But I believe there is a deeper reason. I believe it was because Pythagoras was both a logician and a mystic. He discovered the rule of right-angled triangles and at the same time two of the principal tenets of his society were abstention from beans and the injunction not to sit on a quart measure. Can you credit that? How did he reconcile these things? He could see the numbers in music and was the first to declare their importance. For him the word "theory" meant not a set of hypotheses but rather the passionate and sympathetic contemplation of God's suffering, a form of ecstasy issuing forth in mathematical knowledge. Do you see? He thought with his whole being. He was a repository of reason and unreason, unlike others who came after him who regarded the two as exclusive. A great man, you know, or a great symbol. He stands in a line which extends from Dionysus and Orpheus before him to Plato and Christ, the *Logos*, beyond.

'Now I look at myself and I know that I have long been precluded from the fullness of such contemplation. This is due to the injury I sustained in my youth when your mother was removed from me. Since that time my thinking has been considerably limited, a lower, more cunning thing, much taken up with deception and guile. But you're altogether different, you see. That's what interests me about you. For so long your thinking has been done for you that your mind is as it were a blank, a *tabula rasa*. There are rare and powerful forces at work in it, but you have taken no trouble to comprehend or restrain them. You are a middle-aged infant. No real habits to speak of. Now I, of course, am an old man. There is nothing I can do to recover any innocence or capacities I may once have had. But I have lived and seen and thought much. There are things that I know, special things. Things that can only be given, because I cannot use them myself. But you can, you see. That's the wonder of it. You are there to be given the fullness of life. It's my gift to you, my grandson. I have watched you as I watched your mother, all your life, but never could I come near you. I could never call you my own. But now, you see, we're together, and I'm old and I can give you this thing. It's a great blessing to me. All this time we've been in the mountains, that's what I've been doing, giving you what I know, emptying myself into you. Do you understand? Making you a map, showing you the route. It hurts me, you know, it actually causes me pain, this emptying, this depletion. I'm not complaining, you understand. It is utterly an act of love, given without condition, the only such act I have been able to make during my long life. It is like the relation between an artist and his work. The siphoning of one life and spirit into another. It drains you. It is like a long, slow haemorrhaging. And it humbles and humiliates you and cripples you with self-doubt. All that thrashing about in the darkness. The burden of responsibility is at times intolerable. But I give it to you without regret, my boy. I give it to you because I want you to be free.'

He was smiling at me with an innocent sweetness such as I had never found in him before, his eyes round and as unwary as a child's.

Confusion and gratitude surged within me as I lay on the stone floor, my lip beginning to tremble and my own eyes filling finally with tears that brimmed over and ran down my cheeks. The tears were different than any I had shed before. They were tears of melancholy and of love and thankfulness, fine and exquisite, and I let them flow. Soon I could no longer see through them to my grandfather, his face a blurred smear of pink and white and blue. The chapel was silent, I could not even hear the breathing of the animals, and it seemed as though all life beyond my own had paused. Finally then I heard the sharp hissing sound of rapidly drawn in breath, followed by the grinding of teeth. I saw the outline of my grandfather's head thrown back so that he was facing upwards towards the stars, his body quaking as though convulsed. I cleared the water from my eyes and saw that his face was contorted with pain, veins and tendons erupting everywhere, his arms clutching his ribs. I scurried across the floor to his side.

'Grandfather,' I said. 'What is it? What's happening? Oh my God, this is terrible . . .'

I looked around pleadingly at Atma and the monkey. They were holding their places and wearing stern expressions.

'Please speak to me, Grandfather. I've never seen you like this. I've never seen *anybody* like this. Can't I do something. Do you have pills?'

The pain seemed to fill the whole of the chapel. I had, since we had met, seen him wince and stagger and hold himself still through a passage of pain, but I had regarded these as due to the infirmities of his age and in any case none had been anything like this in scale or degree. He was rocking back and forth and shaking his head, as though he wanted to fly from his body. I thought that it would devour him completely, so intense and enormous was it. His face drained and turned a murky white and he let out a roar, like that of a lion or ape, long and tremendous, a sound that would have filled a plain but which was overwhelming and unearthly in the confines of the chapel. I wanted more than anything for it to end, or to take the pain away from him into my own body.

His watery eyes roved about until they found mine.

'It will pass,' he said.

He spoke with immense effort, his breathing suspended, his voice faint and high, but the terrible convulsiveness of it had abated somewhat and it seemed that the crisis may have passed. I was ashamed as I watched him struggle to compose himself, ashamed at my petulant outbursts, my infantilisms, my cowardice, ashamed at my pathetic dependencies, that a man meant to be in his prime should be tended to and minded as though a small and helpless child by a virtual ancient – a great and powerful ancient, it may be said, but one nevertheless enfeebled by his years. I took him up in my arms and carried him to his bed-roll, laying him down along its length and arranging him as comfortably as I might. Large as he was I had little trouble with the weight. I cushioned his head from the hardness of the floor and lay both our blankets over him so that he would stay warm through what remained of the night.

'Grandfather,' I said. 'Tell me now. Why do you have this pain?'

The pain, I could see, had left its traces on him. There was a tautness to the skin around his eyes and he looked harrowed and disarmed in a way I had never seen before. I reached under the blankets to unlace his boots and began then to rub the soles of his feet. My mother had always rubbed my feet whenever I was poorly.

'There's a cancer in my bones,' he said. 'It's well advanced.'

'Will you die?' I asked.

He made his way onto his side and settled himself into his posture for sleep.

'Yes, I will die. Soon, I think . . .'

His head swivelled round on his pillow then to take a final look at me.

'You're running out of time,' he said, and winked.

Looking up through the hole in the roof I could see that the hard brilliance of the stars had faded and that they looked now like faint white holes in the sky, and that the blackness around them had given way to blue from the first traces of morning light. I did not want my grandfather to die and there was, as he reminded me, our outstanding business, but the book and its missing pages were at least in part a ruse,

I thought, the means by which he brought me to him and kept us together through his final days. I could see too that he had no fear whatsoever of death and that he was awaiting it with interest. As I lay there beside him watching the slow colouring of the sky, there came into my mind the photograph taken by the Judge of my mother and me when I was a boy. I thought then of those happy times, those summers in Kilkenny when the three of us were together and we approximated in some way a family. I had sought with eagerness and trepidation the warm enclosure of its embrace, but we were, of course, at best an equivocal grouping only and in the end it was no more than a mirage, for there had been no real bond and the Judge had been taken from us before his time by the runaway car. The sweetened whiffs of sherry or cognac which drifted from his mouth, the cold rasp of his grey stubble as he kissed me goodnight, these were things about the Judge which had startled me, alien things which I knew were not of or for me, much as I wished to accommodate him and find a place in his life for my mother and me.

Decades were to pass before I found myself drawn into another human life other than my mother. This was my grandfather. And how different it was with him! I could lean over him now or at any time and take in his smell of pipesmoke or cologne, of whiskey or wine or sweat, and know that it was as though these smells were mine. He was my flesh and my blood. Of all the things he had imparted to me during my apprenticeship with him in the mountains, the skills and insights, the range of mind and movement, the animal sensitivity, this thing of family was the finest of them all. All through my life there had been only my mother and me, battling and clutching, turn and turn about, for in twoness there is uncertainty. But now my grandfather made three, and three enclose a space. Three make a triangle, strong and solid without and serene within, and from us there extended backwards many hundreds more to Hervey and beyond, making a great sphere holding a world of its own. My mother of course was missing and I had long been wandering the land in search of her, but she seemed near now and I knew that nothing could ever dislodge her from this fine enclosing space. Could I find her? I could not then know, but I knew at least that in order to do so it would not be through the pictures I had drawn idly in my mind, but rather through the things I had learned in the mountains, my grandfather's gifts, the ability to see and to interpret, the ability to love.

IX

We came down then in the morning, out along the pass that led us by Lugnaquilla, through the Glen of Imaal, down along the Military Road to Rathdangan, and on to Hacketstown and Tinahely and the lowlands once again. The light was bright and hard and the crisp autumn wind tightened my skin and brought water to my eyes. Never before had I seen in Ireland such an extravagance of colour, the peach and flame orange and red like a lobster's claw of the oak leaves, the grass brightly green as it waved in the wind, the sky as luminously blue as my grandfather's eyes. He was out a little way ahead of us, walking smartly and with seeming purpose, though as yet we were without a known destination.

'There's nothing like walking,' I heard him say, 'for feeling the land under your feet.'

I scurried over the intervening distance to be by his side. I had been tentatively delicate from first light, but with the sudden movement a throbbing commenced behind my eyes and arched over the dome of my head to the bottom of my skull and there was a poisonous coursing of ill-being throughout my system from the wine I had taken the previous night. All my fluids seemed to have evaporated.

'How is it you never have a hangover?' I asked.

'Never had a hangover in my life,' he said, fractionally increasing the pace. 'Vigorous walking is the thing.'

He could be monomaniacal about his themes.

'We've walked a very long way,' I said. 'Above a hundred miles, I'd say.'

'We have, we have,' he said. 'And there'll be a hundred more perhaps, who knows. Good walking is a skill. You put your foot on the ground and have to learn how to discover something of yourself in what you see and feel around you. It is devotional, humbling. It requires patience. But it is also generous. You see things at a velocity that is comprehensible. Now I had a magnificent walk in 1921, all the way from Galway to Cork. It was after I left Honor off at Gort to ministrate to Blanchard. I saw astonishing, wondrous things. A seasonally disappearing lake in the Burren, its blue waters rimmed in an orange crust where the sun had scorched the earth. Scores of salmon leaping the weir at Galway. Two eagles with their brood high in the air over Limerick. I saw basking sharks and porpoises lolling in the sun off Kerry Head. I got lost in the empty mountains above Scarriff. On a road outside Ventry I was sold whiskey and plums and goat's milk by a group of bare-legged girls. Do you see? I'd never have known of such things had I not walked among them. I passed through miles of bogland, purple and red, and at dusk I saw a herd of red deer gathered in a silent semi-circle around the ruins of a Norman keep. At Caherciveen I watched an old man touch his bow to his fiddle and produce a sound of the purest innocent delight. Amazing! I wouldn't have thought such a graceful state renderable in any medium. War was with us then too, of course. Vehicles of soldiers and mercenaries prowling vilely about our roads. I remember of all the things I saw at that time the look of smoke-blackened walls. The grey stone walls of the barracks and the red brick of the big houses destroyed by our people and the whitewashed cottages wasted by the military. War like walking has a way of amplifying an impression, of fixing it in the memory . . .'

He looked at me, his right brow raised in his ironical manner, as though inviting me to participate with him in some expanded meditation on his subject. But such was the state of my mind that it was capable of neither penetration nor thinking in any sequence. He on the other hand was in splendid fettle, bearing no traces whatever of the frightening episode in the chapel.

We were entering again into a populated area, with a little row of shops and, set on the bank of a small hill, an estate comprised of tiny houses, each with a rust-streaked satellite dish turned like a sunflower to the sky. It had been some while since I had encountered any concentration of people or commerce with the result that all towns still looked a little strange to me. I could see some elderly men playing cards in the launderette, gathered around the driers for warmth. Further on, another old man went wheezingly by on his bicycle, a gas cylinder leather-strapped to his back. It seemed that everyone here was old.

'Grandfather,' I said. 'I've long been meaning to ask you. That place you have in Dublin. Why do you live there?'

He was silent for a little while as we walked on.

'What an odd question,' he said then.

'But it's ridiculous,' I said. 'It has no features whatsoever. It doesn't suit you at all.'

'It suits me perfectly. It's serviceable, anonymous, bleakly contemporary . . .'

'Come on. You're not those things.'

'And there is another reason too,' he said.

'What?'

'Do you recall the day we met, when we buried your tortoise?'

'Of course I recall it.'

'And afterwards we walked through the city.'

'Yes.'

'At one point we came upon the ruins of some government housing and I told you that an ancestor of mine once owned property on the same site. It was in the Coombe. You did not then know that he was an ancestor of yours also. Do you remember?'

I did. The town planner with the mind as large as Descartes's.

'Well, he was Murrough Synnott. He had his offices and works there, but he lived where I do now, on the estate.'

'Was his the marble archway at the entrance, with the Druid?'

'Right! And the pineapples carved into the pillars. Symbols of prosperity. It's a wonder they were left standing. A developer with a sense of irony, perhaps. Beyond the gate he had eleven acres, with a nine-pin bowling alley, an experimental vineyard and a deer-park in a small wood. In the summer he and his wife took their breakfast under some nut trees accompanied by a harpist who played nearby. Once he took off in a balloon from the lawn and sailed in the air all the way to Athlone. He went about the town in the style of a parrot, with a green cloak and a canary-coloured waistcoat and large rings over his violet gloves. He walked with the unnecessary assistance of a shoulder-high cane! Oh, he was fabulous, comical, brilliant . . . a *gargantuan* personality.'

He feasted like an epicure on the word 'gargantuan', elaborating it theatrically. So vividly did he conjure this man before him and so enraptured was he by the emerging picture that he looked like a boy in love.

'He was rich, then,' I said.

'Well, he was. But there were many who were rich at that time. It was a city of politicals, savants, divines, Huguenot merchants and bankers and lawyers. A *capital*. His business in the Coombe was a glass works, a building which he'd had constructed in the shape of a bottle. They made drinking glasses, water and spirit bottles, cupping glasses and weather glasses. Pier glasses and hand mirrors and windows. There was a place where they made small telescopes designed for looking at pictures in miniature. I think it was a gesture towards Hervey. Do you see? The best of us have tried to make a unity out of our pasts. His accounts I recommend you read and read again. They are unsurpassed. Parodies, entertainments, anatomical and agricultural speculations. There are overheard conversations, paeans to Liberty, invented words and fabulous accounts of meals and wines. There are paragraphs too for the sybarite, written in Latin. And fables! The man had *twelve* children. But above all there are his *visions*. Tremendous visions! Not like yours at all. He had colossal notions for the world around him. He conceived a plan for waste disposal and urban transport by means of underground tunnels. He imported a dead elephant from Africa and had it dissected by a team of doctors before a multitude in College Green. When the grand improving of Dublin was being debated he put forward a scheme for a crystal city centre, with islands of glass outlaying it, a utopia of light and warmth. The man was a wonder, I tell you. He died aged forty-seven under a collapsed gallery while witnessing a performance of "Volpone".'

I did not think he was so much telling me about Murrough Synnott as gaining himself a proximity to him. Was this how a man moved towards death? To have spoken to me as he had over the months I had known him, to have seen and known the things he had imparted to me, his mind, I knew, would have had to have been like a mill, unrelenting and without sentiment, grinding on and on towards purity. But now with the burden of his years upon him, with the sinister poison moving through his body and enfeebling his very structure, with his whole body falling slowly towards sleep, he was, along with his encroaching otherworldliness, enwrapping himself in the sweet fog of nostalgia. He was, I think, by now too tired to study history, but still strong enough to flee towards it from the present.

'My God,' I said. 'What a way to go. What became of the house?'

'The house? *The house?* What do you think?' He had, as I had seen before, suddenly attained such a degree of fury that he looked capable of murder. 'Sold, wrecked, marauded over, despoiled. Its inhabitants sent scattering. Trees from Japan and the Himalayas ploughed under. It happened to them all in one way or another a few years after his death with the Union with England. The Union! You may as well marry a hyena to a swan. They turn everything to carrion. They sucked out the blood and siphoned it into their own island. What became of us? A waterlogged grazing ground for absentee landlords. A European capital become a provincial backwater. And it goes on! This humiliation of the land. Look at Murrough's grounds now. A human chicken coop! Meaningless! Meaningless!'

None of this, I thought, could have been doing him any good.

'But you don't have to live there, Grandfather,' I said.

'What?' He looked suddenly around as though he did not know where he was. 'What do you mean?'

'When we get back, when we accomplish, you know, what we set out to do, we'll all get a place together. You, my mother and me. Somewhere by the sea. Somewhere peaceful . . .'

'Peaceful? Are you *entirely* an idiot? Have you understood nothing of what I have told you? I am precluded from such quotidian comforts. We all are. Did you ever notice your mother experience any peace? Something happened to us when Hervey was chased from the hillside. It happened to me doubly when your mother was taken from me. We lost our access to time. We were condemned to live each other's lives, over and over again. Do you know what I see when I regard the population of our book? Not a line or a parade or a gathering. Something more like a fairground wheel, with the same faces coming around again and again. Utopians, wanderers, ostriches with their heads in the sand. When they move at all it is to throw themselves fruitlessly against a wall which has been built across history. You suggest that we live peacefully? I have yet to discover any means by which to break the spell which keeps us thus ensnared, but manifestly peace is not among them.'

When I turned my eyes again out ahead of us along the road I saw that we were about to collide with a small assembly of about a dozen men and women, gathered around a grotto dedicated to the Virgin. It was newly painted in cream and blue and gold and mementoes of shoes and ribbons and rosaries had been left at the statue's feet. The people were all quite elderly, the men with flat caps and dark suits worn away to a dull sheen at the elbows and knees, the women with shiny handbags and engorged ankles, and from the tea flasks on the roadside and their slouched postures of inertness it appeared that they had been there for a long time. They retreated a little to let us pass. Some kept their heads down and were murmuring over the beads they passed through their fingers, but others had turned towards us and were watching us out of their watery eyes with expressions of sadness and shame. They were startled too, I think, by our alien animals and by the violence of my grandfather's voice.

'Any word yet from the plaster?' he said to them suddenly as we passed. 'Hmmm? Isn't that what you're waiting for? Heavenly utterances?'

His voice was shrill and brittle, a sound like the splintering of glass under intense heat. He was still very angry, and while I was relieved that its fierceness and its weight were for the time directed away from me I nevertheless pitied those men and women, bunching together now and turning away from us.

'Grandfather,' I said. 'You shouldn't mock them. It's what they believe.'

'Believe? That is empty credulity, not belief. Belief is decisive.'

We had reached the far end of the town. The Virgin was looking out over the heads of all of us at the outspreading landscape. There nearest us was a field overbrimming with scrapped cars, rusting and slowly sinking into the boggy earth, their metal panels pleated and smashed, their aerials and wipers and fenders twisted and pointing in all directions. The orange and the burnt red of the rust were like the colours of the oak leaves we had passed in Coolattin Park. Further out was an abandoned house, its roof looted for timber and its walls cracked and waterstained, and beyond it rows of hayricks rotting in a flooded field. Everywhere there was water. It gurgled beneath us through an overgrown ditch, it seeped from the little hillocks and it stood in pools all about us reflecting the brilliant sky. Even the idolators gathered at the Virgin's statue seemed heavy with its intolerable weight. I thought then of the opposite to this ubiquitous wetness. I thought of an Arabian tale that my mother once read to me, a tale of two travellers crossing a great desert, their terrible thirst, their melting shoes, the rocks that were too hot to touch, the bleached lustreless skulls of animals protruding from the sand, the sun that stole all moisture. The sun desiccates, the water rots. But they are, too, the source of all life. All around me was the untameable vitality of the earth. A tree grew within an old telephone kiosk, its branches knocking through its roof and its swelling trunk splitting its seams. Rhododendron and fuchsia and creeping vine poured through the windows of a petrol station, with the strange rusting skeletons of the dispensing tanks still standing in the forecourt. Oat grass grew high through the cracks in the concrete. In the field beyond was an abundance of vetch and white yarrow and knapweed. It was all very beautiful and so minutely did I regard it as we passed that it seemed I could see even the veins in the leaves, as, perhaps, Hervey had seen them through his father's water-filled spheres. This was the wild anarchic growth so loved by Bertrand, to whose eyes the bland geometry of Norman agriculture had long grown tedious. I did not quite know how to encompass it all. I sensed only the mystery that my grandfather was dying as splendidly as the leaves, that my mother was in some suspended state unknown to us and that I was somehow struggling to be born.

We walked on for a time in silence, out again in the wide, unencumbered countryside. All morning we had been moving at a pace greater than the one to which I had grown accustomed, but through it I found that my hangover, as my grandfather had suggested, had been dispersed. He was leaning right into the wind and cutting his way through it. Some powerful current of exhilaration and fury seemed to have taken possession of him on this day, so that by now he was oblivious to the rest of us, not as at other times when he was occupied with a thought, but rather that he was struggling to contain something larger than himself. Maybe he was still in pain and trying to outrace it. Somewhere along this road I heard a sequence of reverberating explosions out ahead of us and off to our right. When we hit a bend they grew greatly louder, causing the monkey to shriek and move around to my offside, and I saw then in a field three heavy black tanks taking target practice with their guns at a gathering of outbuildings in the distance. But my grandfather looked neither to the left nor the right, but bore on out ahead of him through the wind.

At this pace we were soon approaching the outskirts of another straggling village. Just beyond its first two houses, the first a low ranchhouse and the other a bungalow, brightly pink and glittering like granite in the sun, was a nicely built sober grey wall, meeting the road on the left-hand side. Rising above it were two intersecting lines of tall firs that obscured what lay beyond them. Cars were parked in a long line along the wall and across the road I could see a large florid man in a top hat looking down into a small river that had been running beside the road for some distance, watching a group of swans idling in the current. When finally we reached a gap in the wall I was able to look beyond it and see that within there had just taken place a wedding. A modest church built of the same stone as the wall lay behind the quietly jabbering crowd. They were country people, the men slow-moving and too large for their suits, the women nodding animatedly in their clusters. A tiny girl with yellow ringlets and a red face was running about on her own in the long grass amid the gravestones, laughing delightedly and without provocation and throwing carnations upwards into the air. Over by the door the groom was suffering a solitary photographic portrait. He was slope-shouldered and Brylcreemed, his chin was sunk into his chest and his large red hands were folded in front of him over his groin. His forehead was damp with sweat even in the brisk wind. I could not immediately find the bride, but then saw that she was in a corner by the gate smoking a cigarette and talking with a stout young woman with prominent teeth. The hand which held the cigarette was poised upright by her ear, the first two fingers pinching it tightly at the filter while with her thumb she turned her wedding ring around and round. They were standing in the shade, but the sunlight came in through the firs in narrow shafts and one of them fell upon the hand that held the cigarette, forming an egg-shaped pool of light that ranged over her fingers. The ring was a gold band, and as she turned it it gleamed beguilingly in this light, putting me in mind of Morice Regan, watched by Hervey in the Bristol inn as he twisted a gold necklace over his hand and wrist within the glow from the candles.

The monkey and I had lingered a while to watch the wedding guests and we had to sprint ahead to catch up with my grandfather, who with Atma was well advanced into the town. We were overtaken en route by two tall and proud-looking horses, bridled and trimmed in silver and surmounted by two huntsmen identically dressed in long sapphire-coloured coats, white jodhpurs and riding helmets. They passed by us each to one side at great speed and with such terrifying closeness that my ears rang from the clattering of their hoofs on the road. When they had drawn approximately level with my grandfather they halted, dismounted, spat in the dirt, tethered their horses cowboy-style outside a small public house and went into the bar.

'Grandfather,' I said when we had caught himself and Atma up. 'I've just remembered something. That wedding put me in mind of it.'

His strides were still long and steady, as though there was some unravelled tension in his legs driving him on.

'Go on,' he said.

'Well, back in the winter when I was translating, somewhere in the middle of it I saw Hervey.'

'You *saw* Hervey?'

'Yes.'

'My God,' he said. 'I wonder how accurate were your powers at the time. What did he look like?'

'Very dark hair, not tall, solidly built with powerful-looking arms. He had on a belted tunic and no shoes. He had a hairy chest. And he looked happy.'

'Extraordinary. And what was he doing?'

'He had been down at the river where some men were building a bridge and he was walking up the hill towards the tower. He went through the outer gate and got onto a little ridge below the summit where he thought no one could see him. Then he did something very strange. He got down on his knees in the grass and dug a small hole with his hands. Then he took a gold ring from his pocket and buried it in the hole. There was some black earth left over, and do you know what he did? He put the earth into his mouth and he *ate* it.'

The momentum which had been propelling him since the early morning suddenly left him and he stopped in his tracks. He was squinting out along the road ahead of us, but I do not think he was taking anything in.

'Do you suppose it means anything?' I ventured.

'I don't know,' he said. 'Perhaps. Perhaps Hervey was attempting to become wedded to the land.'

I thought of the ring, his look of reverence, his sacramental incantations.

'In the way of being married to another person?' I asked.

'It was something the Celts did. A king, in order publicly to demonstrate his respect and fidelity towards the land over which he held dominion, would enact vows to it as in the ceremony of marriage. If the land in some way failed and did not issue forth in sufficient abundance, then the marriage was deemed to be bad and in some measure the fault of the king. Do you see? It was as though the land were a being in itself. Each field and well and boreen and strand was named and celebrated and recalled for all that had happened on it, so that the name came to contain the whole of its history. It was rather like the relationship between the Athenians and their state. Do you know the *Crito*? When Socrates had been condemned to death, certain disciples of his contrived a plan whereby he could make his escape to Thessaly. But Socrates refused. He told them that he had been condemned by the laws of the state and that as a citizen of that state he could not break his covenant with it. He then imagines himself in dialogue with the voice of the laws of Athens, a voice which he said he heard humming in his ears like the sound of a flute in the ears of the mystic. It tells him that the laws of Athens are just and that he must place justice above all things, above considerations of family and above even life itself. It warns him too of the consequences of breaking faith with the laws. Now it is difficult for us in our stateless country to conceive of such civic attachment, but for Socrates the connection was both intense and primal, like that between the king and his land.'

I thought about this for a moment and my grandfather waited for me to speak.

'If Hervey was wedded to the land where they built the tower, then his marriage was violated by Raymond FitzHenry and his men when they drove him from it.'

'That is correct,' he said. 'Now you understand why we are as we are. We have had inflicted on us a wound which has never healed and for which no retribution has yet been exacted. It has passed on from age to age. We have fought and subverted, wandered in dimness, been made vagrants and dreamed of ideal cities, driven on by the pain from this violation. You know the way it is. A man in pain can think of nothing only how to rid himself of it. And strangely the burden of it seems to grow greater rather than diminish as the generations pass.'

'I can see that,' I said.

We began again to walk, passing out of the town and entering a wide treeless plain, sectioned into small rectangular fields by hedgework and walls. Here and there clusters of beasts lay in the grass. Up from the south was proceeding quickly across the sky a long column of low black and yellow clouds, heavy with rain.

'How is it you never told me of this before?' said my grandfather.

'What?'

'What you saw of Hervey by the tower.'

'Well, you know me,' I said. 'It didn't occur to me that there was anything in it of importance. It came to me like a dream, I gawped at it wonderingly for a while and then I thought no more about it. I never ascribed to it any meaning.'

'I have been looking for the site of Bertrand's settlement intermittently for above half a century. I have been looking for it with greater intensity over the past fifteen years since I deduced the existence of Hugh's missing pages and even more so since I have sensed the atmosphere of my death. But it has not been possible to find it because Hervey does not provide sufficient geographical information in his records. We know that they travelled for two days northwards from Bannow before they came upon the hill, that they were some way to the west of Dermot MacMurrough's headquarters at Ferns and that from the top of his tower on a fine day Milo was able to look upon the sea. We know too that the hill was surrounded by a wood, but then all of Ireland was wooded at the time. Do you see? The imprecision of it has vexed me. I have long known vaguely the quarter of Wexford in which they dwelt, but there are scores of little hills scattered about there. I had no basis upon which to make a choice. But you know precisely the topography, the hill's shape and its proximity to a river. It is a matter of no great difficulty to locate it. We could go there today. We *will* go there today. But think of this. You could long ago have discharged your obligations to me under the terms of our agreement and thereby spared yourself the arduousness of our time in the mountains. You could even now, perhaps, be reunited with your mother.'

'Wait a while,' I said. 'I see what you're at. You believe that Hugh buried the pages in the hill.'

'Of course! It makes perfect sense. We conjectured, did we not, that Hugh being a librarian, while wishing to protect his family from the disturbing sights he had seen in his mind, would nevertheless be unable wilfully to destroy a document. He would, instead, secrete it in a place where it might in the future be retrieved. Now who might have the capacity to do that? We have supposed that only his daughter Anna of all people then living even knew of their existence. He would have trusted her with them, I think. But then it is unlikely that she could have known the location of the hill as neither she nor Hugh had ever been there, and in any case by the time she had discovered that there were pages missing she was too old and tired and broken in love to attempt a journey to find them. As for those who would come later, Hugh knew that even if they were somehow aware that his records were incomplete they would be unable to locate the missing section for the same reason that has been inhibiting me, a lack of geographical specifics. No. He was waiting for someone like himself, someone for whom the limits of reality are not the limits of knowledge as verifiable only by the eyes or by logic. Someone who could see beyond, who perhaps like himself could see across time to a ceremony conducted by his father on the side of the hill. Someone with the webbed hands of an aquatic animal. Someone who bears this sign of the double life.'

'But why there?' I asked him. 'Why the hill?'

'Why would you think? Why would Hervey become wed to it? Because that was their beginning. That is where they were happy. That is where they had peace. And that was their home at least in spirit then and thereafter since the time Raymond FitzHenry drove them from it.'

It had begun to rain. It came at us in grey swelling waves over the plain and was now falling heavily upon our heads. We had come to a halt again in the road and were looking into one another's eyes, my grandfather holding my hands tightly in his own, the water running in streams through his fabulous hair. I could see nothing only his face and shoulders, and even that with distortion, for the lack of food since breakfast had dizzied my head and the rainwater was blurring my eyes. Now and then as we stood there in our still and silent dance, the air around us seeming to hum and whisper in the rain, the sun would break through beneath the column of cloud and fill the plain with an intense golden light. As the light struck my eyes and broke up in the water into reds and yellows and greens it seemed that my grandfather had grown incandescent, that he was passing before me from substance to spirit behind waving and billowing aurora-like curtains of light. It seemed momentarily that if I did not hold him tightly by the arms he would dissolve away entirely into vapour. What we were then in the road and what he had put to me, it was surely as mad and as lucid as anything that had passed in the course of that year. I would take him there to the hill if I could. I would take him anywhere at all.

We struck out again along the road, the rain falling heavily upon us, the monkey burrowing down into my sack through the neck hole for protection. From Carnew a horse trader took us all in his car to Ferns, where we waited edgily for a lift out the Ballycarney road, my grandfather looking to the sky for signs of diminishing light. It had become an unspoken imperative that we get to the hill before close of day. After half an hour or so we made our way back into the town, my grandfather calling into shops and public houses along the way to see if he might solicit a lift to the west. All to no avail. Nothing at all seemed to be moving here in the rain.

'I can get nowhere at all with these people,' he said. 'We'll have to find another means. But I want to show you something first.'

He led us then to the town's castle, a bulked, corroding remains, its clay-coloured stones sleek and gleaming like polished leather from the rain.

'Countrymen of Hervey's built this. Beneath it under the ground is all that is left of the fortress of the man who beckoned them here, the one-time king, Dermot. It was from here that he issued the call heard by Hervey and Milo in Bristol, and it was here that he intended to bring them after they had arrived at Bannow. Do you see? They *crushed* his Irishness into the ground. There is no visible trace here of the life he led.'

There were about the entranceway to the castle an old schoolbus and some cars. He instructed me to mind the road for any sign of movement and he began then to prowl among the vehicles, until on a sudden he was under the bonnet of a car fiddling with its wires and levers until it roared into life. He collected the animals and myself then and we were away, out through the town and then skimming and flying over the puddles and bumps of the Ballycarney road. I was fearful that I might be obstructed somewhat in my search by the poor visibility due to the rain, combined with the fact that I had only seen Hervey and the hill from a single perspective, but the image of it was nevertheless a clear and fresh one in my mind and I was hopeful of finding it if only we could beat the darkness. We continued on through Castledockrell and Templeshambo to Bala Mor, and then north past Black Rock Mountain and alongside the Clody River, diverting all the while into laneways, dirt roads, farmers' tracks, tow paths and the like, spinning and sliding in the mud and coming up yet with nothing. I thought nothing at all of the police, so urgent did our right then seem to the car, until near Bunclody we passed a bomb-blasted barracks, its masonry all fallen in upon the cells and beneath it something still smouldering among the rubble. We went south again, all the way past Tincurry to within sight of Vinegar Hill before we swung back in an arc through Marshalstown and Ballindaggan, encountering hills and rivers in great number along the way but none that I could say that I had seen before. On the far bank of one of these rivers, I believe it was the Urrin, I saw a violinist standing in some brown mud under a tree, playing his violin and screaming. The darkening of the air was accelerating now, as though a sediment was settling in about us beneath the low, still-outpouring clouds. Just above Kiltealy my grandfather stopped at a roadworks and threw a long-handled spade he found there into the back seat with the animals. He roared on again then to the north. Above Templeshambo once more on a small road running beside a river in the direction of a place called Tombrock we were slowed by a man and his dog driving heifers out ahead of them. To my right as we rolled slowly along there came into view a powerful and dark shape, a hill quite near the road, higher than most others we had seen and standing out on its own. I rolled down the window and put my head out, the rain falling upon it and running streamingly down my neck and back. The lines of the picture I had seen in late winter in my mother's room fell now into place with these lines of the Wexford earth and I could see that this was surely it, Bertrand's hill, a little ridge beneath the crest like a child's shoulder, in the fold of which Hervey had conducted his marriage rites.

I pressed my grandfather's arm and told him to pull over. He had not spoken since we had set out from Ferns and he did not do so now. We collected the shovel and our kit bags from the car, leapt a ditch and headed for the hill's slope, the animals keeping to our sides in eager attentiveness. We were again within moments wet to the skin, the rain falling now with remorseless weight, the water flooding over our feet as they sunk into the ground with each climbing step. We were approaching the hill along the same route as I had watched Hervey walk so buoyantly, but where the way for him was open there was now a dense pattern of small empty fields, set apart by ditches and walls and shrubs and rising up the hill, so that it was difficult to move with speed in the darkness and the rain. Passing through a narrow gap near the end, a thorned bramble whipped at me after catching on my grandfather's shoulder and opened a long fine cut under my eye. I could taste the blood as the rain washed it down into my mouth.

Then finally there was a clear way open to us across the grass to the top of the hill. I began to run, as did my grandfather. Somewhere along the way I tripped and staggered and when I looked back I could see the monkey holding some dripping wire up above the grass. But I did not pause, and ran on again after my grandfather. When he reached the flattened-out summit he began to pace about over it, taking in air in short gulps and extending his arms out from his sides like a large bird exercising his wings. When I caught him up he stopped and looked at me.

'Show me,' he said.

We climbed down the short slope and over to Hervey's spot on the ridge and I made ready to dig with the long spade. All light had now drained from the sky entirely and my grandfather held his torch aloft so that I could see. The grass here was long and thick and the strands of it entangled as I lifted the rain-heavy sods, but soon I had opened a wide oval space and my blade pressed easily now through the soft earth. It was rich and black and abundant with mud beetles and worms and centipedes, and I loved the feeling as I dug through it, the taut warm ache in the muscles of my arms, the throbbing in my head as it filled with blood. I dug to the level of my waist, and then to my shoulders. Out of the earth came bits of delf, a beer can, a tiny box containing the skeleton of a fish, a tea caddy, an orb of blue glass, an illustrated silver plate, a fragment of a red blanket, a dog's skull and the rusted ghost of an old rifle, but as finely as my grandfather sifted through the soil he could find no trace of the pages he so keenly sought. I dug on then heartily until I was fully within the earth, the top of the pit I had opened now more than a foot over my head. Then the torch beam wavered and cut out and I saw my grandfather's agitated features looking down at me.

'Sssssttt. Quiet!' he hissed. 'Stop digging. I hear something out there.'

I clambered up the muddy slope to the surface. Atma was in a stiffened posture looking down the hill, his ears cocked, his skin quivering.

'What is it?' I whispered.

The four of us gathered together in a low crouch, squinting through the rain.

'I don't know,' he said.

I heard a sound then, of movement through the grass far down the hill near the walled-off fields, and I saw dimly the outline of a dark shape moving. It was a prowling, stealthy movement, like that of a panther. I nudged my grandfather to show him, but he was looking with concentrated purpose across me, and when I followed the line of his sight I saw another moving shape, like a short wall of hedge coming up the hill towards us. He switched on the beam of his torch again and played it slowly along the ground in this direction, a crawling, weaving pattern in the grass, until it fell gleamingly on a fine point of metal, then down a bright narrow shaft to a radio. Here was a man's shoulder, clothed in military camouflage, and beside it his helmeted head, the features of his face dwarfed by enormous dark goggles. It looked like the head of a fly. I saw all this in the smallest fragment of time, for the beam of my grandfather's light then jerked sharply to the left to reveal a line of four soldiers lying in the grass, their guns pointed at us. When the light fell upon them these guns began to fire, and the guns all around the hill answered them, the bullets whistling in the air and thudding into the earth all about us. I threw the monkey into the pit and scrambled in after him, but as I did I saw my grandfather rise up to his full height.

'GRANDFATHER!' I screamed.

He began to walk towards them in the rain, the guns firing madly. He was smiling.

'It is an illusion,' he said.

He had not gone five feet before the bullets tore into him, slamming into his chest and throwing him back towards me through the air as though he'd been hit by a train. I came out of the hole and lay down by his side behind the pile of earth. He was on his back looking upwards, the rain washing his face. The bullets had shredded his leather coat across his chest and blood was flowing from the wounds.

I held onto his hand and I was weeping.

'Grandfather,' I said. 'Please don't die.'

'I have long been waiting for it,' he said.

The benign, tranquil smile was still on his lips and his eyes were the colour of robins' eggs.

'I love you,' I said, kissing his hand. 'I *need* you.'

'No longer,' he said.

'But the pages,' I said. 'We haven't found them yet. I *know* I can do it. You have to hang on.'

He smiled more broadly now. 'That too is an illusion,' he said. 'But we've had a happy time, you and I.'

He gasped then, trying to suck at the air.

'It's happening,' he said.

'No!' I said.

There was a sound then of water mixing with the air in his throat. It was as though he was drowning from within.

'Grandfather.' I grabbed him by the shoulders. 'I am thinking about my mother now. I see her in you as you must see her in me. We are all of us in each other. I want to go to her now. I want to show her what I have become and to tell her about you. Please tell me what it is you know about her. Won't you? The name of the place you followed her to.'

The liquids were rattling more loudly now in his throat. He arched back his head as if trying to clear it, his mouth opening and closing. I knew that he wanted to speak. But then like the breaking of a spring up through the ground there came not the town name I was waiting for but rather a great wave of blood, up out of his mouth from deep within him and flooding out over his face. It gushed and poured and spilled, washed away by the rain and seeping into the earth. Finally it was spent, and he was dead.

I heard the quick panting of a helicopter then and watched it come towards us over the trees, a huge floodlight fixed to its underside turning about, its beam roving over the hillside until it arrived finally at us. The guns were still firing and the soldiers had begun again to move. They were coming from all sides, it seemed, and I could see no means of escape. I took the torch from my grandfather's hand and threw it with the kit bags down into the pit. The monkey was still there, screeching wildly and without cease at the helicopter, which hovered now above us illuminating the whole of the hilltop. I made some grabs for Atma but he leapt clear each time, for he would not leave my grandfather. I stood up then and jumped into the hole but, strange to say, when I hit the base of it it broke through, and I fell into darkness, as though I had been swallowed by the earth.

X

I was in a cavern with graves. It was long and narrow, with its floor and walls paved in large flat stones, and it ended somewhere beyond the darkness. The air here was dry and stale, though now little eddies of rain-cooled wind and the smell of wet earth were wafting through it. The light from the helicopter came in fitfully with the wind through the hole above my head, spilling into the darkness so that I could see among the tufted white tubers and dead roots sticking out through the gaps in the walls several protrusions of bone, a splintered clavicle, the rounded end of a thigh or arm bone, the curving white parallels of a ribcage. I dug the kit bags and torch out from the pile of earth onto which I had fallen. The monkey was squatted down waiting for me on the stone floor at the edge of the light, smeared in mud. He looked bald and thin and terribly frail, and he was shivering a little from the cold. Above me I could hear blasts of static from the soldiers' radios getting nearer and the revving of land vehicles ascending the hill. I got up then and walked down into the grave. I was aching a little in my back and chest from the fall, and a cut had opened up on my leg just below the knee. I thought of a cut I had sustained on another perilous journey, through the outer reaches of the Judge's house when a nail on the stairway had torn into my flesh and I had watched the blood seep into my white cotton socks. When I reached the monkey I turned on the beam of the torch to see how we might go on. The tunnel was long and narrow, with gaps between the stones in the wall leading off to small round rooms, and it ended in a low, stone-arched doorway passing on to I knew not where. Had Hervey run weeping along this same dim tunnel, his manuscript tied to his body? As we walked towards the little doorway I saw that the stones along the walls still bore faintly the tracings of engravings. I stopped then and turned the beam on them. Here were squat figures with tunics and beards and wild, cavernous eyes, a chain of animals forming a ring, each devouring the other, mad, spiralling lines such as had been worked in gold into the leather cover of our book, running here about the borders of the stones in an infinite complexity and seeming without beginning or end. The soldiers were now above the hole. There was the shouting of orders and the sounds of their vehicles. We began to run. I looked above me for any sign of the leakage of light and a way back to the outside world but there was nothing. When we got to the end I got down on my knees and passed through the little doorway. Here was another rounded chamber, like the others we had passed but larger, with a vaulted ceiling and its walls paved with illustrated stones. In the centre was a high pile of bones, blackened with smoke, tiny hands and enormous spines, the long heads of horses and cattle, the grinning skulls of humans. There was a short burst of rifle fire and then something landed on the pile of earth beneath the hole. It made a dull sound like that of a foot landing into the side of a dead animal. Within moments then there was a flash of light and a fierce explosion and the whole of the tunnel at the far end crumbled and gave way and collapsed finally in a great heap of earth. I came back out of the chamber. No longer could I hear the helicopter or the vehicles or the shouts of the soldiers. I ran back down along the tunnel, examining one by one the small rooms that led off to the side, but the walls of each of them were dense and immovable. The monkey had stayed behind in the end-chamber and I could see him through the doorway walking fretfully around its perimeter. I entered it then and sat down, taking him up in my arms to keep him warm. We sat for a long time in this way, rocking back and forth in our entombed silence. Then I felt once along the hairs at the back of my neck and again a second time within the folds and slopes of my ear a faint bestirring of air, a small gentle gust no more forceful than the breath of a child steaming a window-pane, cool as though freshened with rain and unlike the air of the dead elsewhere in the cavern. I tried to trace it to its source, but it is a difficult matter to follow brief movements of air. I looked carefully round me. The paving-stones along the walls with their haunted men and their frantic lines reached to a height of some three feet and above them rose the domed ceiling, its mud surface smeared and hardened and glazed. I could see no fissures that would let in the air of the world and when I drummed over it with a pair of bones it betrayed no hollowness whatever. I could see however that while the stones were recessed into the earth rather than set upon it, thereby presenting a continuity of surface, there was a single one of them, quite near to where the monkey and I had been sitting, which was set at an angle and protruding along one side. I moved along its edge with my palm and finally felt near the floor a soft billowing of cool air. I dug at it with my fingers and levered it with the heavy rib of what might have been an ox or a bull and smashed at it with a stone the size of a canonball until at last it gave way, fell over, and broke into pieces on the floor. And there it was, a small hole opening onto an even narrower tunnel that led along the ground a distance of some ten feet from this grave out to the Wexford countryside. The monkey peered in but seemed not to like the look of it and backed away. Could I possibly get through it? It was hanging with roots and littered with stones and it narrowed here and there to dimensions which from this distance I could not accurately calculate. I threw the kit bags in and with the longest bone I could find pushed them along as I lay outstretched in the tunnel until they reached the exit hole at the far end. I withdrew the bone then and entered again, squirming along wormwise, my arms doubled up so that my hands were pressed flat beneath my shoulders, but as I reached a point just over halfway the walls narrowed and I found I could proceed no further. The earth here hadn't the brittleness it had within and I thought I could break through but the harder I pressed the more I buried myself, the earth furrowing under my shoulders and building up around my neck, so that I had to retreat, a difficult manoeuvre as I had little means by which to propel myself. Once in the chamber again I took off my sack, sweaters, various undergarments and sandals, so that I stood naked but for my socks, rolled them all together in a ball and pushed them through to the kit bags. I reasoned that as I was widest now at the shoulders rather than the waist I could attain the most narrowness by inching along with my arms pressed flat against my sides, a means of movement for which the sole power derived from the muscles at the base of my back. I entered thus again and proceeded along until I arrived at the narrowing, my shoulders sliding into the furrows they had made previously and forward movement seemingly impossible. The dangling roots waved about in my face, the stones beneath me dug into my flesh and clods of earth fell from the ceiling so that I wondered would the whole of it collapse over me. The monkey was holding fearfully onto my ankle at my rear, his little fingernails embedded in my skin. The pressure of the earth on my chest was terrible so that I could take only the shallowest of breaths and if I moved forward at all it seemed that the walls were pressing into me and would crush me entirely. I struggled through to the level of my bicep and knew that from here it would be impossible to go back. I drained all the air from my lungs and with the full strength of my back and my legs and my feet I surged forward in a great heave. More earth fell about my neck from above but still I remained where I was. I tried again. Then again a third time and I was through, my face fallen against my rolled-up sack and within a foot or two of the open air. I pushed it along with the kit bags out ahead of me with the bridge of my nose and my brow until I was out again in the fresh wet grass. I lay in it for a while with the monkey, letting the rain, falling softly now, wash over my body.

Above me, the military were occupying the hilltop. They were not from my point of vantage visible apart from the appearance now and then of a silhouetted soldier, but the whole of the area glowed with the white and yellow lights of their illuminations, as though it had been stricken with radiation. There was a ditch a dozen or so yards away from me, and it was not a difficult matter for myself and the monkey to get down into it unseen and move along it in a low crouch, past the fields, under the road and across an open area of grass to a line of trees and the flowing river where long ago Hervey had watched the men with the colourful hair and flowing robes building a bridge with stone. I sat among some rocks on its bank and looked up at the hill through the trees. The helicopter was parked on the summit, its blades slowly stirring the air, and a pair of armoured land vehicles were idling on the slope. Some two score of soldiers prowled about among the beams of light, their goggles down over their eyes, the upraised aerials of their radios wagging in the air like the feelers of ants, their shadows huge on the grass. I could hear nothing at all of their doings. There was only the sound of the flowing water and of the movements of the monkey above in the trees. Then at a point just above the land vehicles, near, I would say, to where I had tripped over the wire, there was a tremendous blaze of light, as though a great star had exploded somewhere under the hill, illuminating the whole of the area, the fields and stone walls and the trees, in a fierce red glow. There was a trembling in the earth and then there reached me a fearsome gale of hot wind and the awesome roar of the blast. Doors and rifles and shoulder packs were thrown up into the air. There were flying heads and limbs and great sods of earth arcing way above me and then raining down all about the hillside. Atma too was there, his broken body sailing high above the ground. The noise of it hummed for a time in the air, a kind of long, pulsating echo. And then again there was stillness.

I got into the river and lay down on my back. I rested the kit bags on my chest and let the river carry me along, past fields and forests and little towns, the monkey keeping pace with me among the trees or on the ground. I ate some food and slept finally in an old boathouse by the side of the river, and when I woke in the morning I went through my grandfather's effects. There were his Euripides, a bottle of cologne, some clothing, tools of different sorts and several thousand pounds in cash. I made my way over to Carlow, where I had a haircut and shave and bought a tweed suit and hat. I had a fine dinner of river trout and potatoes and asparagus in a hotel and afterwards as I drank my wine I opened the book. I wanted to see the handwriting of my forebears.

Here was Hugh's, spare and intellectual, and Anna's, regular and upright and then looping and sloping at all angles as her loneliness besieged her. Ronan's was wide-gapped but meticulous and the hand of his son Conal, master of the macabre, was tight, minuscule and black and had a brittle, spindly look, like the dripping of candle wax. There were childish hands, misspellings, codes. Murrough included with his writings drawings of his glass city and a caricature of Bishop Berkeley. My grandfather's own father had handset his bland horticultural observations in a medieval typeface on vellum, and my grandfather himself included some musical scores, accounts of his time in prison and writings about his travels in Italy and South America before ending with a long and terrible meditation on my mother's birth and the denial of his fatherhood. His handwriting was broad and strong, but I thought I could see even in its vigour the doubt and pain that had brought him low. After him came my mother, not a narrative at all but a page on which she practised her signature with its newly discovered surname of Synnott. I remembered sitting down before the book so long ago in my mother's room and sensing its strange holiness – its hypnotic lines, mysterious smells and hidden messages – but now it seemed its pages were as of my own skin, that they formed a greater skin which enclosed the sphere that held me and all the others and all the time that could ever be.

Before I put the book away I looked again at Anna's account. I wanted to see what she had to say about her father's manuscript, those errant pages my grandfather had died for. I followed her narrative through the torn silk hangings and bleeding walls and melting bronze of the invasion, her flight from the giant and Bruce's ravening hordes to her sanctuary in the home of her brother, but when I looked for her addendum about the twelve missing pages which he had told me about I could find nothing at all. It did not exist. Her nephew Ronan makes the next entry in the book, and he notes that Anna died within days of arriving at their home. I could see it now, my grandfather's grand jest, this last illusion to which he had referred as he lay dying on the hillside. Here he was laughing beyond the grave, and I laughed with him there in the dining-room of the hotel. He had invented Hugh's missing manuscript and its fevered prophecy in order to keep me by his side, to give me his gifts of thought and love and history, an invention like the diguises he had worn to watch over my mother, but altogether his most fabulous and intricate of all.

I drank more wine and wondered a while what those pages might have contained had Hugh been able to look out through time into the future and written about it. Was there such a thing? I had once asked my grandfather about the nature of prophecy. 'Prophecy,' he said, 'is Divine History. All time is there for you, if you can but get to it.' In his feigned speculations about them my grandfather had suggested that the pages must have described a terrible vista, too terrible for Hugh's family to see, but my grandfather like myself now could see back across that vista and of course it was terrible – Hugh's own blazing library, his grandson Ronan, broken-backed and bleeding on a rock, those epochs of uncertainty, decay and dispossession, all the misplaced hopes, mistimed inventions and ingratiating tergiversations in the face of mute, brutal power, the great ferris wheel of his descendants described by my grandfather, circling sadly in the air, and now, more recently, a fat man in a sack and his elderly companion and their menagerie walking in the high ground. And there was my mother too. I seemed to see her there in Hugh's agonising vision, with her red hair and in her black cloak, ever wandering, over Bertrand's hilltop, at Ronan's festival of music, through Murrough's imaginary city of glass and in the valley with the ringfort where her mother and father first kissed, confused, beautiful, searching for she knew not what, driven on uncomprehendingly. How badly still I wanted her with me.

In the morning I hired a driver and we headed out west and south, down across Kilkenny and into Waterford. At Dungarvan we paused a while by the bay and watched a young man drifting alone in his rowboat towards Ring, singing and talking and writing in a little book. We kept to the coast then, past Youghal and along the whole length of Cork. I had no destination that I knew of. My grandfather had toured here while my mother was in Honor's womb, and I suppose I may have thought that I might see my mother herself walking happily in the sand. Beyond Bantry I got out and made my way high above the bay in the mountains. The stones were glazed in ice. White wraiths of mist drifted by and caught me up and the streams around me bubbled and roared. I began to cry. I lost the bay and the ancient path over which we had been walking. All around me were plunging slopes and immensities and I was without rules or signs or guide or even a person or place to call my own. I fell onto the ground and screamed until I felt the monkey's hands on my temples and his cheek pressed to the back of my head. I got up then and began again to walk, past Glengariff and out towards Kerry. Somewhere I heard a wild, reverberating roar, strange and vast like the call of a beast, and when I looked round me I saw far below at the base of a ravine a solitary trombonist playing up to the echoing mountainsides. Evening came down and we had to keep to a paved road. At Kenmare we took a meal and I hired another car. We drove through the night, here and there about Kerry, past Tralee and onto the west coast, up along the Shannon estuary and into Clare. Sometime in the morning we came to Gort. I could find not even a stone of Blanchard's church, but the vicarage was still there, its walls crowded in with bushes and tall grass. In the hallway a sheep looked at me in terrified stupefaction and then vaulted out the scullery window. The drawing-room, where Blanchard had enthused before the fire and Miss McInnerney's cockatoo had sung from its cage, was filled with potatoes. There were potatoes too in the dining-room and still more piled high upstairs in the room overlooking the drive where Honor had given birth to my mother. There were no deeds attesting to this event here in Gort, nor were there any above in the records office in Galway. It was as though she had been born in the air, her name writ in smoke.

I hired another car at Galway and we angled eastwards. I had not slept or eaten at all and sometimes as I looked out the car window I began to dream. Rocks walked and the walls of houses rippled. Sometimes I thought I had been talking with the driver but I could not be sure, and sometimes I saw bats flying at the windscreen. My mind thickened with things. Eagles, rings, shepherds' huts, letters of the alphabet. I heard Atma barking and the whistling of bullets. They were all together inside my head, but after a while they played themselves out and I was clear again.

Somewhere in the Midlands I began to think with some method about my mother. I thought too of how Hervey had sought for Milo and my grandfather had sought for me and how I in the same manner was searching for her. What was it caused people so to search? I thought of the fantasy put forward by Aristophanes at the Symposium, of the round, double-faced creatures, divided into two by Zeus, like an egg by a hair, condemning them to prowl over the earth in search of their lost halves to regain thus their union. But from whom could my mother have been divided? I thought of the placenames I had heard after she had been retrieved from her wanderings – Pomeroy, Magilligan, Claudy, Buncrana, Dungiven. I did not know these places and as we drove through the flat expanses I looked at them on a map. In the midst of them was a name I recognized from my grandfather's narrative, Eglinton, a small place out beyond Derry, the home of the Reverend Blanchard's housemaid, Miss McInnerney. But why would my mother have been looking for her? I did not think my mother could have known her except in the earliest stages of her infancy, and in any case there was little chance that the woman was still alive. I thought of how she had listened to my mother's movements within the womb, of her strange comings and goings, her whiskey and her vegetables, and the little black-haired girl with her arms around her knees when my grandfather had come looking for my mother. I could fathom no pattern or meaning in any of this, but I had aught else to go on.

As we went northwards the bunkers and patrols and observation posts thickened. I changed the car for a coach at Monaghan, and when we got to the border, by the blockhouses and the barbed wire, some soldiers boarded it with a circular file of photographs and looked into all our faces. After they had passed me by I heard from the back of the coach a brief commotion, a shouted expletive and a noise as of an axe splintering wood. There followed then a low moan. I turned to look and saw an elderly man being attended by other passengers, blood and broken teeth falling from his mouth. There was blood too on the rifle butt of a passing soldier. Further on, Strabane was in flames. In Derry there were thousands in the streets beneath a pair of circling helicopters, listening to a man with a beard. I took a taxi from here through the Waterside and out the Limavady road. It was a still afternoon, the sun shining weakly from our rear over the wide farmlands. The driver turned in over a little rivulet and put us out at a meeting of roads. This was Eglinton, he said.

I stood with the monkey beside the Orange Hall, the town stretching out to the right and the left. It was a place of vast oaks and silence. Some of the trees I found bore small plaques plated in silver and commemorating the crowning of kings and queens over in England. We walked on then into the town. I called into a few places along the way, a hotel, a greengrocer's and a garage, but the people I met there were young and wore the uniforms of their trades, and none of them had heard of Miss McInnerney. Outside a supermarket I stopped a vicar mounting his bicycle, but he was new to the parish and he was acquainted with no one of that name. I walked back the way I came, the streets empty, the evening coming gently in, on past the hall, until I heard ringing out behind me a sharp, elegant click, as of a stone on wood, and turning saw a field of perfect grass, filled with silent cricketers in their white flannels. I stood with the monkey and watched a while, this game I had never seen, so polite and so vicious. Beyond was the old part of town and the big houses, smiling lions and pillars of rose-coloured brick at their entrances, the trees here huge and blazing in their colours. I came then to a lane of small cottages, at the near end of which was a post office. Within, behind a worn mahogany counter piled high with ledgers and stamp books, was a tiny woman of greatly advanced years, her hair as white as my grandfather's, her eyes blue behind her spectacles, her face an animation of pouches and lines and creases. On her left hand there was a leather glove-like contrivance that protected only her thumb and gave her the look of a gambler. She was shuffling papers and talking to herself, but the door was locked and I could not gain entrance. I walked a little way down the lane. Glass decanters and polished sideboards could be seen through the windows and one of the houses bore the gold plaque of a dental surgeon. Further on, near the end, suspended by chains over a window that reached to the ground and rocking a little in the faint evening breeze, was an outsized pair of spectacles. I hastened towards them, my pulse quickening. Here, in the window, were displayed the wares and implements of the optician, long familiar to me from my mother's years of collecting, an ophthalmoscope, a Victorian eye chart, rows of spectacles on a plastic rack, an old rotogravure print of Aristotle dissecting the eye of an ape, photographs of smiling, handsome women wearing glasses. But the photographs were faded and over everything there lay a thick film of dust.

I heard the rattling of keys then and saw the woman from the post office enter the lane. She made her way arthritically around the corner, her legs rigidly bowed, her whole body swinging as though hinged. I quickly caught her up.

From her I learned that a Hatta McInnerney, a vicar's housekeeper, had indeed lived there after coming up from Galway, but that she had been dead some twenty years. She was buried above in the church yard. Her sister Edith too was dead, and Edith's husband Archie, and their daughter Violet passed away only that previous spring. There was only one left in Eglinton belonging to Hatta, and that was Violet's son Tommy, Tommy Bridge.

'Where do I find him?' I asked her.

She took me by the arm and ambled and creaked her way around the corner.

'There,' she said, pointing. 'Above the glasses.'

There were the swaying, enormous spectacles under which I had just been standing.

'There? The optician's?'

'That's right.'

'But it's abandoned. I saw it. It's covered in dust.'

She came at me low, her head stopping conspiratorially by my chest. She smelled of old leather and rose-water, and she spoke in a loud whisper.

'He hasn't shifted from the place since his mother died,' she said. 'She ran the business there for above forty years until her heart gave way. They had a nice house out the country but when she went he moved into the rooms above. Keeps everything as it was when she was there.'

'Do you think could he help me?' I asked.

'Maybe he could. He knew Hatta well when he was a boy. He's the last of them anyway.'

'What do I do?'

'Just knock on the shop door. But give him a wee minute to come down. He's slow on his feet.'

The monkey was there with our bags on the window ledge taking in the last of the day's light. As we set off down the lane I felt a dizziness coming on and I had to brace myself for a time against a wall, but I recovered then and we continued on. When we arrived at the optician's I rang the bell and waited, as she had told me. The day was going out, the light now pale and watery so that the shadows had no lines. After a time I heard footsteps moving on a bare stairwell, a hollow, uneven sound, as though the steps were being taken each by each. He came in then through double doors at the back of the shop and made his way slowly around a glass counter, the spectacles there within all fallen from their racks in upon each other, an entanglement of plastic and wire. He had a limp. He was lean and delicate and he wore a black suit, but he had a look too of some neglect, the laces of his left shoe dangling open and the early growth of a beard spreading over his face. As he came towards me and I looked at him through the glass I had the sensation that I had seen him before, a sensation that compounded and intensified as he came more clearly into view, the hollows and high elegant bones of his brow and cheek, the fine lines of intelligence around his lips, his round, beautiful eyes.

He opened the door and put his head out.

'Yes?' he said. His voice was soft, hardly more than a breath.

I looked at him wonderingly for a time.

'You had an aunt,' I said then. 'I mean a great-aunt. Hatta McInnerney. The woman at the post office told me.'

'Yes,' he said. 'I had. Long ago. She's dead now.'

'I know that,' I said. I was finding it difficult to assemble my thoughts. His voice I could not place, but I felt overpoweringly that I knew the rest of him well, his face, his movements, his look of sadness and innocence. I thought of people I had known, so few to have known really in a life as long as mine, but I could not readily find him among them. He was looking at me closely.

'Are you all right?' he said.

'I'm a little dizzy,' I said. 'I've been on the road a long while. Do you think – ahh – would you mind if I came in for a moment?'

He let me pass and put out a chair for me. I moved towards it unsteadily, a reel beginning to twist a little in my head.

'I liked Aunty Hatta,' I heard him say.

'Did you? I thought she'd have been a good woman. My grandfather told me about her the night before he died.' I tried to speak as deliberately as I could, but it felt as though the skin was stretched back over my ears, my speech echoing, the words at a far distance from the thoughts. 'She knew my grandmother,' I said. 'Did she . . . do you ever remember your aunt speak of her? They were friends, I think. It was down in Galway.'

'No,' he said. 'I don't think she did. I was only ten when she died. Why do you ask?'

'I don't know entirely,' I said. It was as though in my mind a thought was pursuing a word unknown to it, that I was clutching at things as yet not visible. 'That's the difficulty of it. What I am really doing is trying to find my mother. It is, after a fashion, all that I have been doing since the winter, when she disappeared. But in all that time I have yet to discover anything of substance to guide me. She left when I was away and never returned.'

He came gently nearer, his eyes intense.

'I know that pain,' he said. 'It has been with me since the spring when my mother died.'

'I heard that,' I said. 'I'm very sorry.'

'You think she came here, your mother, to Eglinton?'

'She may have,' I said. 'She may have come here looking for her past. She never really had a past before. Nor did I. It was in the winter that she discovered the nature of this past, who her parents were and who came before them. She read about it all in a book. Your aunt was there when my mother was born, in the vicarage in Galway.'

He ran his hand agitatedly through his hair.

'I wish I could help you,' he said. 'But she never spoke of it. She had secrets, so she did. About her youth, about Galway. My grandmother told me that when she was there she nearly married a fisherman, a Catholic, but someone put a stop to it. Some things came out towards the end, though, when her mind was going. She told me things that no one else told me. She told me that my mother was adopted.'

I did not seem immediately to hear this. The sense of vertigo that had beset me was accelerating and I felt within my head the opening of splits and fissures. I heard water falling there, as though my skull had become a leaking dam, a great weight pressing in upon it. Still, though, there was this feeling of pursuit.

'Your mother?' I said finally. I do not know did I yell these words. 'She was *adopted*?'

I attempted to look at Tommy Bridge. He was pacing about in front of me, his stiffened leg dragging over the floorboards. His head was a globe of blue glass. I saw within it my mother dancing in her wedding gown, roses trailing from her hand. I saw my grandfather as a young man standing on a rock, the sea foaming about his ankles. I saw Miss McInnerney running to her car. I saw wars and people weeping, Bertrand with his spectacles and I saw the faces of Tommy Bridge in the blue glass in a succession back towards his infancy. The waters were now flooding in mightily and I abandoned myself to them. I knew that I would find him somewhere if I kept on. I saw again the great procession with Hervey at the head carrying the flag. I saw the piper with the buckyrose in his hatband and the head of a falcon and my grandfather with his wings looking down upon them all. Next came the corpses and the stretcher-bearers, those faces which had passed before me when I lay in my grandfather's bath. Here were Ronan and Hugh and Murrough and myself. And here at the back was Tommy Bridge. He was limping along the road carrying his burden to the jade-coloured field just as he was limping before me in his mother's shop. I had it now, that synchronous activity put forward to me by my grandfather in his kitchen the night before we had set out, those streams of the mind moving in harmonious consort, that forcing through the pressure of thought of what is buried up into the light. I had too my mother's riddle. I thought of Miss McInnerney's childless sister. I thought of the great eye that had hung over my mother's bed, of Honor's troubled dreams obliterating her birth-giving, of the little black-haired girl in Gort, and of my mother's agony on the grass before the Judge's bonfire. I thought too of the double hoofbeats I had heard while my grandfather told me his terrible tale. They were the beating of hearts.

'Your mother,' I asked him. 'Did she come from the south?'

'I think so,' he said. 'I don't know where exactly.'

'Did your Aunt Hatta bring her here?'

'She did.'

'And your father, was he called Tommy too?'

'He was. That's right.'

'And you,' I said. 'Were you born on Hallowe'en?'

He smiled, his eyes glowing like moons.

'Yes,' he said. 'I was.'

'And tell me this,' I said. 'Do you know this rhyme?

Willy, Willy, Harry, Stee,
Harry, Dick, John, Harry Three,
One, Two, Three Ned, Richard Two,
Henry Four, Five, Six – then who?'

He joined me then and we concluded the remaining verses together.

'*Ned the Fourth and Dick the Bad,*
Harry's Twain and Ned the Lad,
Mary, Bessie, James the Vain,
Charley, Charley, James Again,
William and Mary, Anna Gloria,
Four Georges, William and Victoria,
Edward the Seventh and then –
    George the Fifth in 1910.'

I stood to face him. I felt as I had when I emerged from the shepherd's hut in the mountains.

'We're cousins so,' I said.

'What?' he said. He stumbled back on his bad leg.

'You and I, we're cousins.'

'How can this be?'

'My mother and your mother, they were twins.'

'You're sure? How do you know this?'

'There were signs. Things my mother did. Other things. One time in Dublin someone called my mother Violet. My grandfather taught me how to read the signs. "A greater operation of mind", he called it. It took me a long while to learn it. Strange to say, though, he didn't know about it himself. He was away at the time of the birth. My mother didn't know and I don't suppose yours did either, because they were taken from each other just after they were born. Not even our grandmother knew. She fitted through it all and when she woke up she had nothing. I think probably that in all the world only Hatta and the doctor and the Reverend Blanchard ever knew what happened that day. It was not even recorded. Hatta stole your mother and took her north because she pitied her sister who lacked a child of her own. Blanchard went the other way and found a home for my mother in

Limerick. It was a wild time, a small pause in a war. Anything could happen.'

He made his way about the room, his hands pressed to the sides of his head. I could see that he was thinking hard, assembling for himself his new past.

'This is a wonder,' he said, stopping before me. He looked fervently into my face. 'These holes we've lived with. Mysteries. What else do you know about me?'

'I know that you lived in a house by a mill. I know that your mother supplied glasses to a woman called Foster. And I know that your father had guns.'

'That's right! That's right! Miraculous! My father was a policeman. Of sorts. It seemed they were all policemen in those days. He had many guns. My mother hated them. She was a member of the operatic society . . . I wonder were they alike at all, your mother and mine?'

'She used collect lenses. And sing.'

'No!'

'She did. And she used come here, but in a kind of a trance. She was looking for your mother, but she didn't know that she was and I don't suppose she ever found her.'

'She didn't. No. It's tragic. They could have filled each other up.'

'I thought, you know, she might have come here again. She knows a little more of the story now, not all of it, not about her lost twin, but about her real mother and father and Miss McInnerney. Maybe you saw her. Red hair, but greying. Probably confused-looking.'

'Confused?' He smiled. 'There's no one confused here.'

'And she might have been wearing a long black cloak. Here, look. I'll show you.' I went into the kit bags and brought out the little photograph of my mother and me taken by the Judge. 'See? That's her. You can't see her that well, I know, because it's an old photograph and her head is thrown back a bit. But you get the idea. I mean she must have looked something like your mother.'

'My mother's hair was black.'

'Well, the features then.'

He turned on a small lamp and looked carefully for a time at the photograph. And then up at me.

'There was a woman,' he said. 'In the winter, like you said. She stayed in the hotel there for a week or so, but she came and went. I saw her in the churchyard once, maybe by Aunty Hatta's grave, I don't know. I didn't pay much attention to her. But she came by here several times. She'd stop and look at the things in the window. My mother was transfixed. She couldn't take her eyes off her. She'd say, "There's that woman again. I wonder who she is. Hasn't she lovely hair?" And so on. Well,' he said. 'She looked something like this picture. And she looked like my mother too.'

'Is there any more?' I said.

'My mother followed her once. She didn't go to the hotel, or anywhere else. She went to the big house above, the Colonel's. My mother found out later that the Colonel's wife had taken her on as a cook. Would that be right, would you say?'

'It would. It was all she could do, poor woman. Serve people. Bright as she was. And then?'

'That's all. My mother died a while later. I never saw the woman again.'

'*No!*' I shouted, the air ringing after me like a tuning fork. There was my mother in the lane beyond the spectacles and the glass, tantalising, a spectre, smiling as in the chalk drawing she had left on the mirror in her room, looking at the artefacts of the eye, and taken now again by the drifting mists. 'I'm sorry,' I said. 'But there must be more. The Colonel, or his wife, whoever it was she was working for, they must know something.'

'They might all right,' he said.

'Couldn't you phone them?' I said.

'I could, I suppose.' We looked at each other, searching, and I saw what it was that made the round pools of his eyes so beautiful, this look he had of agonising receptivity, of rapture denied.

He went through the doors then and back up the stairs, dragging his damaged leg, his progress painfully slow. I could do nothing to still the pounding in my heart, the throbbing in my head, the tightening in my chest. I saw then hanging by a nail on the wall a photograph framed in dark wood of a woman in a white optician's coat, its collar high above her neck. Here was Violet, my mother's twin. I took it from its place and brought it to the monkey. Her long dark hair was wound round and piled high on her head, she had a wide, severe brow – another point, she was, like me, on the long line that twisted and writhed downwards from Hervey and Emer, a look in her face more of method than of anarchy, those forces pondered over by Bertrand, but with my grandfather's sensual lips and a look somewhere in her eyes of the wounds suffered by her son.

'You can keep that,' I heard him say.

He was standing in the doorway.

'I spoke with the Colonel. His wife is away, he said. He also said that the woman who worked for them, your mother, was taken ill in the spring. They brought her to hospital. He doesn't know much more about it. His wife used to visit for a while, but they lost track of her. He told me the name of the hospital, though . . . I'll take you there.'

We all went out then and got into Tommy Bridge's car. It was night now, the air cool and alive with small breezes and currents, the stars distant and gentle. We drove on, back the way I came, over the flatlands and farms and past the slumbering animals to the city and my mother. At the hospital we all got out, the monkey and I and Tommy Bridge. We went up the stairwell and down the long corridors and finally to the place where my mother lay. A nurse told me she was dying, a day or two she had no more, her body wasted by chemicals and radiation and cancer, her mind emptied and the pain held away by the oblivion of morphine. I saw her then in her gown on the white sheets. She was tiny now, my mother, her limbs and body shrunken, all her wild red hair nearly all gone away, her white scalp shining under the fluorescent lights, her face smiling a little, her eyes open and uncomprehending. We went to her then and sat around her on the bed, the three of us, Tommy Bridge to one side of her and I to the other. I took her right hand and Tommy took the left and then we joined hands ourselves to make a ring with the monkey sitting in the middle on her lap. I told her then the story of her father, this great man, of our wanderings in the mountains of Ireland and the privations and disciplines he had imposed on me, of his vast looming brain that had watched over me and tutored and fashioned me, and of the strength of his love for her. I told her too of the soldiers who had

228

stalked us on the hillside and who had taken his life, of the great fire
that had taken theirs, Bertrand's hill, this place where the story had
begun and been lost and which might now be reclaimed. On and on I
went, Tommy Bridge looking on wonderingly the while, and in the
telling of it I felt freedom. My mother had the pouch now with the
monkey's jewellery and was decorating him with his bangles and
necklace. She was happy in her task, beyond recognising, beyond
speech. She was back in the warm fluids of Honor's womb, untouched
by pain. When I stopped speaking I began to weep. She was passing
from me, taking with her the last of the things that bound me. I took
her up in my arms and kissed her and sang to her, songs my
grandfather had taught me, the sounds humming through me and into
her, my tears streaming down over her head. I saw my hand huge on
her arm, the frail webbing stretched still between my fingers, this sign
of doubleness, a doubleness that I saw everywhere within and without
me, in my mother's dying and being born, in my holding her aged
infant body, both son to her and father, in her falling towards the
peace of the earth where Violet lay, her double, in those twins in time,
Hugh of the webbed hands and I, he the first and I the first again, in
those who wandered like my mother as all before her had done since
our days on the hill, in those who had taught, like Bertrand and my
grandfather, and too in those double things, my life of fact and that
other life that ran along beside it, the river of pictures that I saw and
was now understanding. I saw it too in Bertrand's dream, the complementariness of opposites that he had fashioned around the tower on
the hill, that doubleness that had been riven apart and was now one
within me. I held my mother closer and sang and wept more over her
head, this head that I could now see lay on the stretcher beneath the
green flag beside another head, that of Violet, her twin, there in the
great procession that moved past the angels over the winding road and
down to the still field and the grave that awaited them. Outside the
hospital I heard shots in the night and the wailing of sirens but I also
heard out ahead of me and, too, ahead of the marchers their silencing.
They were all of them marching, the Synnotts, the dreamers and
warriors, the bickering farmers and the saints with their wagging
beards, the falcon and Hervey and Tommy Bridge and I and all the

others, gathering now in a ring around the grave and lowering there into the earth the bodies of Violet and my mother, the two of them one, the nightmare ending, the fairground wheel ceasing, the eyes seeing, the journey done. As they all pass from me now I write these words on the final page of the great long book of my family, I fasten closed its covers with their gold fittings and I look up into the light.